RUNNING SCARED

VANIA RHEAULT

BOOKS BY VANIA RHEAULT

To my mother.
She always knew I could do it,
but I'm sorry I didn't while she was alive.
Mom, this one's for you.

Created with Vellum

CHAPTER ONE

"I WAS SO embarrassed," Marta Braddock murmured, cupping the icy mug between her palms.

Ian Butler laughed, drying a glass with a white terrycloth towel.

To see Marta sitting in his bar sipping a frosted mug of beer made him believe miracles could happen after all.

He'd have bet the bar, hell, the whole building, it would never have happened in a million years.

Marta being in Minnesota was a dream—and a second chance.

The bar was empty as usual, not even his friends Dane and Brett stopped by on a regular basis anymore. But he'd rather spend time with Marta any day of the week, and he winked at her, enjoying her story. "Then what happened?"

"Luckily, she wasn't angry. I mean, how many redheaded Hollys work at the university? It was easy to stick my foot in my mouth bringing up Dane, but she was gracious about it."

"What did she say?"

He hadn't been this content in a long time. When Brett

told him Marta was moving back to Minnesota, it was like a wish he'd never dare say aloud was granted, and suddenly his whole world was open to him again.

Casually, he leaned a hip against the bar, resting his elbow on the polished wood, propping his chin on his fist.

Her eyes danced in the lights that showcased the bottles in front of the mirrored wall.

She looked as he remembered her: brown shaggy hair, usually pulled back with a running headband, brown eyes, plump lips.

Marta rarely fussed with makeup, complaining she would only sweat it off, and she usually did.

Tonight, she wore a nylon running skirt with a Tower City Marathon tank top. A Tower City Marathon running jacket hung from the back of her stool.

She looked like the life-long runner she was, her face showing the wear and tear of what she did for a living, lined from strain and sun exposure, her eyes hardened from the vicious training schedule she endured to keep in shape.

Or had that been Brett and what he'd done to her?

Ian rolled his shoulders in an attempt to ease his stress. He didn't like thinking about Marta's history with Brett, but he could never seem to help himself.

"She invited me for coffee later this week. I'll probably go because it'll be nice to know people on campus. I'm going to be spending a lot of time there."

"It's great you're making friends right out of the gate."

"She's not usually there after spring semester, but she needed to offer a summer course. How about you? Any plans for this summer?"

Ian never made plans.

Stacking glasses under the bar, he shook his head.

"Nothing. I'll help you move into your apartment.

That's the most exciting thing I've got going on right now."

He tried to play it cool, but he was looking forward to spending time with her a lot more than he should. And it wasn't entirely true—there were things that needed his attention—but he didn't want to load her down with his problems.

Like the twenty-one-year-old delinquent slamming her way into the bar.

"Hey, where've you been?"

"Leave me alone!"

Sadie, Ian's little sister by thirteen years, crashed through a door that opened to a stairway leading to their living quarters on the second floor.

"What was that about?" Marta asked, eyebrows raised as a door upstairs crashed.

Normally they wouldn't have been able to hear Sadie's display of temper, but tonight the jukebox had run out of quarters, and neither he nor Marta had fed the machine to keep it going.

The silence was welcome, and often when the bar was empty, he cleaned in the quiet, or used the time to catch up on his reading.

It wasn't good for business, but he preferred it when no one was around.

"My sister, Sadie. She's bitter our parents aren't coming back from their permanent vacation. They prefer their house in Georgia to the apartment upstairs, and they have no interest in moving back—it's too cold."

Marta took another sip of her beer.

"How do you think you're going to fare this winter?" he asked.

Marta shifted on her stool and stuck her tongue out at him. "I used to live here, remember?"

Yeah, he remembered.

He could recall every second of their time at the university.

Every study group, every pizza run, every drunken sleepover.

Dane and Liz, Dane's girlfriend back then, and Brett and Marta. Ian and whatever chick he'd been hanging with at the time.

His years at the university had been bittersweet because every moment he spent with Marta was another second he knew she would never be his.

AFTER LEAVING IAN'S, Marta quietly closed the door to Dane and Nikki's apartment. She'd been sleeping on the couch while she decided what to do.

After talking to her landlady in California, she decided to sublet her apartment and have her personal things shipped to her.

She didn't fancy pulling a U-Haul half way across the country, and paying UPS shipping on the few things she wanted to keep with her seemed like a small price to pay for the convenience of not having to fly back to California one more time.

With Dane's help, she'd secured his old apartment next door, since he lived with Nikki, his fiancée, now. But she needed to furnish the empty apartment, and Ian's offer to help had been welcome.

Dane and Nikki were busy with the store, and well, she didn't feel right hanging around Brett.

Not now he and Alyssa were engaged.

Ian's offer had been a surprise, since he seemed busy

with his own situation, but she'd taken him up on it anyway and tomorrow they would go shopping. It might be an all-day endeavor, but she didn't mind spending time with him. In fact, she was looking forward to it.

She wanted to find out where all his rough edges had come from. He was a lot different than the kid she'd gone to school with.

"Hey, where were you?"

Dane shuffled into the kitchen wearing plaid lounging pants and nothing else. The sun had started to bronze his skin from his long hours of outdoor running.

Marta wasn't allowed the privilege of running topless, and her skin was lined with the funky sports bra tan she always seemed to have going on. "I was at Ian's."

"Oh?" Dane filled a glass with water, downing it in a few smooth swallows.

Marta waited until he was done and looking at her again before she answered. "Yeah. It was okay. I haven't kept up with him like I have with you and Brett."

"He's been waiting for you to come back."

Marta kicked off her running shoes, and feeling at home, made herself a peanut butter and honey sandwich.

Before her shopping spree in the morning, she needed to go for a run, and the protein in the peanut butter and carbs from the bread and honey would give her some much-needed energy. "I doubt that. He doesn't seem like the type to settle down. While we were in school, he dated women like we went through running shoes."

Dane leaned his ass against the counter and crossed his arms against his chest. "Yeah. Because you weren't available. He would have settled down if you hadn't been with Brett."

Taking a huge bite of her sandwich, Marta jerked a

shoulder and met Dane's brown eyes.

She'd never felt any attraction to him whatsoever, and standing in his kitchen with him in his pajamas did nothing for her.

Even thinking about Brett only brought a burn to her throat and an ache to her heart. She hadn't been attracted to him for a long time, even though that had been one of Alyssa's biggest fears when she came back to Minnesota.

Alyssa had always expected Marta and Brett to get back together, but that never would have happened. No, that had run its course, and she had nothing now but the slight shiver she felt whenever Ian looked at her with his steely grey eyes.

But that wasn't lust or desire, or even simple arousal.

It was unease, and maybe just a little bit of fear.

"He's been okay, hasn't he? He's not the same person he was in school."

Dane spoke through a yawn. "None of us are. Do you have plans tomorrow?"

"I'm going shopping with Ian. It's time I filled up my apartment and got out of your hair."

"What did I tell you? He's whipped. There's no man in his right mind who would voluntarily go shopping for a whole day."

"Then I won't bring up the day we spent looking at flowers," Nikki said from the hallway that led to the bedrooms. "Leave her alone and come back to bed. Good-night, Marta." Nikki pulled Dane's arm.

"You said you weren't going to tell anyone," Dane said, his voice growing fainter before the door to their bedroom closed.

Marta smothered a laugh around a bite of her sandwich. It was nice to see her friends happy and in solid relationships.

It was too bad she wouldn't be one of them.

"THERE IS NO man in his right mind who would do this," Ian grumbled as he trailed Marta through Target, mumbling his thanks to the caffeine gods as he sipped the largest Americano Starbucks sold. "Explain to me again what you're doing?"

In an aisle of the kitchen area, Marta stopped pushing her cart. Studying a set of plates, bowls and coffee mugs, she said, "I'm subletting my apartment in Napa, and my parents are keeping my car. It seemed better to start over than to haul everything I own up here. I don't know how long this coaching thing will last, and if I have to go home, I'll pack it up and take it with me or donate it."

It wasn't lost on Marta she still called California home, but for her it would take a lot more than a job and a new apartment to consider Minnesota her place in the world.

She'd enjoyed her time at the university and it was nice to drive north and visit her aunt and uncle whenever she liked, but her parents and most of her memories were still in California.

"Besides, the university is paying my moving expenses, so why not?"

What they'd give her wouldn't pay for everything she'd need to start over, but it wouldn't have covered all of her moving expenses, either.

Bathroom things and kitchenware filled her cart, and she added the box of blue plates to the mix. "I need silver-ware, then I think I'm done."

"Done, *here*," Ian said.

"Well, yeah. I thought we'd do lunch then go to the

furniture store. You know, Dane's old apartment is pretty big. I have room for a treadmill."

"No."

Marta laughed at Ian's scowl. "'No', as in I don't need a treadmill, or 'no', as in you won't go with me to the sports store so I can buy one."

"Both. Aren't you going to run at the school? They have treadmills."

Marta studied a coffee mug bragging Caffeinated Queen. "That's true. But I'm not going to be there every day. Maybe I'll want to run at the apartment—especially when it gets cold outside."

"Dane, Nikki, and Brett run outside in the winter." Ian took a sip of coffee.

"When are you going to start running?" Marta said, casting Ian a look out of the corners of her eyes.

Ian sputtered, and coffee dribbled down his chin. "Marta."

She smirked. "What? Exercise is good for you."

"When are you going to *stop* running and get a life?"

Marta looked away to hide the hurt on her face. She'd had a chance, once, to have a life. To have a normal life so many women seemed to want.

She hadn't wanted it then, and foolishly thinking she never would, she'd taken her own choice away.

A full life didn't have to mean babies and marriage, but she was thirty-three years old, and for a woman her age, that meant getting married and starting a family, or start adopting cats.

"That would be counter-productive to my being in Minnesota, then, wouldn't it?" she asked.

Her new job coaching track at the Minnesota State University, Tower City, depended on her running. Many coaches rode bike alongside the students they coached, but she wouldn't be one of them. If they had a long run scheduled, then she would be running right there with them.

She believed nothing would inspire them and spur them on like her participating.

It's what made her time running so special at the university—her coach had done the same for her and her teammates.

After loading her purchases into the trunk of Ian's car, they settled into a booth at Grill, a steakhouse near Dane's running store.

That was one perk of moving back to Tower City—being part of the growing running community and helping plan the Tower City Marathon.

Brett was the director of the giant race and had built it up from scratch.

Dane and Nikki ran the Tower City Running Company shoe and running equipment store. They were all runners, even Brett's fiancée, Alyssa, and they pitched in to give Tower City a close-knit running community.

Hoping he didn't notice, Marta studied Ian over the edge of her leather-bound menu.

They were all runners, except Ian. In college, he hadn't hung out with them because of running, rather, they'd been business majors, and he used his degree to keep Butler's Bar —BB's for short—running after his parents' interest in the bar waned.

"How's business?" she asked after they gave the waitress their drink orders.

Ian set his menu aside and ran a pink packet of sweetener along the backs of his fingers. "It's not bad. Sadie hates helping out, but she's twenty-one and not going to school. I make her work, which doesn't sit well with her but—" He looked away. "Sorry. You don't need to hear about my mess. I just wish she had some direction."

Marta covered Ian's hand with hers. He squeezed her fingers in return, and she was surprised when her heart picked up speed.

She'd never thought of Ian like that, not back in school when she'd been with Brett, and filled with guilt, she pulled her hand back, resting it on the cushioned bench. "I remember being that age. It's difficult knowing what you want to do when you're that young."

Ian continued to run the packet along his hand, making it flip between his long fingers. "That's not true. You knew exactly where you were going."

Marta wished they were still holding hands, but given they were only friends, that would be totally inappropriate. "But I had running. What does Sadie have?"

"Not running. A deadbeat boyfriend. That's about it."

"Then she should find something."

Interrupting their conversation, their waitress brought them waters and coffees and pulled a pad out of her black apron to take their orders.

Marta was starving after shopping and her early morning run, which she'd went on alone. She remained the group's sole hardcore runner; not even Brett ran his own marathon anymore.

After the waitress moved to another table, Ian picked up their conversation while he added the packet of sweetener he'd been playing with to his coffee.

"That's easier said than done. Not everyone wants to jump right back into classes after graduating high school. I let Sadie take some time off, and she liked it. Too much. Now she has no interest, and with her free time, she gets into trouble."

Marta didn't have any experience with girls her age except she used to be one, and Sadie sounded a lot different from herself. "Ship her to your parents then."

"I wish I could. But enough about her. Tell me what you've got going on for the next little while."

Marta told him about the things she had lined up.

She'd have to stay with Dane and Nikki until her furniture arrived. In the fall, she'd help Brett and Nikki with the first annual Tower City women's race, while, of course, the Fall Semester at the university began and she'd start her coaching job.

Her days would be full of training and accompanying her students to meets all over the tristate area. And, if she was lucky, even further.

"It will be nice to have you here," Ian murmured, turning his coffee cup on its saucer.

Marta's cheeks flushed. She wouldn't have given Ian the time of day in school, not like that, but now his words and the look in his eyes when his gaze found hers stirred her heart.

But she remembered what she'd done. Ian deserved better, better than the little she could give him. He'd want a family, children, and she couldn't give him that.

She sighed, relieved when the waitress brought their entrees.

IAN KNEW HE'D said something wrong because Marta fell quiet during their meal and didn't say anything as he paid their bill.

In silence, he drove them to a discount furniture store. He didn't know why telling her it was nice having her back was wrong. It was the truth. He had no one to hang out with, and he was hoping Marta would fill some of his free time.

He wasn't using her, but what would he be doing now if he wasn't testing recliners and couches? He'd be in his apartment above the bar listening to Sadie's stereo blaring.

It was his only saving grace she lived in her own apartment. But even though the walls were thick, they still didn't completely block out the music Sadie played. After waking up past noon, of course.

"This one's nice," he said, settling into a dark green couch. Maybe he could talk her into letting him kill time at her place during the day. There weren't many evenings he wasn't bartending.

Marta sat next to him, hugging her purse to her stomach. "Yeah, it's not bad."

She was such a runner, he thought, shaking his head in amusement at her black and pink running leggings and matching neon pink running shirt. The ever-present running shoes were on her feet. She'd tried to put on a little makeup, but her hair was in its usual mess, making her look like she'd taken an afternoon romp in bed.

He tried to lean away when her scent reached his nose, but the armrest blocked him in and there was nowhere to go. Christ, he didn't need a hard-on in the middle of the store.

He'd hoped the years that had gone by would have faded his feelings from so long ago.

But it seemed the saying, "absence makes the heart grow fonder" was true in his case, and instead of the feelings going away, when he'd seen her at Dane and Nikki's engagement party a couple months ago, they'd strengthened to intolerable levels.

Marta moved on to the beds, and he reluctantly followed her to the back of the store where wall-to-wall mattresses were on display.

Shoving his hands into the pockets of his jeans, he watched her flop from mattress to mattress. "Aren't they all the same?" he asked, rolling a piece of gum between his teeth with his tongue, focusing on the minty flavor.

Stay down.

Speaking to the ceiling she said, "No. Firm, medium, soft. You know."

"Like the Three Little Bears."

She lifted to her elbows. "Yeah. Like that. Try this one."

"I'm good." The last thing he needed was to lie on a bed with Marta because it was the only thing he wanted to do.

"I need your opinion," she said, lying back, shoving a plastic-covered pillow underneath her head.

"I won't be the one sleeping in your bed." He snapped his mouth shut.

"Can you just come over here?"

He clenched his jaw, mortified he slipped. "Fine."

Gingerly, he lay next to her, the plastic crackling under his body. There was enough room that they both lay comfortably side-by-side on the queen-sized mattress.

He adjusted, wiggling his ass, feeling weird to be on a bed with his shoes on, and his hand brushed hers. To prevent it from happening again, he laced his fingers and tucked them under his head.

"How's this?" she asked.

He resented her acting so nonchalant about their hands touching when the contact set his whole body on fire.

Rolling to his side, he propped his head in his hand and studied her face.

So much strain, so much pain.

She didn't think anyone could see it, but he did—the toll her career put on her body.

Running was like modeling, football, or baseball. You were old at thirty. It's probably why she took the coaching job, because she knew her time running competitively was coming to an end.

He wished he could make her life easier; he wished she would find something different to do. Wanting to give her something, anything, he leaned down and kissed her, rubbing his lips across hers in a light, feathery kiss.

"Can I help you?"

Dressed in a three-piece suit, a salesman stood at the end of the mattress frowning at their public display of affection.

Marta rolled off the bed and treated the salesman to a dazzling smile, her hands clasped behind her. "We'll take it."

MARTA WANDERED THROUGH what used to be the business building of the city's state university—her alma mater. She'd been devastated to find out they had almost razed that section of the school to construct a new wing, but at the last minute they'd turned the hall into additional classrooms for English.

With the help of a donor, the university had purchased an old parking lot and built an entirely new business center instead.

The rooms were the same, the smell of must and dust the same, and it seemed as if there was the same carpeting peeling away from the floor.

It was in these rooms she'd met Brett, given him her heart.

She'd been too young for it, to be that much in love, and with such a damaged man. Her heart had paid the price, and little had she known, so had Ian.

She'd been too oblivious to see the affection he'd held for her, but she'd seen it yesterday, he'd made sure of it when he kissed her.

Her lips fizzed at the thought, and she traced her upper lip, lost in the memory.

"There you are."

Marta tore her eyes away from an empty classroom that still had an old chalkboard attached to the wall. The desks had been moved away giving the janitor space to vacuum the floor.

"Holly, hi."

"I saw you come into the building, but I was across campus, and in these heels . . ." she trailed off, lifting a foot. She wore strappy sandals with a four-inch heel in a color matching the bright green sundress she wore.

Holly Carole made Marta feel like a dwarf and a freak. She'd never had any sense of style, instead always relieved her running clothes came in matching colors.

And heels. Good Lord.

Holly's heels made Marta's feet ache just looking at them.

"Are you free for that cup of coffee?" Holly asked, gripping a black binder close to her chest.

Having finished a meeting with Coach Wesley and the Athletics Director of the university, Gregory Spaulding, she'd wandered campus, concerned by just what her new position was going to entail.

Due to their exceptional track program, the university

was losing prospective students to another school four hours away, and the athletics director dumped it on Marta's shoulders to make the track program at the Minnesota State University, Tower City more appealing.

She had no idea how she was going to accomplish that, and the situation worried her.

"Sure," Marta said, and she trotted down the short stairway to the main hallway.

"Are you settling in all right?" Holly asked, leading her outside into the sunshine.

"Not too terribly," she said. "I found an apartment quickly—I moved into Dane's because he's living with Nik —" Marta clamped a hand over her mouth, horrified. How many times could she be so stupid?

"God, Marta. You don't have to feel like that every time Dane's name comes up. He's a mutual acquaintance. It's bound to happen."

"You're too understanding," she muttered, following Holly into the student exchange.

The building had been renovated since Marta went to school there.

The top floor was now an open space designed for studying and hanging out with friends, complete with a huge flat screen TV that played soap operas and talk shows.

The ground floor contained a Starbucks and a sit-down restaurant staffed by work-study students, and in the basement, a non-alcoholic dance club was open to students on the weekends.

In the café Marta ordered a skinny vanilla latte, and she sat at a small round table across from Holly.

"I don't mind talking about Dane. I'm glad he's happy," Holly said, smoothing her hair. "Don't you have an ex you care about?"

She thought about Brett. They were friends, but he was engaged to Alyssa now. It wasn't her place to care about him.

Marta shook her head.

Leaning forward, Holly said, "Someone in the present then?"

"Maybe."

She took a sip of her latte. She didn't want to talk about Ian, either, but Holly tilted her head and narrowed her eyes. The other woman wouldn't let her off the hook.

"Is he in California? Is he a runner like you?"

"No to both. He's here in Tower City. He runs a bar downtown."

Holly laughed, the smooth sound frothing from her coral-painted lips. "Didn't you luck out then, when the school offered you a position? New job, new apartment, new guy. You've got your hands full."

When Holly put it that way, she did sound like she had a lot going on. But her apartment was put together, and she didn't see Ian as much as she would have liked—he was always at the bar.

Coaching would take most of her time once she started, but she still had four weeks before attending the first practice.

Coach Wesley would show her the ropes and introduce her to the kids.

If the athletics director had his way, she'd be present at more meetings like the one she'd gone to that morning, but she hoped she wouldn't have to do that. Promotion was supposed to be the public relations department responsibility, not hers.

"Not really," Marta said, watching two stick-thin blonde girls wearing backpacks and holding folders order coffees.

They must have been on their way to a summer class. "Ian is busy at the bar all the time."

"Ian Butler?" Holly asked before taking a sip of her coffee.

"Yeah," Marta said, surprised. "How did you know?"

"Dane and I dated for three years. I know who his friends are. When you said a bar downtown, I didn't know you were talking about BB's. How is Ian doing?"

Marta pictured the gruff look in Ian's grey eyes and the tense line of his scruffy jaw. "He's changed a lot from the boy I knew in college."

"Has he fallen on hard times?"

A long time ago Marta had resigned herself to the fact she would never be close to Alyssa, and Nikki was Alyssa's best friend. Marta needed to make her own friends in Tower City, and she decided to confide in Holly as a start.

"Not that way." Marta tapped her short, unpainted fingernails on the sticky green lacquer of the table. "Dane said he'd had a crush on me in school, and I broke his heart when I moved to California."

Holly's brown eyes sparkled. "And he's waited for you all these years."

"I wouldn't go that far."

"But he *is* still single."

"Yeah."

"And he still wants you."

Marta thought of Ian's kiss in the furniture store. "Yeah."

"Then girl, what are you waiting for?"

SHE KNEW WHY she was waiting, and it wasn't good.

What would Ian say when he found out the truth?

Maybe he already knew, but Marta doubted it.

She'd told Alyssa, and she hoped revealing her secret helped Alyssa and Brett move past the roadblocks in their relationship.

Ian wouldn't be so receptive if he knew; she was sure of it. It was probably better if she didn't become close to him. He'd ultimately want something she couldn't give.

As she lay in bed that night, she thought of Ian's kiss. His lips had been warm and firm, kind of like the no-nonsense person he'd grown into.

He'd lost a lot of the fun, and as she woke up her phone to check the time, she hoped it wasn't because of her. She refused to believe he was still single because he'd been waiting for her.

Her phone chimed with a text. She bobbled it—the wind chimes sounded louder in the middle of the night—and she dropped it onto the floor.

It was almost two in the morning, and no one delivered good news in the middle of the night.

Leaning over the edge of the bed, she grabbed the phone off the carpet.

Are you awake? Ian's text asked.

Yeah.

It wasn't unusual for Ian to be awake at this hour—his bar didn't close until two. She tried to make herself relax, and she flopped onto her back to hold her phone more easily.

Sadie hasn't been in all night, and she was supposed to work her shift. I haven't seen her since yesterday. Can you help me look for her?

Of course.

Marta hoped it wasn't anything serious.

Sadie was twenty-one and had the right to go off on her own. But it was late, and if Ian hadn't seen her since yesterday . . .

Thanks. I'll pick you up in ten minutes.

Do you want me to ask Dane and Nikki to help? Marta pushed Send, then slid out of bed to change.

No, thanks. I'm going to drive around—I don't want to be alone.

Okay, I'll be ready.

In the dark, under the summer moon, Marta paced nervously in front of her building waiting for Ian to pick her up.

The humid air pressed down on her, and sweat slid down her back. She choose a star and wished with all her strength they would find Sadie safe, and that everything would be okay.

IAN WASN'T HAPPY he'd resorted to texting Marta.

He could have called Brett, or Dane, like Marta suggested, but bothering them in the middle of the night didn't feel right.

Besides, he preferred spending time with her, and her presence calmed him. He relaxed his death grip on the steering wheel as she adjusted her seatbelt.

"What's going on?" she asked as he drove out of her building's parking lot.

The residential area was dark—everyone was sleeping, not even a squirrel ran across the street looking for a game of tag or a midnight snack.

"I try not to be too hard on her—she's technically an

adult," Ian said, casting Marta a quick look out of the corner of his eye.

Sadie was the same age now as they'd been when they attended the university, and knowing how wild they'd acted at that age didn't give him any reassurances.

"But usually she's not this careless. She won't answer my texts, and her line goes straight to voicemail."

"Has she done this before?" Marta asked, looking out the passenger window.

"Not for such a long time."

"Where are we going to look?"

"I know a few of her hiding spots."

It might take a while to check all the places he had in mind, but he hoped she would turn up at one of them.

"She's probably fine."

"That's all you got for me?"

"Well, I'm not going to offer false hope." Marta shifted in her seat. "Tower City isn't crime-free. Even Nikki ran into trouble last year. You never know."

Ian had forgotten about Nikki walking into the middle of two thieves stealing from Dane's store, and a chill traveled down his spine. Just because he didn't see crime happening didn't mean it wasn't there.

The idea made him sick.

"Yeah, you're right—and Sadie has her share of luck finding trouble."

"I can't imagine how hard it's been to keep tabs on her."

Ian turned onto a street lined with older apartment buildings. "It hasn't been easy, but I love her," he murmured, scanning the buildings, looking for the address where Sadie's on again, off again, boyfriend lived.

"I don't know if that makes it better or worse."

"It makes it worse, Marta. Caring for someone always makes it worse."

In the soft glow of the streetlights, Marta swallowed. She was thinking about them—how he'd been in love with her.

The subject was a huge elephant in his little car.

"We can talk about it," Ian said, parking in an empty space. He didn't care if it belonged to anyone or not—he wouldn't be around long enough to be in anyone's way.

Marta followed him up the cracked sidewalk littered with weeds and empty beer cans. "Talk about what? Where are we?"

"How I felt about you in college."

Ian looked over his shoulder, a smile lurking around the corners of his mouth.

He didn't know what it was about her that made him want her so much. She'd rolled out of bed to help him, and it showed. Dressed in sloppy running pants and a Tower City Marathon t-shirt should have made her look unkept, but the clothes made her look adorable and her messy hair pushed away from her face with a running headband added to her appeal.

Before she could respond, he opened the glass door of the building. "Sadie's boyfriend lives here. I figured instead of driving all over hell and back, I'd try the sure thing first."

"Why did you ask me to come with you if you knew where she was?"

"Because if she's here and she's hurt, I'll need you to keep me from killing the son of a bitch."

Ian used his car key to jiggle the deadbolt loose just enough to pull the door open.

"Nice."

"Nothing I haven't had to do before."

Trent wouldn't let him in otherwise; they'd been through this more than once.

He followed the sounds of a party up two flights of stairs and down a beige-carpeted hallway.

The building wasn't terrible as apartments went, but there were nicer ones to choose from if you needed a place to live. At least he knew there wasn't a meth lab set up in the bathroom. That honor went to complexes across town and to the sleazy trailer park north of the city.

He pounded on the door and then turned the knob, the scent of pot and the thumping bass of music hitting him in the face the moment the door cracked open.

Kids crowded the kitchen mixing drinks from an obscene amount of alcoholic choices lining the counter, and none of them gave him or Marta a second glance.

He didn't see Sadie.

The pot smell grew stronger in the little living room. A movie he didn't recognize played on the huge flat screen TV. Kids were lying everywhere—on the couch, in beanbag chairs, or on the floor—doped out and watching TV while they sipped drinks.

"Anyone know where Trent is?" Ian shouted.

"In the bedroom, man," said a guy who sat in a recliner with a half-naked woman draped across his lap.

"Were we this bad?" he asked Marta over the music.

"Worse," she yelled, covering her ears.

In the bathroom, a keg sat in a stained white bathtub, and a young punk sitting on the closed toilet held a fistful of cash. A stack of red Solo cups sat next to him on the sink vanity. "A dollar a cup," the guy mumbled around a cigarette dangling from his lips.

Ian grimaced. "No thanks. I'm looking for Trent or Sadie."

"Trent's in his bedroom." His eyes moved away when a young woman wearing Daisy Dukes and a pink tank top hedged around Ian with an empty cup.

Ian stepped back, and his ass bumped into Marta. "Sorry."

"No, that's okay. I was looking . . ."

Across the hall, a bedroom door gaped wide open. On the unmade bed, a naked woman with ratty blonde hair sat on top of an equally naked male. They were too drunk or stoned to care everyone could see what they were doing. Or maybe it was everyone else who didn't care.

Ian did.

"Son of a bitch." He ripped Trent out of the bed, toppling the woman off the mattress and onto the floor where she landed in a heap and started crying.

"What the fuck?" Trent whipped his head around as if he didn't recognize where he was.

"Where's Sadie, asshole?" Ian grasped the lowlife by the shoulders and pushed him against a poster of a hot new country band.

"Sadie?" Trent asked.

His pupils were dilated, but his eyes didn't see a goddamned thing.

"What the fuck?"

"I'm looking for my sister, moron. Where is she?" Ian shook Trent's shoulders, and his head banged against the wall. It didn't anything to sober him up.

Ian couldn't understand what his sister saw in the scumbag he had pinned against the wall.

Trent colored his hair jet black and wore the same colored eyeliner smeared under his eyes. Scrawny, his ribs stuck out under pasty white skin, and he smelled like sex, cigarettes, and booze.

Trent jerked away and pulled a pair of dirty grey sweat-pants off a floor cluttered with crusted dishes and beer cans.

"I fuckin' don't know," he said as he unsteadily lifted one foot and then the other to pull his pants up.

Ian was grateful he didn't have to see his little dick anymore. It probably wasn't any bigger than his brain.

Trent sat on the edge of the bed, his eyes flickering between Ian and the sobbing still coming from the floor. "We had a fight about Gabby," he said nodding his head at the girl, tears running in rivers down her face, "and she took off."

"She didn't go home," Ian said through clenched teeth.

His sister's disappearance made more sense now.

"I fuckin' don't know. I haven't heard from her. Now get the fuck out. I need a drink."

Ian grabbed Marta's hand and led her through the apartment that seemed even more crowded than it had when they'd arrived.

It was difficult for Ian to hold onto his anger when he could empathize with his sister so strongly.

Nothing like having your heart broken to make you go off the deep end.

Marta's skin felt smooth and warm in his grasp, and Ian enjoyed the contact as they walked through the hallway and down the stairs, the music fading behind them.

Reluctantly, he dropped her hand to pull his cell phone out of his pocket.

He dialed 911 and gave the dispatch the address. "There's a party in this building. Pot. Lots of it. Maybe some underaged drinking."

"What's your name, sir?" the bored-sounding female asked.

"Tim Smith."

Ian disconnected the call before she could ask him anymore questions. He would already be on Sadie's shit list for looking for her, but if she found out he called the cops on her boyfriend, she'd never talk to him again.

"Tim Smith?" Marta asked, her lips twitching.

"I didn't want to give my name. Let's go. I have a few other places to look. If I don't find her, I'll have to call the cops. Even if they don't do anything about it, at least my call will be on record."

It wasn't until he was driving down the empty street when Marta spoke. "How long have you been taking care of her?"

Ian grinned in satisfaction when a bright red light flashed in his rear-view mirror. It must have been a slow night in Tower City for the cops to respond so quickly to a kegger.

"Since she turned seventeen. One winter Dad tangled with a snowplow and lost, and it soured him on living here. Some of Mom's family lives in Georgia, and they decided to move down toward Savannah. Sadie didn't want to change schools right before her senior year of high school. I could understand that, and I said I'd watch out for her. She was okay for a while, but a girl that age needs a mom."

Ian turned the car around a corner.

"She needed guidance. She started yelling at me all the time, said I couldn't stand in for Mom and Dad, that I couldn't boss her around."

"And by then it was too late to send her to your parents?"

"I couldn't force her onto a plane. Still can't. At this point, the only thing I can do is give up, and I won't do that. I don't have it in me."

Ian thought that could be true of Marta, too.

She didn't say anything, which was fine. He didn't know where he stood with her, and he didn't know her feelings about Brett, either. She could still be in love with him, and he couldn't compete. He couldn't then, and he couldn't now.

Marta living in Tower City again was more than what he thought he'd ever have, and Ian didn't want to press the subject. He couldn't live with himself if he made her run like Brett did.

"You're a good person," Marta murmured, breaking the silence.

The heaviness that had accompanied them on the way to Trent's apartment returned.

And one day, hopefully good enough for you.

MARTA WAS TORN between hoping he meant her, too, as well as his sister, and not wanting to read too much into the things he said.

Eleven years was a long time to wait for someone.

"Where are we going next?" Marta asked, smothering a yawn. The late, or early, hour was catching up with her.

"We're here," Ian said, pulling into the empty parking lot of a city park near the university.

"Oh, my God." Marta scrambled out of the car. "I haven't been here for years."

When everyone grew tired of hanging out in the dorms, the city park was a refuge, rain, shine, or snow.

She'd come here frequently with Brett to run the trails, go for a picnic, or to sunbathe in the summer sunshine. Sometimes they all went along—the group of them—and spent the day playing Frisbee and drinking beer they smuggled into the park.

"It hasn't changed much," Ian said, taking her hand again and leading her down a darkened path. "It's still a place to get drunk, hide from your parents—and the cops. Sadie likes to come here, and if she had a fight with Trent, I bet she'd run here to lick her wounds."

Nothing was different, except some of the grilling and bathroom shelters looked repaired, and the playground equipment had been updated. The rest looked the same, from the acres of lush grass to the bridge that spanned the Ruby River.

Marta cocked her head, listening for any indication they weren't alone. She heard nothing but the early morning wind in the trees and the strumming of vehicles from the poor slobs already on their way to work, or the lucky ones finally going home.

The sky was losing its blackness, but the sun still had at least an hour before it would treat them to a stunning Minnesota summer sunrise.

Walking on a trail she used to run frequently alone and with Brett, she held Ian's hand. To outsiders catching a quick look, they could have been lovers taking a leisurely stroll—hands clasped, arms brushing in a familiarity they hadn't lost despite the years between them.

"It's so quiet," she said, to break the unnerving silence. "Do you think Sadie's here?"

Ian squeezed her hand. "I don't know, but thanks for helping me."

"I don't mind." She paused. This wasn't the time or place to ask, but the words left her mouth before she could stop them. "Do you think one day you'll want kids?"

With her heart in her throat, Marta waited for a

response. Not that it mattered any—or she tried to pretend it didn't.

"Prob—Wait. Did you hear that?"

Marta couldn't hear anything over the blood rushing in her ears. "No. What?"

"Listen."

Marta heard it then—a squeaking, a sniffling, like a young girl trying to hold back her tears.

"I think that's Sadie, over by the skating rink."

Ian took off toward the wooden ring full of grass and weeds this time of year. She peered through the glimmer of darkness, and a figure sat perched on a bench near the warming house.

He knelt, gathered the crying brunette against his chest, and she rested her head on his shoulder.

Marta envied Ian's sister. Envied her the comfort she was able to find in someone's arms.

When she'd fled to California, she'd had nothing and no one. Or she felt like she hadn't. Her parents had done their best, but at that age, nothing but time could have repaired her broken heart.

Cradling Sadie in his arms, Ian stood, adjusted his sister's weight before taking a step forward.

"She's hungry and scared, but she'll be okay. I'll drop you at your apartment before I take her home."

Marta sat in the cramped backseat while Sadie sniffled in front of her.

The sun was breaking over the horizon when Ian pulled into her parking lot.

"Thanks for helping—I appreciate it."

"It's no problem," she said, opening the car door, the squeak breaking through the still morning. "I'm just glad you found her."

"Me, too. I'll call you later."

Wearily, wishing she were still with them, Marta stood in the quiet as Ian drove away.

———

"WHAT YOU DID was stupid and selfish," Ian yelled at Sadie later that day.

He hadn't gone to bed after dropping Marta at her apartment. He'd been too pissed to calm down enough to sleep.

He stood behind the bar, tired, grouchy, and feeling hungover. Pissed to be in the middle of another useless sparring match, he glowered at her across the gleaming black floor.

"What I do is my own goddamned business." She slammed a chair onto the floor with such force it fell over.

"Not when you make me sick with worry. All you had to do was answer your phone."

He rubbed his forehead with the back of his hand, all the fight leaving him. His sister was old enough to take care of herself. Only, he couldn't bring himself to wash his hands of her because she felt like their mom and dad already had.

"It died."

That was all she said, and his temper rose again. "Then come home, work your shift like the grownup you keep telling me you are. You want me to treat you like an adult—you have to earn it."

When she turned her back to him and began placing the remaining chairs onto the floor, albeit more calmly, he knew that would be all he'd get out of her.

Ian sighed, prepared for another long, boring shift.

CHAPTER TWO

"WE HIRED YOU because Coach Wesley thinks you would be an asset to the university. I'm having a difficult time believing that, Miss Braddock."

Marta flinched.

The Athletics Director, Gregory Spaulding, splayed his hands against the clean blotter laying on a desk that looked like it was worth more than two years of her running earnings.

Spaulding's secretary had been called her into his office for an impromptu meeting. Poor timing, her head reeled from lack of sleep.

"Shouldn't we wait for Coach Wesley?" she asked, looking around Spaulding's office, unable to meet the man's eyes.

"He won't be joining us." He snapped his fingers in front of her face. "Look at me. I wanted to speak to you alone. Coach Wesley and I have differing opinions on how the track team should be handled. We're hemorrhaging students, and I'm taking this opportunity to rectify that."

Her cheeks heated in shame, humiliated to be treated

like a dog with the attention span of a toddler. "What can I do?"

"Coach Wesley assured me your name was enough to bring recognition to our team. It's not. We could have had Libbie Layne, but I took Wesley at his word you'd be good for the university. I was brought in to shape up the entire athletics department—not only track. Our football team hasn't won a game in years. Basketball, men's and women's, is in the toilet. This isn't the same school as it was twenty years ago, even ten years ago."

Marta nodded, not trusting herself to speak. They'd chosen her over Libbie Layne—a marathon goddess from Minnesota—whom Marta had lost to on more than one occasion. "

I'm willing to do whatever you need me to do, sir," she murmured, scared of the man and the rage simmering in the heat of his icy blue eyes.

"Damn straight you will," Spaulding hollered, slamming his fist on the desk making a dish of paperclips dance. "You run, I think you know how, you run your ass to the PR department and tell them to do their goddamn jobs. I want press releases, a fucking press conference. I want the Tower City Journal to do a write-up."

He sucked in a breath and with shaking hands smoothed his tie. "Coach Wesley went to bat for you—don't make him regret it. Now get out."

Marta didn't need to be told twice, and she scrambled from her seat like a scared little kid being dismissed from the principal's office.

She ran down the hallway past locker rooms and weight rooms, past the pool. The chemical scent of chlorine plugged her nose, and she took a deep breath when she made it outside, the reddish-brown track spread out before her.

Wiping her eyes, she leaned against the building.

She'd never been spoken to like that before—never by someone in the industry. She knew Coach Wesley hadn't been privy to Spaulding's meeting with her. There was no way the mild-mannered coach would ever let someone raise his voice to her like that.

Not wanting to risk Spaulding's wrath if he caught her crying and loitering outside, she walked across campus to the building that housed the administration offices.

Sleep deprivation hadn't helped her deal with Spaulding's abuse. She should have taken a nap before meeting him.

She found a restroom and splashed cold water onto her face rinsing away her tears. The chill against her skin woke her up, and she hoped the people in the public relations office made coffee.

When Marta asked if there was someone she could speak with, the secretary explained Mr. Spaulding had called ahead, and someone was already waiting to meet with her.

The tall curvy woman ushered Marta into a conference room, the windows looking over the campus's square, and blessedly gave her a mug and a carafe full of coffee. As Marta sipped, she prepared to spend the afternoon sorting out her future.

DRAINED, MARTA SANK into the seat of her beat-up car. She shouldn't have been in such a hurry to choose a vehicle; she didn't think the car would make it through the winter.

Plus she'd need to plug it in—Dane's apartment hadn't come with a garage.

That was another choice she was regretting, but it had been convenient to move into the empty space instead of starting a new search.

Closing her eyes in defeat, she rested her head against the back of the seat. There were a lot of things she was regretting now.

Marta drove to Ian's, turning the radio to a station playing pop music, hoping the cheery beat would lift her spirits.

After navigating the rush hour traffic, Marta parked in front of BB's.

She looked forward to a glass of wine and some conversation with Ian, and she groaned when Sadie stood behind the bar, sprinkling change into the register.

It didn't look like the girl was dropping the coins into the correct slots, letting them rain from her palm in a steady stream, the silver and copper falling where they may.

Sadie looked up when the door opened, and she frowned at her.

After the humiliating meeting she'd just endured, she wasn't about to sit through another. If things turned ugly, she'd bail, simple as that.

"I was looking for Ian," Marta said, approaching the bar.

"I figured," Sadie said, slamming the register shut. "He's upstairs."

Not letting Sadie's attitude deter her, Marta slid onto a stool.

She'd been building up to a glass of Moscato, and now there was nothing she wanted more. Her mouth watered, already tasting the sweetness on her tongue. "Would you mind if I ordered a glass of wine? Is Ian coming down?"

"I'm not a fucking bartender, so he better." Sadie pulled a wineglass from underneath the bar.

Sadie fill it with a very expensive red.

The girl either wanted to charge her twenty bucks or couldn't tell a glass of good wine from a cup of Kool-Aid.

"Thanks."

"Uh." Sadie pulled her phone out of the back pocket of her jeans.

Taking a sip, the fruity flavor fizzed pleasantly in her mouth, and Marta welcomed the buzz as the liquid slid to her stomach.

When Sadie didn't make a move to abandon her, Marta flailed in the silence. "Men, huh?" she asked, attempting some kind of camaraderie.

"Assholes," Sadie said without bothering to look away from her phone.

Sadie was a pretty girl—slim, decent boobs. Her hair sparkled either from health or dye, and her skin shone clear and luminescent.

Unlike hers when she'd been Sadie's age.

By the time Marta turned twenty-one, the sun had marked her skin with a permanent tan.

Sadie's features fit her face, except Marta didn't share the appeal all the earrings in her ears.

"Done staring?"

"Just remembering what it was like to be your age," Marta said, then took a huge gulp of wine. She didn't care how expensive it was. This wasn't the time to sip and savor.

"It sucks," Sadie said, finally meeting Marta's gaze.

The hurt in Sadie's eyes took Marta aback, but the girl would shun any sympathy, and she kept it tucked away.

"Only if you let it." Maybe Marta could instill some

wisdom in the poor girl; Sadie didn't have a consistent female role model.

"What can I do?"

"Take control. Stop living for other people."

"There's nothing to take control of," Sadie said, shoving her phone into her pocket. "My life is a pile of shit."

With that, she slammed out of the bar.

Alone, she watched Sadie stomp down the sidewalk until the window gave her up and Marta couldn't see her anymore.

WITH A SHAKING hand, Ian disconnected the call. He'd taken it alone knowing it would be bad, and it was.

He didn't know what to do—he couldn't very well say no. But he had no business saying yes. Sure, he could pass it off and someone else could do what he wasn't willing to do, but that wouldn't make him any kind of man he would be proud to be.

Marta had asked him if he wanted kids. He hadn't answered her which was just as well because he didn't know. It's not like he was in the position of choosing. She was the closest thing he had to a girlfriend, and that wasn't saying much.

Although, he hadn't been the best at trying to reconnect since she'd come back.

He better head downstairs.

Sadie wasn't dependable, and he shouldn't have left her in charge for as long as he had. He didn't have much of a choice though—he'd already played phone tag with the social worker for too long.

It didn't shock him Sadie no longer stood behind the

bar, but he was surprised to see Marta sipping a glass of wine.

The place was empty, which was both good and bad. Good because there wouldn't have been anyone to serve them, bad because every day the ink in the books turned redder and redder.

"Hey, what are you doing here? Have you been alone long?"

"No. Sadie took off a couple minutes ago. No one's been in."

He expected that.

Taking his place behind the bar, a position more comfortable to him than an old pair of jeans, Ian fell into his evening routine. "What's up? I didn't expect to see you today."

He never expected to see her, and it was something he should fix—soon. He should ask her out on a date.

Or something.

Get a handle on how she felt about him, if she even thought of him at all. Maybe he'd been friend-zoned and didn't even know it.

"I had a bad meeting at the university. The athletics director is on my ass about the school's reputation. Like it's my fault the athletics department is going down the tubes." Marta took another sip of wine.

Ian noticed it then, the extra strain. It blended so well with the tension always present on her face that he'd missed it, but it was evident now.

Her eyes widened for a moment when he took her hand, but she didn't pull away, instead giving him a squeeze in return.

"What are they asking you to do?"

"The usual. A press conference, a write up in the paper.

Remind everyone why they chose me, get my name out there. The university is bleeding students, and apparently, I'm supposed to slap a Band-Aid on it and stop it. I don't know how they expect me to do that, but I said I'd do everything I could. Spaulding wasn't impressed."

"Are you thinking you don't want to do that anymore?" Ian asked. From the shelf behind him, he pulled out a bottle of wine to top off her glass.

"I don't have much of a choice. I moved here to coach. What would I do if I didn't?"

"What would you want to do?"

"Can I tell you a secret?"

"Yeah, sure," Ian said, pleased she was willing to confide in him.

"Sometimes I wish I could not run."

That wasn't what he expected her to say, and Ian tried not to let his mouth hang open. "Then don't."

Marta took a gulp of wine. "I've been a runner my whole life. I've sacrificed . . . things . . . to be where I am. What would those sacrifices mean if I gave up now?"

Looking away, Ian said, "I guess you would have to figure that out. We all make sacrifices—sometimes they're worth it, and you gain something better. Sometimes they're not, and you lose."

He didn't like where the conversation was going. He'd made sacrifices, too, gave up hopes and dreams, time he would never get back. He was thirty-four years old, managing a bar that wasn't his, living in an apartment he didn't own.

"I gave up some important shit, Ian. I have to make it count."

"You don't have to prove anything to me, love," Ian whispered, hating the tears pooling in her eyes.

"No, only to myself. And I'm the toughest critic of them all."

IAN CLOSED EARLY. He rarely did, unless there was an emergency, or he wasn't feeling well and there wasn't anyone to take his place.

But in the five years since he'd run BB's, those times had been few and far between. It wasn't like he'd be losing any customers, and at nine that night, without guilt, he flipped the sign to Closed. His tread heavy on the narrow stairway leading up to his apartment, he retired for the evening.

Sadie hadn't come back after abandoning the bar, more than likely galavanting around town, up to her ass in trouble.

It was sad to say, but right now, Ian was too tired to care. She'd have to find her own way home; he was too worn-out to do anything about it.

He put off calling his mom and dad, the other situation weighing more heavily on his mind.

The social worker he spoke with earlier hadn't given him much time to think about it, only a day or two to make his decision.

He wished there was an easy answer, an easy way out.

But there never was.

MARTA WOKE THE next morning to Nikki bouncing on her bed.

Groaning, she rolled over. "Go to work or something."

"Or something. Margie is working the store today, and

Dane and I have the day off. Wanna go to the park and have a picnic? Maybe play some Frisbee? Alyssa and Brett will be there, and Dane is texting Ian. It'll be fun. We haven't all been together since the engagement party."

Pulling a pillow over her head, Marta couldn't think of anything less fun. Hanging out with Alyssa and Brett while they made goo-goo eyes at each other didn't sound appealing, neither did watching Dane and Nikki do the "in love" thing.

She and Ian were the only two not paired up, and she didn't want him to feel like everyone was pushing them together.

Still, she did want to be included, wanted to make friends, hang out with the old crowd. Holly couldn't be her only friend in Tower City.

"Can't we do it at a normal hour? What time is it?"

"It's eleven o'clock. Dane and I already had a run. We should have asked you to go, sorry."

Marta peeked from beneath the pillow. "It's okay. I wouldn't have wanted to anyway. I was out the night before helping Ian look for his sister and didn't get any sleep, then I went to a couple of meetings on campus yesterday. I was done in."

"Really?" Nikki asked, frowning. "Did you find her? Is she okay?"

She sat up and adjusted her t-shirt; she didn't need her boobs hanging out of the droopy neckline. "Yeah. She had a fight with her boyfriend. We found her in the park of all places, and Ian brought her home. Sadie's not a very happy girl."

"It's a tough age. I didn't go to university right away like you guys did, and I found my own share of trouble. If you need me to talk to her, I can."

"Thanks. I tried to talk to her yesterday when I stopped to see Ian after my stupid meetings. She's at that age where you can't tell her anything she doesn't already know."

"I know that age all too well. Well, come on. It's gorgeous outside. We have a cooler—you can put your snacks in ours. We want to leave in about an hour, is that okay?"

It gave Marta enough time to make coffee and shower. "Yeah, thanks. I'll come over when I'm ready."

"Great! See you in a bit."

Marta made coffee and took a mug to sip on while she stood under the hot spray.

She didn't have much food and was only able to smear some peanut butter onto two heels of bread. Hoping the others would share some chips or fruit, she filled a bottle with tap water. She was about to wander down the hall to Dane's and Nikki's apartment when her cell phone rang.

"Hello?" she asked, puzzled, not recognizing the number.

"Miss Braddock?"

Marta winced. She recognized the voice of Gregory Spaulding, and it was not a great start to her day. But the sooner she accepted Spaulding was a part of her professional life, the easier it would be to deal with him.

"Yes, speaking, Mr. Spaulding, what can I do for you?"

"The press conference is scheduled for tomorrow morning at ten. You're to be there with a smile pasted on your pretty little face. You're going to talk about how happy you are to be at the university and lay out your plans for the track department."

Marta gulped. Beyond accepting the position, she didn't have any plans for the track department. This was her first coaching job, and she didn't know what she was doing. She'd need to talk with Coach Wesley.

Before she could form the thought into words, Spaulding said, "You'll meet with myself and Coach Wesley before the press conference, and we'll go over everything. Just show up and say what we tell you to say."

Opening her mouth to respond, she was cut off by her cell phone beeping.

Spaulding had hung up on her.

Tomorrow wasn't going to be a very good day.

Ian inhaled the fresh air, enjoying the sun warming his face. He didn't spend as much time outside as the rest of his friends. Being the only non-runner in the group should have made him feel excluded, but it didn't. He'd always listened to the gripes they had about Tower City's running community, Brett's marathon, and Dane's store. It seemed to be part of the bartender package, paying attention with half an ear when people bitched about the day-to-day. He didn't have anything to contribute in the way of running or any aspect of it, and he didn't want to change that.

Alyssa took to it, he thought, watching her throw a Frisbee to the dog she and Brett had found a few months ago at a state park near Tower City. Looking at the dog now, he never would have guessed it'd been close to starved, not with the way he barked happily, showing more interest in chasing butterflies than the Frisbee Alyssa was trying to teach him to catch.

"How's life treating you?" Brett asked, handing Ian a beer they smuggled into the park, like old times.

They had tucked themselves into a corner of the grass

not wanting to bother anybody, and Ian glanced at Marta and Nikki lying on their sides on the ground, watching Alyssa and Hunter play.

"Not bad, not good. Same old, same old," Ian said truthfully. He debated telling Brett and Dane about the phone call he received yesterday.

"An agent picked up our book," Brett said before Ian could say anything more.

"That's great!" Dane clinked his beer bottle with Brett's. "You knew it was good."

"Well, it's good because of Alyssa."

"You two had a bumpy start, huh," Ian asked, fishing for advice. When it came to Marta, he was flopping like a walleye out of water.

"Yeah, but" —Brett lowered his voice— "mostly it was because of Marta."

"You two have a lot of history."

"Yeah, and most of it's bad," Brett said, watching Alyssa laugh over Hunter's antics. "And the deal with my parents didn't help, but Alyssa hung in there."

"Are you going to ask Marta out, now that she's back?" Dane asked Ian, pushing his running sunglasses to the top of his head.

"No. Well, when we were furniture shopping I kissed her—"

Brett and Dane laughed.

"It's not funny. She never said anything about it afterward, and I never tried again."

Brett scoffed. "You have no idea how she feels about you, do you?"

Scowling, Ian said, "I'm still trying to figure out how she feels about *you*."

"She doesn't feel anything for me. We've been over for years."

"Being over doesn't mean she's not still in love with you."

"She's not. But I'm not saying she's ready for a relationship. I have no idea about that. You'll have to ask her yourself."

"I can't. At least, I shouldn't. I got a phone call yesterday. A distant cousin of mine was in a car accident last week. She was killed instantly."

"Sorry to hear that," Dane said. He took a swig of his beer and rested his forearms on his knees.

"What does that have to do with Marta?" Brett asked.

Ian wet his mouth with the last of his beer. "Well, ah, my cousin had her shit together and had a will, you know? And well," he cleared this throat, "she named me guardian of her kid."

"How ARE YOU settling into the city again?" Nikki asked Marta as they watched Alyssa play with Hunter. Tired of lying on the hard ground, they sat at a picnic table not far from the guys who were drinking beer and talking about God knew what.

Marta didn't like the worried look on Ian's face, and she wondered if Sadie was giving him a hard time again.

"It's okay. The apartment is fine, and I like the city, but . . . I don't know. I don't feel at home here."

Nikki rubbed Marta's back. "Homesick for California?"

"Maybe."

Marta grimaced when Nikki bumped her shoulder and said, "No, it's something else. What is it?"

She debated telling Nikki the whole story: the university, the press conference. She didn't know why she was worried about it, because she'd done press conferences before; she'd been the center of attention plenty of times.

If she believed the hype, she was a pillar of the running community, not only in Tower City but The Running Community, and with that came responsibilities of being a role model.

She didn't dope, didn't party, and she didn't do anything stupid. Being scrutinized came with the territory. But she couldn't pinpoint what was bothering her now, except she didn't like the way Spaulding treated her.

"I'm having some issues with the athletics director at the university. He's put a lot on my shoulders, and I don't know if I can do what he wants me to do."

Wiping sweat from her forehead, Alyssa sat next to Nikki and grabbed a bottle of water from the cooler at Nikki's feet.

Marta hadn't hung around Alyssa much since she'd been back.

She didn't feel comfortable around Alyssa, and she still hung onto a small amount of resentment Alyssa spilled her secrets to Brett the first chance she got.

It all worked out for the best, and she needed to put bitter feelings away. She needed to try if she wanted to be included in these kinds of things.

She scrambled for something to say to start a conversation with Alyssa, but Nikki asked, "What's he expecting you to do?"

Marta cast another glance at Ian. Now he was laughing at something Brett said.

Good.

"Turn the athletics department around. Raise enrollment and track participation. He wanted Libbie Layne, but Coach Wesley asked the school to take me on instead. I can't do what Libbie Layne could do for the school. Knowing that now, I wish they would've gone with her."

Nikki whistled.

"Who's Libbie Layne?" Alyssa asked.

"One of the top female runners in the industry. She was born and raised in Minnesota and would have been a perfect pick. She wants to coach somewhere?" Nikki said, leaning to the side to scratch Hunter's head.

"I have no idea. I know she's been struggling with injuries, that could be why she's looking into doing something else. She's getting old like me. She's not as fast as she used to be," Marta said.

"What are they making you do?"

"A press conference is scheduled for tomorrow. Athletics Director Spaulding and Coach Wesley are coming up with ideas to promote the track team. I met with the public relations department and they have other promotional events planned for me. I don't know if I'm a big enough name in the industry to do what they think I can do."

Marta took a deep breath and tried to calm her racing heart. It would all work out. To take her mind off the entire situation, she asked Nikki, "How are wedding things coming along?"

Nikki brightened. "Good. I wanted to ask if you would be a bridesmaid. It'll be perfect. Alyssa's my maid of honor, and Brett is Dane's best man. I know he's going to ask Ian to be a groomsman, and you could pair with him. My sister is going to be my last bridesmaid. Dane is going to have to find another groomsman, but I don't think he'll have any trouble. His dad was talking about a cousin Dane used to be close to." She shrugged. "I'm not sure. But it would be really cool if you said yes."

Out of the corner of her eye, Marta noticed Alyssa scowl. She'd need to clear the air with Brett's fiancée sooner rather than later. She had enough going on at the school she didn't want to put up with conflicts in her personal life, too.

"Can you give me a couple days to think about it?"

"Sure, but don't take too long. I was hoping to start looking for dresses for you guys soon. I finally picked out my wedding dress, so I kind of got a feel for what I want you guys to wear."

"Do you have your colors picked out?" Marta asked.

It warmed her heart to see Dane and Nikki so happy. Marta had known Dane's ex, and while she hadn't seen how Liz had treated him—she'd been in California when Liz and Dane married—she'd heard the horror stories from Brett.

"No, not yet. Maybe one day we can meet at the bridal shop. Some dresses, I think, look better in certain colors, so I'm keeping an open mind."

"I'll let you know as soon as I can. Probably after the press conference. I'll have a better idea if I'll be able to spare the time. I don't want to commit if I can't do it." Marta squeezed Nikki's hand.

"That sounds good, but we're all busy. I'll be on my own with a lot of the wedding details with the marathon going on around that time," Nikki said.

"How's that going?" Marta asked Alyssa, taking the opportunity to draw the woman into conversation. "Your idea to have the high school kids take the pictures turned out fantastic."

Alyssa squinted at her. "You mean he hasn't told you?"

"We don't talk that much," she said, trying to keep the annoyance out of her voice.

"I'm, umm, going to the bathroom," Nikki mumbled, then took off.

What a coward, Marta thought with envy as Nikki sprinted over the brilliant green grass, Hunter chasing her to the shelter where the public restrooms were located.

"Brett doesn't want to direct the marathon anymore," Alyssa said, playing with the white cap of her water bottle. "We're thinking of starting a family, and he doesn't want to put up with that if we have a baby."

Painful prickles ran along Marta's skin.

She'd known all along Brett and Alyssa would one day have children, but she hadn't been aware she'd be around to watch it. "Then what would he do for work?"

Alyssa glanced at the three men who were now throwing the Frisbee she'd been using to play with Hunter.

"Something else, anything else. There's no rush for him to decide—I make enough to support us both. I don't think he understands that gives him the freedom to choose. He's always been on his own, you know?" She blushed.

Of course Marta knew Brett had always been alone. Even when Marta and Brett had been together he'd been alone, unwilling to let her close to him, and eventually, that ruined them.

"Who will direct the marathon?"

"Maybe Dane." Alyssa lowered her voice even though there was no one around to hear. "Nikki told me she wants to have a baby right after the wedding, but if they only count on the profits from Dane's store, they would have a hard time of it."

Alyssa looked over Marta's shoulder, and Marta turned to watch Nikki, who'd come out of the restroom, play a game of tug of war over a stick with Hunter.

"The money Dane would make directing the marathon would help them out," Marta said, filling in the gaps.

"Yeah. With Nikki's and Dane's parents living here, they wouldn't have to pay for childcare. Nikki would manage the store, and Dane would direct the marathon. It could work for them." As Nikki neared, Alyssa whispered, "Don't tell her I told you. She'd be embarrassed. Talking about money is so gauche."

"I understand. Listen Brett and I aren't as close as you seem to think we are."

Alyssa brushed a lock of hair away from her face. "I know. I'm sorry. Brett is still" —Alyssa raised her eyes to the sky, and then back to the wooden table— "hurt over what happened between you two. Talking about having a baby with me is a big step."

"But it's one I'm happy you guys are thinking about taking. I only want him to be happy. I don't resent him for what happened. We were kids and we've both moved on."

She'd tried to move on. But that didn't mean she had.

Not wanting to be the cause of any problems between Brett and Alyssa, she said, "I think you need to be more worried about the lasting effect of how Brett's parents treated him. Him knocking me up wasn't the reason we didn't make it. It was what he'd grown up with all his life that ended us."

"I know, I'm sorry. I . . . you were his only real relationship before me, and it's difficult not to be jealous of your history."

"There's no reason for that. We had more than our share of problems, and we didn't work out. It's a miracle we're still friends, but in the long run that helped, don't you think?"

"Yeah, you're right. It will just take us time to settle into our relationship. How are you and Ian?"

"Yeah, how are you and Ian?" Nikki said, plopping onto the bench next to Marta smelling of sunscreen and sweat.

Marta looked away. She was more comfortable talking about other people than she was talking about her self. "What about us? The fact that there is no us?"

"No, the fact he can't keep his eyes off you?" Nikki asked.

"I don't know what you mean."

"He was so distracted by you earlier the Frisbee beaned him on the side of his head." Nikki giggled.

"I haven't noticed," Marta muttered, her cheeks pinking.

With eyebrows raised, Nikki said, "Then you better start because he's coming this way."

It was a pleasure for Ian to watch Marta talk and laugh with Alyssa and Nikki. The more welcome she felt in Tower City, the less of a chance there was of her leaving to go home to California.

Now the thought entered his mind, he realized that had been a worry since Brett told him she was moving here. No one would put up with the harsh winters if they didn't have to. He didn't want to think about what he would do if Marta left him again.

"Hey, can we talk?"

He sounded more serious than he meant to, but he needed her advice. And there was something worrying her, he could tell by the look in her eyes, and he wanted to find out what it was.

"Yeah, sure."

"Bring the dog," Alyssa called after them.

With the way Hunter was already running across the expanse of grass toward the bridge spanning the Ruby River, they didn't have much choice.

As they followed the dog, albeit more slowly, Ian had to laugh at Marta's clothes.

She wore her usual running outfit—her tennis shoes, compression socks stopping at her knees, a black and pink running skirt and a pink racerback tank with a black sports bra underneath. A black and pink running headband held her hair in place, and sunglasses rested on the top of her head.

The last time he'd seen her wear regular clothes was at Dane's and Nikki's engagement party. She'd looked like a real person, not a mannequin for a sports store. He wished she'd dress like that more often. Human.

She was much more than a runner, but that was all she seemed to see in herself.

"So . . . what's up?" Marta asked, kicking at a pinecone from one of the evergreen trees liberally dotting the park.

"I need your advice."

"With Sadie?"

Ian shoved his hands into the pockets of his basketball shorts. "No. I was on the phone yesterday when you came in. I found out some news, and I need to make a decision about something important."

They stood off to the side of the path, and a group of kids raced past them on bikes, flying over the bridge.

Being a kid had been so easy, and he envied them, probably biking to one kid's house where his mother would feed them peanut butter and jelly sandwiches and then they would wash them down with chocolate milk before zipping out of the house to the next adventure.

He stopped on the middle of the bridge and focused on the murky water flowing under them.

"Whatever I can do to help, let me know," Marta said, leaning against the thick metal rails made to keep stupid people from falling into the river or jumping off for fun.

"Do you mean that?" Ian asked. He prayed she did because if he took this on, he would need it.

Sadie was more trouble than help; Ian wouldn't find it there, no matter how much he begged.

"Yeah, sure. Of course. We're friends, aren't we?"

Ian rested his shoulder against the rail and pinned Marta with his gaze. "I don't know, Marta, are we? Where have you been all these years? You kept in touch with Dane and Brett, but you didn't give a shit about me, huh? Barely an email, not even a phone call in over ten years."

"Where is this coming from?" Marta took a step back.

Ian sighed. "I don't know. It's not your fault I was in love with you. What was I to you, anyway? A drinking buddy? A study buddy? Brett did whatever he did, and you took off. I can't blame you for not looking back."

Marta stared at the water, resting her wrists on the rail, and she twisted her fingers together. "I asked about you, you know. Every time I talked to Dane or Brett, I asked how you were doing. I didn't forget about you—I honestly didn't know how you felt until Dane told me, and that wasn't even that long ago."

"So what exactly do you feel for me now? Friendship? More? Are we going to move from study buddies to fuck buddies?"

"I don't need to listen to this," she snapped. "I didn't know, and I wouldn't have known what to do with it even if

I had. Brett hurt me, and I ran. I wasn't thinking beyond that, okay? Stop blaming me for a relationship we didn't have."

"I'm sorry," he said, running his fingers along the orange rust of the coarse handrail. "Believing you hadn't given me a second thought hurt more than I realized."

"I did think about you, but I was licking my wounds in California and trying to build a life. Yet, here I am, back in Minnesota, so apparently that didn't work so well. What do you want with me? What do you want me to do?"

"Kiss me," he said, pulling her lithe body into his arms.

Running made her so tiny, so thin, hugging her was almost like holding a child, and he took advantage of her weight and height, boosting her onto the rail. She wrapped her legs around his hips pulling him closer.

Her lips were soft, and she tasted of nothing but her. Not of the beer they'd brought, not of any kind of food.

No, he thought as she devoured her warmth, she tasted of only herself, the pain of the past, the bitterness of broken dreams, of her shredded heart. He tasted all that on his tongue, and he wanted to eat her whole, from the outside in, and repair the damage the world had done to her.

Ian broke the kiss before he drowned.

Gasping, Marta rested her forehead against his shoulder. "What was that?" she whispered.

He wanted to answer, "Love." At least, it was for him. Always had been, always would be.

He didn't know what it was for her. While he caught his breath, he watched the birds as they flew overhead and the clouds cover the sun.

"It was just a kiss," he finally said when the silence stretched too thin.

"Right. It was only a kiss."

She let her legs fall from his waist, but she let him hold her in place, keeping her from sliding off the narrow perch. When she ran her fingers along his arms, the hair on the nape of his neck stood on end and his stomach rolled in desire.

He could take her here, just like this. Slowly. Savoring.

Showing her eleven years of loneliness in one heated session of lovemaking.

"What did you want to talk about?" Marta asked, gripping his elbows for balance.

He rested his forearms against the metal on both sides of her hips. "The day you were at the bar with Sadie, I was upstairs."

"Yeah, I remember," she said, meeting his eyes and smoothing a hand through his hair.

He leaned into her touch, took the support she offered. "A social worker called me—"

"Hey, you guys! It's getting late," Dane called to them, his hands cupped around his mouth, his voice carrying across the grass. "We need to get going."

Ian grabbed his cell phone out of his back pocket. "Shit. It *is* late. I need to head back and open the bar."

"But what were you going to tell me?" Marta asked as she landed on the splintered wood of the bridge. "What about a social worker? Is Sadie in trouble?"

"No, nothing like that, though I wouldn't have been surprised," Ian said, grabbing her hand. "Can we talk tomorrow? Before the bar opens? Can we do breakfast or something?"

Marta shook her head. "No, I can't. I need to be at the university for a press conference."

"I'll go with you. What time?"

"You don't need to be there."

Ian grinned, shaking off the prior intimacy. They were back to standing on the solid ground of friendship.

"And what? Miss my favorite famous runner in action? I don't think so."

"Fine, if you want to crawl out of bed for it. I need to be there at nine to prepare, and the conference starts at ten o'clock."

"I can do that. Then we'll go to breakfast."

"I'll let you buy me brunch. I'll need booze after that."

"Sure thing," Ian agreed, following their friends to the parking lot.

MARTA'S STOMACH PITCHED as Ian parked his car in the university parking lot.

The press conference was being held at the student exchange, and unfortunately, they were early enough Ian had been able to park in the lot attached to the building. They wouldn't have to walk far, and she'd been counting on the few extra minutes to prepare.

She sat in the seat, but she couldn't make herself unlatch the seatbelt.

"It's going to be okay," Ian said covering her hand with his.

His rich voice didn't soothe her, or the way he rubbed his thumb along her knuckles. "I hope so. I don't have a good feeling about this."

"What can they say? It's just an official announcement you're going to coach the track team. It's not a big deal, is it?"

It *didn't* sound like a big deal, not when he put it that way.

But Ian hadn't been there the day Spaulding yelled at her, practically placing the blame on her that the athletics department at Minnesota State University, Tower City, had been in decline for the past several years.

Marta didn't think it was fair they were pinning the school's reputation and future on her coaching there, and she wished if that's what they'd been thinking, Coach Wesley would have been honest with her from the beginning.

"I hope it doesn't turn into one."

"It'll be fine," he said, opening his door.

Carefully, Marta stepped out of the car.

She'd tried her best to look professional wearing a sky-blue pencil skirt and a cream-colored silk tank top underneath the blazer that matched the skirt.

The plain nude pumps on her feet felt strange and placed pressure on parts of her legs her running shoes didn't. She couldn't understand how women like Holly wore dress shoes day after day, and she took baby steps trying to keep from stumbling over the campus's cobblestone sidewalks. What a wreck she would look like if she had to speak at the press conference with skinned-up knees.

"There you are—we've been waiting," Gregory Spaulding barked at her when Ian opened the door for them at the student exchange. "I hope you used your brains and didn't try the athletic building first; we don't have much time. We'll talk in a meeting room upstairs."

Hating Ian had to witness the way Spaulding treated her, she colored and refused to meet Ian's eyes even after he gave her a comforting squeeze to her shoulder.

"Asshole," he muttered into her ear, and she bit back a small smile.

She locked her gaze onto the carpeted stairs, and she followed the athletics director to the top floor.

Ian went with her, a hand at her lower back. She was grateful for the support—but it felt odd, too. Brett wasn't the only one who'd been alone since they'd broken up. She was used to doing things on her own, but she had to admit, not having to felt nice.

People crowded the space. Someone wore a perfume that didn't agree with Marta's stomach, and she swallowed back her nervous nausea.

Campus maintenance workers had built a dais for the podium and were removing the campus furniture to make space for the audience.

"I'll find you after it's over," Marta said and leaned into Ian's strong presence as he kissed her cheek.

"It'll be fine. Good luck."

In a chilly room on an uncomfortable plastic chair, she sat through the briefing with Spaulding and Coach Wesley.

The coach seemed to have aged significantly since she'd seen him last, and though it shouldn't have, it made Marta feel slightly better Spaulding was being as hard on Coach Wesley as he was on her.

It wasn't fair; she knew the track team was doing well for the size of the university, even if they weren't placing at any of the meets.

It wasn't Coach Wesley's fault cutbacks in all the departments across the university were instigating the lowered enrollment. It didn't matter if the athletic department was top-notch if students couldn't take the classes they wanted.

Marta certainly understood it looked good for her to be circling back to the university after a successful career in running, even if she hadn't made it all the way.

The university was Marta's alma mater and she'd graduated with honors. It was probably the reason she'd been
given the position over Libbie Layne who hadn't attended
the university, and it was a realization that hit home as
Spaulding went over the points he would make during his
speech.

"There will be a question and answer, and then we'll be
done. Later, a reporter from the Journal will be contacting
you for an interview, and we're going to set something up
for the first practice of the season. Maybe another interview
or a news clip. We need to keep the athletics department
fresh on people's minds. We haven't been given a donation
in quite some time. There is a lot riding on this, Miss Braddock," Spaulding said, that ever-present glint to his eyes.

Marta cast a glance at Coach Wesley's pallid face. She
worried for her former coach, but before she could reassure
him, Spaulding clapped his hands together.

Coach Wesley flinched.

"It's time to start. Say the right things, and smile. I'll
take care of the rest."

That didn't alleviate Marta's fears, but she followed
Spaulding, dressed in one of his usual suits, and Coach
Wesley—who was dressed as she wished to be in warm up
gear—to the dais and the podium where the school's mascot,
a red dragon with orange flaming from its mouth, blazed on
the front.

She caught Ian's eye—he'd chosen a seat in the back
away from the crowd—and he shot her the thumbs up. She
wished she possessed half his confidence.

Standing near the podium, she tried to ignore Spaulding
belittle Coach Wesley in vicious whispers, spit gathering at
the corners of his mouth.

Instead, she watched the crews for the local television

stations set up their cameras and microphones. The journalists from some of the smaller towns located around Tower City played with their hand-held recorders to record bits for their sports pages.

"We're going to get started," Gregory Spaulding said into the microphone, raising his hands for the crowd's attention.

The room quieted, and cameras started filming.

Marta plastered a smile on her face and barely heard what Spaulding said through the static in her ears.

When he opened the floor to questions, Marta stood on a wooden block behind the podium to give her the height she needed to look into the audience.

"You didn't make it to the Olympics," one cold-hearted reporter said. "How do you feel about that?"

Marta stumbled through the answer.

If only she could speak the truth. Tell the reporter, tell the whole room, what she'd given up for that dream.

What the Olympics had meant to her.

What she could have had right now had she made different choices.

It was something she'd tell Ian one day. That he was still in love with her was obvious, but he would change his mind about their future once he knew the truth.

Marta swallowed. She tried to find him through the sea of camera flashes and the reporters who were standing rather than sitting, but she couldn't.

She'd felt something in their kiss yesterday—not from him, she already knew what he felt for her. No, it had been something in her own heart, something that had responded to the resentment he'd kept inside him all this time.

A question from a different reporter jerked her back into focus.

"What makes you qualified to coach?"

Marta listed the marathons she'd won over the past few years, the records she'd broken during her time at the school.

Even without making it into the Olympics, her history sounded impressive, and she was gratified to hear a murmur of approval ripple through the room.

"Will you be able to hack the cold since you've spent so much time in California?" one reporter asked, laughing.

Relieved the worst was over, Marta parried back and forth with the reporter.

When the banter ran out, a different reporter on the opposite side of the room asked, "From what you've said, you haven't run a race for a while. Which is your next big one?"

Marta opened her mouth to say she wouldn't be running any races while she was coaching—training took too much time—when Spaulding took the microphone.

Nudging her out of the way, he almost knocked her off the wooden block.

"We've decided Miss Braddock will race in the Minnesota Lady Slipper Marathon in October. It's one of the largest races in the country. To celebrate her winning time, the university will fund a track scholarship to be awarded to an exemplary student who wishes to pursue track at this level."

The room erupted into cheers and more questions, but stunned, Marta clung to the podium for support, her tongue glued to the roof of her mouth.

Sweat trickled down her back.

The Lady Slipper Marathon rivaled the Boston Marathon in terms of participants and quality of runners.

The elites who planned the race into their schedules

trained for months hoping to win the one hundred-thou-sand-dollar prize.

October was three months away.

There was no way Marta would be fit enough to run the race, not even for a slim chance of winning.

Especially not when she would be busy when fall semester started at the end of August.

Coach Wesley grabbed her arm.

Marta swung toward him to lash out—the least he could have done was warn her running a prestigious marathon would be be part of the job description—when his pasty lips opened and closed, and his eyes rolled into the back of his head.

He collapsed onto the floor, the dais trembling beneath them.

Dropping to her knees, she yelled to anyone who would listen, "Call 911. He's having a heart attack."

CHAPTER THREE

I AN HERDED MARTA to his car and gently pushed her inside.

He'd darted through the crowd to reach her and found her kneeling beside the old guy's body while two others, he didn't know where they'd come from, performed CPR.

The coach hadn't died, and Marta stayed with him until the EMTs took him away.

The press conference attendees scattered after that, not even the grouchy guy who'd pounced on Marta when they arrived stayed to say anything more, disappearing through the crowd and waving off any questions thrown at him.

It had been a fight for Ian, too, to drag Marta away from the reporters who wanted a statement, but he put his arm around her, glared at anyone who approached them, and led her to his car.

In shock, Marta sat in the passenger seat, staring into space.

Occasionally he would pat her knee or squeeze her hand, but nothing elicited a response.

He didn't want to leave her alone, and he brought her to

the bar, his arm encircling her waste as he urged her up the stairs to his apartment.

When it was clear she couldn't do anything for herself, he undressed her.

He unbuttoned her blazer, peeled the blouse over her head, unzipped her skirt, and tugged it down her legs, over her feet. He drew back the comforter on his bed, and pressing his fingertips into her shoulder, forced her onto the mattress, needing her to rest.

Her blank eyes worried him.

He wanted to ask her what she was thinking, though her passive expression made it evident she wouldn't answer, even if he tried.

Ian tucked the blankets around her as he would a child he was putting to bed and murmured, "Will you be all right?"

He smoothed her hair back, and he blew a sigh of relief when her eyes focused.

"Ian," she whispered, and she ran her hand along his cheek.

He read desire in her eyes, and his cock stiffened.

"Please."

Dredging up all the willpower he could to ward off the want in her voice, the tears running into her hair, he said, "Not like this."

Ian closed the bedroom door, and her sobs followed him down the hall.

***

IAN WENT DOWNSTAIRS, sure his resolve wouldn't last if he had to listen to her cry, and he called Brett and Dane. Both promised to come as soon as they could, and they arrived within minutes of each other.

Though it wasn't even noon, Ian had beer at the ready, and some for himself, too, though he had to keep his head straight to open the bar.

"Do you have any idea how fast she would need to run to win?" Brett asked incredulously after Ian finished telling them what happened that morning.

Ian shook his head. He didn't follow the sport—he had his own interests and they didn't include running. He could barely make it up the stairs to his apartment after a long shift.

"Look at it this way," Dane said, after wiping his mouth with the back of his hand, "the woman who won the Boston Marathon in the women's division was a Kenyan who ran less than a six-minute mile—for twenty-six miles."

The speed and distance didn't register with Ian. "Is that fast?"

Brett groaned. "I don't know how to break it down any clearer. Twenty-six miles at a six-minute mile is only two and a half hours, roughly. When I was at my fastest, I could only run *thirteen* miles in that amount of time. That type of training is excruciating. I don't know what kind of training Marta's been doing, but it's not that kind. She would *need* a coach—not be one."

"So she has no shot at winning?" Ian asked, placing fresh bottles of beer in front of his friends.

He owed them for dropping whatever it was they'd been doing to come listen. He had nowhere to turn for this kind of thing; he would have to forget he was talking to Marta's ex.

"None. She might place in the top ten, maybe—but she won't win. There were a few elite women who didn't run

Boston in April who may show up. It won't stop Marta from trying, though."

"Then there's nothing I can do?"

"Be there for her. Try to understand the predicament she's in. When we were in college, her whole life was running, eating, sleeping, and studying. If I wanted to spend time with her, we studied. Sometimes she would party with us to celebrate a winning meet, but it wasn't that often. Now, if she tries to win that race, all she's going to do is run and sleep. There won't be time in her life for much else. Take it or leave it."

"I don't know what you mean," Ian muttered.

"Don't give me that shit. I know you love her—"

"No fighting," Dane said, lifting a hand in warning.

Brett shoved Dane's shoulder. "I don't care, asshole."

He popped a small pretzel into his mouth. Tucking it into his cheek Brett said, "I would rather it be you, one of my friends, than some schmuck I don't know. At least I know you'll take care of her."

"I want to," Ian said, "but she won't let me. And I got enough on my mind without worring about Marta literally running herself into the ground."

"What are you going to do about your cousin's kid?" Dane asked.

"I wanted to talk to Marta to get her take on it, but we're going to have to handle our own problems."

"That's bullshit. If you want to be with her, then stick with her. Our women," Brett said, gesturing between himself and Dane, "tried to run out on us—"

"Speak for yourself," Dane interrupted. "You did plenty of running."

"All right. Fine. We're all good at running, except you, you pansy," Brett said to Ian. "You love Marta, you stick with her because it sounds like this university stuff could go to shit real fast. She's not going to win that race, and she knows it, too. What it will do for her position, for her reputation at the school, I don't know. But we'll all be there for her. All of us. Tell us what you need, and you'll have it."

Ian appreciated his friends' support.

He was afraid it wouldn't be enough.

———

IAN ORDERED TAKE out and closed the bar for an hour to feed Marta dinner.

As he carried the cartons from the Italian place down the street past his sister's apartment, he wondered where Sadie was. He hadn't seen her since she abandoned Marta in the bar, and it didn't bode well for what Sadie was doing or where she could be.

"Marta?" he said when he opened his apartment door.

"In here," her tired voice replied, and Ian found her where he left her that morning.

"I thought you'd be hungry," he said, holding up the white bag. The air filled with the scents of garlic and butter, and his heart rate slowed when a smile tried to lift her lips.

"I am, thank you. I was trying to get up the energy to get dressed and go home."

"You don't have to do that. Here, I'll let you eat in my bed as long as you don't get breadstick crumbs in my sheets."

"Deal. What did you order me?"

Ian sat on the bed and untied the handles of the plastic bag. Steam rose from the opening, and his stomach rumbled. "I ordered your favorite, of course. Veggie lasagna. You still eat that, right?"

"Yeah, it's still my favorite."

"Good."

Marta opened her mouth but then shut it again.

"What? You can talk to me, you know." Ian pulled out the paper plates the restaurant included in the delivery and dished up salad slathered in Italian dressing.

"Can you turn the TV on? The six o'clock news is about to start, and I want to see if they show the press conference."

Marta didn't need a reminder of what happened, but he'd rather she watch it with him than alone. He was surprised she hadn't searched for it on her phone, but it looked like she'd been sleeping all day—her eyelids drooped with fatigue, her hair tangled from his pillow.

Marta tucked his black sheet around her breasts, revealing only the cream straps of her bra. She took the plate and white plastic fork. "Thanks. This looks good."

Ian wanted to touch her in some way but held back. "I owed you a meal. We didn't get to the brunch I promised you," he said, looking for the remote.

They watched the commercials and other news stories while they crunched on salad and breadsticks. Ian had just unboxed their main entrees when the press conference began to air.

On his small screen, she watched the conference. He didn't care about seeing it again—he'd been there in person, and he didn't want to see the strain on Marta's face, the worry, the shock when that prick announced she'd be running, and winning, the Lady Slipper Marathon.

But the cheering crowd directed his attention to the news program, and Marta, the Marta on screen, looked like death warmed over. "Who was the guy who had the heart attack? Why was he there?"

"He's the coach I'm taking over for. He was my coach while I was in school."

"I'm sorry."

A female news anchor updated the audience on the coach's health saying he was stable and was expected to make a full recovery.

The news program ended, giving way to the theme song of *Jeopardy!* and Ian turned the TV off. They ate in silence, sitting in the light coming through his bedroom window.

"Ian, about this morning . . ."

Ian gave in to touching her then, brushing his fingertips from her temples down her cheek to her jaw. "I wanted to, but I would never take advantage of you that way."

She looked away.

"What have you decided about the marathon?" Ian asked, changing the subject and spearing a shrimp in his shrimp fettuccini.

When they made love, it would be because she wanted him as much as he wanted her. Not because she was looking for sympathy, empathy, compassion, things she would have accepted from anyone.

He didn't kid himself—she would have poured her desperation into anyone who would have let her. The knowledge didn't make him love her any less, but it made him even more determined to make her see it was Ian she needed, and no one else.

"I'm going to train and run it, of course," Marta said, surprised.

"Like Brett said you would."

"You talked to Brett?"

"Yeah, I asked Dane and Brett to stop by. I had no idea what that asshole's announcement meant for you, and Brett explained it. To be honest, it doesn't sound good."

Marta wiped her mouth with a paper napkin, her plate sliding precariously on her lap. "I've been training, though I haven't competed in a while—I can use that in my favor. I have almost three months; all I can do is try my best."

Ian's cell rang, the generic ringtone cutting through the silence. He didn't recognize the number, and he debated whether to answer it, when Marta said, "You should answer that. I need to get home, anyway."

Holding up a hand to keep her from sneaking away, Ian answered. "Hello? Yeah, speaking."

Marta began cleaning up their dinner from his bed, shoving the trash into the empty plastic bag their meals had come in.

Ian sighed. "Yeah, I'll be right there."

"What's wrong?" Marta asked, looking up from a black Styrofoam container.

Ian fell back onto his bed, tossing his phone on the comforter instead of throwing it across the room in frustration. "Sadie's in jail and needs me to bail her out."

WHILE SHE DRESSED for her evening run, Marta hoped things had gone well for Ian. She'd wanted to go with him to the police station, but he waved her off saying it was a family matter, and he needed to take care of it on his own.

That stung, even though she had no right for it to.

She wasn't his family. Marta wished she could forget she hadn't been honest with Ian about what had happened between her and Brett. She needed to confess soon, but it was difficult to do because he wouldn't talk to her anymore.

The way he'd taken care of her after the press conference had been sweet of him, but it shouldn't have surprised her. That's the way he was.

She'd miss that.

As she buckled her GPS watch onto her wrist, a knock sounded on her door. She didn't think it would be Ian; he was probably reading Sadie the riot act right now.

"Hey," Dane said, "going for a run?"

"Doesn't it look like it?" she asked, surprised Dane had taken the time to pop in. Nikki, the marathon, and his store took up all his time, though not necessarily in that order.

She pulled her running shoes out of the closet.

"Like you don't always dress like that."

Grinning, she sank to the floor to tie her shoes. "Point taken. What's up?"

"Well, I wanted to talk to you for a second, but I can while we run. I haven't gone today."

"Oh, but I was going to *run*."

She needed to start training as soon as possible. First on the list was figuring out how far she could go. Afterward, she would focus on speed work and then combine the two.

"I can handle it. I'm in better shape than Brett these days. Let me change."

He disappeared down the hallway before she could argue.

They met outside and walked in silence for the first ten minutes.

Her feet dragged, mentally exhausted after the press conference. The responsibility of winning the marathon weighed on her like a ton of bricks. She would have to start sleeping more if she was going to seriously train for the race.

"What's going on with you?" she asked as they started a light run. This speed would never cut it, but Marta had to be smart and start thinking like a coach.

Digging out her old running plans from other marathons would remind her what she needed to do, what her body could handle, and she made a note to herself to look for them later. She hoped the notes made it with her to Minnesota.

"Nothing much. Wedding stuff. Nikki told me she asked you to be a bridesmaid. I think she wants everyone to meet up soon to look at dresses or something."

"Well, I can't do it now, obviously," Marta said.

She drew in a breath and tried to appreciate being outside. The paths behind her apartment building were the best thing about where she chose to live. She could run through the park a million times and the scenery wouldn't bore her.

"Sure you can. We're not getting married until next year. By then you'll be comfortable in your coaching job, the marathon will be long over. Just because you have this crap to deal with now doesn't mean you can't be in our wedding. You have plenty of time."

"True." She couldn't imagine finding a dress would take much time out of her training schedule. "Yeah, I guess so. You can tell Nikki I'll do it, then."

"Awesome. So, that's crazy about Ian and his cousin, huh?"

"He hasn't told me anything." Marta gave him a quick look before picking up speed.

They were running eight-minute miles, and while that wasn't bad, it wasn't good. They were only three miles into their run, though, and she had to remember to balance speed with distance.

Visiting Coach Wesley in the hospital would be a good idea; she would never turn down his advice.

"I guess you've had a lot going on," Dane said, then

sucked in air through his nose. "A cousin he hadn't been in contact with, I think, ever, died in a car accident—"

"Oh, that's too bad."

"Yeah, there's more. She named Ian guardian of her child."

Marta dodged a stick in her path. "Really? There's no other family? Ian's parents?"

Dane wiped at his forehead. "I don't know; he didn't get into it much except a social worker has been pressuring him to make a decision. He's really torn up about it. He runs the bar for his mom and dad, watches his sister. Now someone wants to give him a baby."

Marta glanced at her watch. Six miles in.

Another ten at the speed they were going, and she would consider the run a success.

"He was going to tell me, I think, at the park, but we had to leave. Alyssa said Brett doesn't want to direct the marathon anymore."

"Yeah. He's been at it a long time. I can't say I blame him, really, and each year it seems to grow a little bigger. Besides, his book grabbed a huge advance."

Marta had forgotten about Brett and Alyssa's book, but she was happy things were working out for them. "That's great! What's going on with you and the store? It's not turning out how you thought?"

Dane blew out a breath. "Seriously, I thought it would be making more money by now. And a Fabulous Footwear is moving into the Tower City Shopping Center. At least with the other stores in the area, they carry more sporting goods, not focusing so much on shoes, you know, and those types of stores have never hurt me. But this new store accepts the mall coupons and gift cards. I'm going to have to wait and see how it pans out."

"Seems natural you would run the marathon if Brett steps down. Nikki already does the women's race, and you've been helping Brett for years." Marta made the thought seem like hers; she didn't want Dane to know Alyssa was talking behind their backs.

"I don't know how long I would want to do that, either. Nikki wants to have a baby; she says she's getting old." Dane huffed a laugh. "But I don't want to be worrying about the store and the marathon all the time. I would never get a break, and I want time to be a dad. I know how important that is."

This was news to Marta. She assumed it was a done deal because of Nikki's and Dane's financial situation.

"Well, who would do it?"

"There'd be someone who would step up. Brett has plenty of volunteers who wouldn't mind doing it."

"But no one would love it as much as you two."

"Probably not. But don't you get tired sometimes?"

"I can't afford to get tired."

She'd made that choice a long time ago.

"You can't keep fucking around," Ian yelled at his sister, slamming into his apartment after a tense drive home from the police station.

"This wasn't my fault," Sadie cried, wiping tears from her cheeks.

"It's never your fault." he threw his keys onto the kitchen table.

Sadie had wanted to hide in her apartment, but with a grip of steel on her arm, he'd steered her toward his and locked the door behind them.

"I was in the wrong place at the wrong time."

"That's what you always say. If you would work at the bar like you're supposed to, if you would maybe go to school, stop staying out all night, you would never be in the wrong place at the wrong time because you would never be in the wrong place. This needs to stop. I didn't have to bail you out, and maybe I shouldn't have. The bar has been closed most of the evening. What would Dad say?"

"Who gives a shit what Mom and Dad would say? It's not like they care about us."

Ian sank into a chair.

Sadie's hair hung in greasy strands, and he could smell her fear and anger; she needed a shower and a decent meal.

She hadn't wanted to call him, but an officer called on her behalf after listening to her cry all afternoon.

"That's not true," he said.

But it was.

He didn't hear from his parents much, and Sadie probably heard from them less than he did.

Ian called his dad to give him the reports about the bar, and that was only if he could get a hold of the man between rounds of golf.

His parents didn't mean to be cruel or unkind—they figured they'd given their kids a decent upbringing, and it was their turn to live their lives now their kids were old enough to take care of themselves.

That was hardly heartless, and like Marta pointed out, they could hop onto a plane if he and Sadie wanted to see them more.

"There's nothing stopping you from moving to Georgia. Savannah is supposed to be a nice city. And they're not even an hour away from the beach. You could turn into a little beach bunny," he said, trying to draw a smile from her.

It didn't work.

"If you fucking don't want me here, then tell me."

"It's not that I don't want you here. You're my sister, and I love you. But you need to stop acting like a child. Get your shit together."

Sadie scoffed. "Like you do, brother of mine?"

She slammed out of his apartment, and three seconds later music shook his walls.

Awesome.

Ian knew he should go downstairs and open the bar, but he didn't care. He had too much on his mind to give a shit if the one or two people who might have dropped in went elsewhere for their beer.

He pulled off his white button-down dress shirt, shucked his jeans from his legs, and fell into bed.

Marta's scent enveloped him, and holding the pillow she'd slept on to his nose, he took a deep breath.

He'd wanted to spend time with her, to reconnect. But it wasn't possible, not when he was at the bar all the time, and now she was going to be running her ass off for a goddamned marathon.

That was something he should have asked Brett and Dane when they'd been there earlier—what was it like to have such a passion for something? Ian had never felt a passion, an obsession like that for something, well, not for anything besides Marta.

He took over the bar because at the time he didn't have anything else to do. He'd graduated along with the others, but he didn't find a job like Dane and Brett. After Marta left, he'd been in a bad way, he'd only hidden it so no one knew.

Sadie hadn't been far off the mark accusing him of not having his shit together.

His cell phone rang.

Maybe it was Marta calling to see how Sadie was doing, or to ask him if he wanted to hang out. He dug into his pocket for his phone, but his hope disintegrated when he recognized the social worker's phone number.

"Hello."

"Mr. Butler, I apologize for calling so late. I'm at the office a little longer than usual to do some last-minute paperwork. Anyway, I was hoping you'd given a little more thought to Shyla's care."

Ian covered his eyes with the crook of his elbow. "I'm sorry, Miss Gibson, I want to, I really do."

The social worker sighed. "I've heard that tone more than once, Mr. Butler. No one seems to think they can take care of a child, but then they find it's not that difficult. She wouldn't be yours—you would receive a stipend. You'd be her guardian, nothing more."

If the social worker wanted to comfort Ian, she'd missed the mark. If he took Shyla, she would be his. He would be in it all the way or not at all.

When he didn't respond, Miss Gibson ended the call with, "I will give you one more day. Please, Mr. Butler—I've seen children enter the foster care system. Some thrive, and some . . . do not. I'm not going to pretend it's a system that isn't broken. But we do the best we can. Goodnight."

Feeling guilty a little girl was depending on him to take care of her, and knowing he was failing miserably, he poured himself a drink.

IAN WOKE TO his phone ringing. People needed to leave him alone. His head pounded, and with a groan, he rolled over and grabbed his phone off the nightstand. "Hello," he mumbled.

"You owe me breakfast."

Marta's voice penetrated the fog in is brain, and he smiled as he stretched. "People" could leave him alone. He'd talk to Marta anytime. "Didn't I say brunch? Brunch is later. What time is it?"

"It's already ten o'clock. Come on, get your lazy ass out of bed, and I'll pick you up in an hour."

She hung up before he could respond.

He rubbed his face and stumbled into the kitchen to make coffee.

After a shower, he dressed and headed downstairs to wait outside. The coffee and shower did little to make his headache disappear, and he pushed his sunglasses over his eyes before falling into the passenger seat of Marta's car.

"You look like crap," Marta said and made *tsking* noises with her tongue.

"It was a late night last night," he said.

"You bailed out Sadie, then? What'd she do, anyway?"

"She was at a party and they were doing drugs. I don't know if she was doing any, but someone called the cops on them."

"Sounds like someone else I know," Marta said, laughing, giving him an elbow to his shoulder.

"I was pissed. Where are we going anyway?"

"A little café downtown makes a delicious brunch, and they serve bottomless mimosas."

They were silent the rest of the way and didn't speak until they settled into a corner booth. After ordering the brunch buffet and giving the waitress their menus, Marta took his hand. "Hey, are you really okay? Did you get more bad news or something last night?"

Ian scoffed. "Sadie is enough, but no, I got another call from a social worker who—"

"Dane told me about that. Some cousin willed you her baby. That's odd."

"Yeah, I've been wanting to talk to you, get your opinion. I mean, I'm not father material, am I? Yet, I can't stand the thought of that little girl staying in foster care."

As they walked along the buffet and dished up their plates, Marta asked, "Tell me about her. How old is she? What about her father? Can't your parents take her?"

Ian filled her in on what he knew. "She's two, and she was in daycare when my cousin was in the accident. At least we can be grateful her life was spared. Her name is Shyla, and she's in with a foster care family while I decide. She's having a tough time—Shyla, that is. Misses her mom, cries a lot. That's to be expected." Ian pursed his lips. "They're giving me time to think about it. They contacted my parents probably thinking I'll say no, but it didn't do them any good. They don't want anything to do with it. My dad said if I didn't do it, no one in the family would. Sadie can't—she can't even take care of herself."

He took a bite of his scrambled eggs.

"I think you should do it."

Ian choked. "Really? What do I have to offer a kid?"

"You have to ask?" Marta said. "Come on. A stable home, someone who would love her—family. This could even turn Sadie around. Give her purpose."

"Or it could backfire, and she'd accuse me of trying to make her do more. Last night wasn't very pleasant."

"Where does Shyla live?"

"In Colorado. The social worker would fly her here. She'd look around my place, interview me, you know, make sure I was fit, then she'd drop her off, and Shyla would be mine. I guess it would be that easy."

"Well, I think you should do it. Poor little thing. She needs you."

Ian met Marta's eyes. "I wish you did."

"I'm not a child."

"Sometimes you look like one," Ian said, lifting her head with two fingers under her chin. "The look in your eyes when you think no one is watching. How uncertain you seem at times. Marta, I want you to know with the marathon and things going down at the school, I'll always be here for you. I've always wanted to be. You've just never let me."

Marta pushed a kiss to his knuckles. "I appreciate that, but you have enough on your plate without worrying about me."

He couldn't tell her that worry and stress came with being in love with someone.

"Whatever you say."

He scooped more eggs into his mouth before they turned cold.

"How much longer do you have to decide about Shyla? She sounds adorable."

Ian chuckled. "It's kind of funny. The social worker emailed me some pictures of her, and she looks exactly like Sadie if she would keep her hair blonde and stop dyeing it that god-awful black mess. She's a Butler, that's for sure."

"Then you *have* to take her, Ian. Don't let this be a mistake that will follow you for the rest of your life."

Ian lifted his gaze from his plate to find Marta's eyes full of tears. "We all make mistakes. It's part of growing up, it's part of life. You can't blame yourself for mistakes you've made. You need to move on."

"Could you move on when you look in a mirror every day and see, time after time, everything you've done, everything you failed to do, there, in your eyes, mocking you? How do you move on from that?" Marta wiped her cheeks with her napkin then slid out of the booth. "I'll meet you outside."

Head lowered, shoulders hunched, she hurried to the door. After giving her a few moments to pull herself together, Ian paid the check and met her at the car.

She drove him home without a single word.

IAN WANTED TO call the social worker and tell her to start processing the paperwork or whatever she had to do to get the ball rolling, but first he had to let someone else know.

He pounded on Sadie's door, for once the apartment quiet, but there was no answer, either.

"Sadie," he yelled, hammering his fist against the wood. At least he didn't have to worry about disturbing anyone.

Frustrated by lack of response, Ian turned the doorknob and stepped inside.

"Jesus Christ, Ian," Sadie snapped, pulling a long-sleeve pajama shirt over her head.

She wasn't fast enough.

Purple bruises covered her back.

"What the fuck, Sadie?" Ian said, gently cradling her face in his hands. "What are all those bruises? Who the fuck did that to you?"

"Mind your own fucking business," she said, wrenching away.

"Hate to break it to you, sis, but you *are* my business." Ian sank onto her unmade bed. The blankets stank like cigarette smoke and stale perfume. "If you've got some guy pounding on you, I want to know. You don't have to stay in an abusive relationship. I can help you."

Exhausted, he rubbed his face.

"You don't know what you're talking about."

"I probably don't."

He hadn't known anyone who'd been hurt that way before.

"What'd you come barging in here for, anyway? Can't you leave me alone for one second?"

"No, I can't. Then where would I find all my fun?"

On her way to the kitchen, Sadie gave him the finger.

She started to make coffee, and Ian sank into a kitchen chair in gratitude. They would need it.

"I haven't told you, but I've been talking to a social worker."

Sadie stilled, the spoon stuck in the plastic carton of grounds. "About me?"

"No, not about you. You're an adult, what am I going to say to them? I haven't told you about this because I wasn't sure what I was going to do. We had a cousin, a few times removed or however that works—"

"Had?"

"Will you let me tell the story?"

Ian smoothed crumbs off the table's surface. At least her kitchen was relatively clean, and he didn't have to worry about dying from mold poisoning or some shit from dirty dishes.

"Yes, had. She was in a car accident. Her daughter was at daycare, and she's okay, but our cousin died in the crash."

The coffee dripped in that comforting way it had, the hot plate hissing as it seared off the water from the bottom of the carafe.

"So what does that have to do with us?" Sadie asked, pulling mugs out of her cabinet.

"It doesn't have anything to do with you, well, maybe it does. She named me the guardian of her child, her daughter, Shyla. She's with a foster family right now until I make up my mind."

"That's fucked up."

"I know it is, and I've taken longer to make a decision than the social worker is happy with. But in the end, I decided I can't leave her with strangers. Even the social worker admitted that doesn't always turn out."

"You're going to be a dad?" Sadie asked, snickering.

"I haven't worked anything out yet. Like how I'm supposed to take care of her and the bar" —Ian pinned her with his stare— "and you."

"I don't need you taking care of me," Sadie snapped, pouring coffee.

"Ah, yeah, you do. You don't work, you don't go to school. You fuck around all day and night with no motivation, no goals. Now you're letting someone beat you up. It sounds like you need a social worker after all."

Ian took a sip of coffee, burning his tongue.

"I got it under control."

"See the thing is, you don't. And the social worker is going to fly Shyla here and snoop around. She's going to look at our apartments, look at the bar. She won't leave Shyla with us if she thinks we can't take care of her. If I do this, you've got to promise me you'll clean up. I might as well tell the social worker not to bother if you can't."

"How in the hell did this become my responsibility?" Sadie flopped into a chair and crossed her arms over her chest.

"It's not. I'm only asking you to please look like you've

got your shit together while she's here. Then go back to Trent and keep getting your brains bashed in if that's what you want."

Imagining his sister voluntarily hanging around a guy who liked hurting her made him want to puke, but he knew the more he tried to keep her from doing something, the more determined she would be to do it.

If he kept his nose out of it, maybe that would knock the wind out of her sails and she would dump Trent on her own.

"Whatever."

Feeling like an old man, Ian stood, his bones creaking with the weight of resentment and responsibility. "See, if you went to school, you could improve your vocabulary."

"Fuck off."

"You keep proving me right." He quickly closed the door behind him in case she threw something at him.

Downstairs, Ian prepared to open for the day.

He dialed the social worker and listened to the line ring as he flipped on the lights.

There wasn't much to do in way of opening.

The bar didn't serve food, and it took a huge load off Ian's responsibilities. He didn't have to deal with cooks, inspections, ordering supplies. It was enough he had to make sure they never ran out of booze, though that wasn't much of a worry when there weren't any customers.

"Miss Gibson," Ian said when she answered the phone.

"Mr. Butler, I'm happy to hear from you. You have good news for me, I hope."

"Actually, I do. You can bring Shyla here at your convenience. I can't let her grow up in the system. My cousin chose me for a reason, and I don't want to let her down."

Miss Gibson blew out a breath, and to Ian it sounded like static through the phone line.

"That's fantastic, Mr. Butler. I can't begin to tell you how relieved I am you've decided to take this on. She'll have a real chance at a normal life if she can find stability in your home. I'm going to email you a checklist of the things you'll need to have done before Shyla arrives. You'll need to have a bedroom for her, furniture. I'll include her clothing size so you can supplement her wardrobe. Your cousin was struggling financially, and Shyla doesn't have much. She would love some toys, I think. That kind of thing."

Ian tipped his head back and stared at the ceiling. He did have a spare bedroom he could turn into Shyla's room, he didn't have a problem with that. But all that shopping.

"I'll do whatever it is you need me to do."

"I know you will." The social worker's voice oozed warmth. "I'll process the paperwork as quickly as I can and make the flight arrangements. I believe I can book a direct flight from Denver to Tower City."

"I'll pick you up at the airport and take you where you need to go."

If he needed to make a good impression, he might as well start now.

"I appreciate that, Mr. Butler. That reminds me, Shyla will need a car seat."

Ian stifled a groan.

"I'll be in touch."

He couldn't wait.

MARTA FELT TERRIBLE for running out on Ian during brunch. He'd upset her telling her to move on.

There were some things that couldn't be undone, no matter how much she wanted it. Sometimes mistakes stayed with you forever, and this was one of those times.

After she dropped Ian at home, she called the hospital and asked how Coach Wesley was doing and if he was accepting visitors. The nurse at the nurses' station said he was weak but stable, and visitors were allowed to stay for ten minutes at a time.

Marta didn't take the time to change from the running clothes she'd worn to brunch and drove to the hospital. Her car made rattling sounds when she hit sixty miles per hour, and she bit back a growl of frustration.

Things weren't going her way since moving to Minnesota.

The only good thing was Ian, but that wasn't going very well, either.

Choking back tears, she parked her car in the visitors' lot and through the maze of waxed, gleaming floors, found Coach Wesley's room.

The nurses had cleared his room letting him eat lunch in peace, and she found him alone, an empty tray on the small table, staring out the window. He lay in a reclined position, his head resting on a fluffy pillow.

"Coach."

"Oh, God, Marta," Coach Wesley choked. "I had no idea. No idea."

Marta hurried to his bedside and grabbed his hand, being careful not to jar his IV. "I know. I saw it in your eyes."

"Back out. Get away from Spaulding and the school as fast as you can."

Marta sat in the padded chair beside the bed. "I can't. I've started training—"

The coach licked his dry, chapped lips. "You won't win, you know that, don't you?"

She looked down at her hand grasping his. "I have to try. Coach, this is my life."

"Marta, look at me."

Marta met his faded green eyes that were swamped with compassion and sadness.

"I remember the way you used to be back then, determined to make a name for yourself. All three of you, and you did a good job of that. Dane and his store, Brett and the marathon. Yeah," he said, when Marta's eyes widened, "I've kept tabs on all of you. You and your little group. I remember you and Brett. You were so close and then one day you weren't. You never had the same spark in your eyes, your running suffered. You lost your joy. What happened between you two all those years ago?"

Marta swallowed around a lump in her throat. "It was nothing. It's still nothing. Brett's okay. He's written a book, and he's directing the marathon. He's engaged, you know."

"But not to you."

Marta smiled, but it didn't reach her eyes. "No, not to me. We've both moved on, Coach. Things happen. The Lady Slipper—"

Coach Wesley started coughing. "Can you—" he gestured to a Styrofoam cup sitting on the table next to the bed.

Marta held the cup for him, guiding the straw to his mouth.

He took several long sips before turning his head away.

"This marathon won't prove anything," Coach Wesley rasped. "Spaulding, he won't be happy, even if you win. There will always be something else. He's gunning for you —you need to be careful."

Beads of sweat gathered at his temples, and his lips trembled.

Marta's ten minutes were almost up, and she gripped his hand in goodbye.

"I've run, and coached running, all my life. I don't have a wife, I don't have children. I don't have family."

"The running community—"

"Has been my family, and they've been wonderful to me, but they aren't a substitute for love. You've given so much to the sport, too much. Do you want to end up like me, some old man with nothing? I'm going to die in this hospital bed, alone. Don't end up like me, please."

Marta leaned over and kissed his cheek. "You aren't going to die. I need you to write a new running plan for me to help me win this marathon. What I have from before won't work now. I'm getting old, and I haven't competed this way in years."

Coach Wesley shook his head. "You haven't listened to a word I've said. There's more to life than running."

"Not to me, there isn't."

"Then you need to find something, someone, before it's too late."

After a long run later that evening, Marta was trying to relax in the bath when Brett texted her.

Coach Wesley passed away half an hour after Marta left his room.

CHAPTER FOUR

"HE'S NOT HERE. He's downstairs."

Marta looked down the hall to Sadie, who was peeking around the doorjamb of her apartment.

"I tried that, but the door is locked."

"It's ten o'clock in the morning. Who's going to want to drink now?"

Marta could think of at least one—she certainly wouldn't have turned down a big glass of wine if one had been presented to her. "Right."

"Go back down the stairs and turn right. Follow the hallway and that'll lead you to the bar's storage room. You can get in that way."

"Thanks. How have you been? Jail treat you okay?"

"Better than this dump." Sadie shut the door in Marta's face.

Stifling a chuckle, Marta followed Sadie's directions and found herself in a small room stacked with beer boxes and small pallets of wine and hard liquor.

"Ian?"

"In here."

She followed his voice to the front of the bar where he was counting liquor bottles.

"Hey, you. I didn't expect to see you around."

Marta grimaced. "I know. I'm sorry about how I acted yesterday. Things haven't been going well for me."

"Ah-huh."

He looked good in faded jeans, a light blue button-down shirt, and a dark blue tie. His dark blond hair was brushed away from his face, and his grey eyes snapped with pleasure.

A knot that had been twisting in her gut loosened.

He was glad to see her.

"Coach Wesley died yesterday. Brett texted me last night."

Ian looked up from a number he was recording in a little notebook. "I'm sorry. I know you respected him."

"Yeah. He told me . . . well, that doesn't matter. Anyway, did you decide anything about Shyla? That's her name, right?"

"Yeah. I called the social worker after you dropped me off yesterday and said I'd take her. She emailed me a list of things I'm going to need to do before they fly here. I was going to ask you if you could, ah, help me shop for her. You know, maybe return the favor for dragging me all over when you needed furniture."

"Yeah, sure," Marta said, surprised he asked. It wasn't like they'd been getting along. "Today? Tomorrow? Tomorrow evening is Coach Wesley's funeral."

"I'll go with you."

"What about the bar?"

Ian blew out a breath. "I'm starting to care less and less about this place."

Marta sat on a stool as Ian counted bottles in a cooler

that looked like a stainless-steel refrigerator. "What would you do if you didn't manage this place? What *did* you do after school?"

"Nothing much. Worked job to job. Took care of Sadie, made sure she went to school, helped her with her homework. I could tell, even by then, our parents were checking out, and a few years later it got worse when my dad slid into that snowplow. It scared the shit out of him, and the crash totaled his car. It was torture for them to stay for as long as they did. Taking over the bar, well, I wasn't doing anything else, and I didn't care one way or the other. But I didn't think I'd be doing this indefinitely."

He mixed her a mimosa, and she gratefully took a long sip. With the way the conversation went at brunch the day before, she hadn't enjoyed the one she'd ordered.

"What would you do if you could do anything at all?"

Ian scoffed. "I don't have time to breathe much less think of a new career path. And having Shyla here will make it worse. Until she gets used to me and realizes this is going to be her home, it will be tough for a while."

"What does Sadie think? Did you tell her? Will she help you?"

Marta wanted to do what she could to help, too, but she didn't want to promise anything she couldn't give.

Coach Wesley's voice echoed through her mind, warning her to find meaning in something other than running or she would end up alone.

There was a man standing in front of her who loved her, and she could love him back if she let herself.

Tears sprang to Ian's eyes, and he looked away.

"Ian? What is it?" Marta asked, alarmed.

Gripping the edge of the bar, he whispered, "I walked in on her because she didn't answer the door, you know? I wanted to talk to her about Shyla. She was dressing, and," he cleared his throat, "her back was covered in bruises. I think her boyfriend is beating her up."

Marta covered her mouth, horrified. "Oh, my God."

Ian sighed. "I know. She denied it, of course. I have to take one thing at a time. She didn't give me any pushback for wanting to take Shyla. If she can behave while the social worker is here, that'll be a blessing. Then I can figure out the rest."

"I'll help as much as I can." Marta clamped her mouth shut. She hadn't wanted to offer her time, her help. But the despair in Ian's eyes had her promising anything she could to make it disappear.

Ian tried to smile. "I know you will. Has that prick contacted you since the conference?"

"No, thank God. But I have no doubt Spaulding will milk Coach Wesley's death. And now I'm in a bad spot. I was counting on him to ease my way into the position. I've never coached before, I don't know any of the kids."

Ian brought her hands to his lips. "How about we run away," he mumbled against her skin. "We'll run away and leave all this behind us."

"You can't do that. People need you here," Marta said, trembling from the heat of his mouth as his breath caressed the backs of her hands.

"Sometimes I wish they didn't. Sometimes I wish I were on my own—live for myself, you know? It's nice not to have responsibilities. I feel like I've always kept track of Sadie, and now I'll have Shyla for the next sixteen years." Releasing her hands, he turned away and resumed counting bottles.

Marta held in a breath and tried not to cry.

She couldn't tell Ian how much she needed him, not

now. He'd made it clear he didn't need her dumping her problems on him.

Marta was on her own—just like she'd always been.

MARTA WOKE EARLY to run before her shopping trip with Ian. Gregory Spaulding hadn't contacted her since the press conference, and his silence both worried and relieved her. She feared what he was doing behind her back.

Ian's idea to run away was a pleasant thought, and as she ran through the park, the sun casting a shimmery glow over the trees, she mulled over the idea of moving back to California.

She wouldn't be giving up anything—only a crappy job she regretted taking and friends she could stay in touch with online.

As she breathed deeply and checked her speed on her watch, she admitted she was lying to herself.

Leaving Minnesota would be difficult.

She'd committed to being in Nikki's and Dane's wedding, and Ian was counting on her to help with Shyla. Living in Minnesota had turned into more than just coaching at the college.

Ian would appreciate seeing her look like a regular person in public, and Marta dressed in a denim skirt and a plain white t-shirt. Even she could admit wearing her running attire all the time bordered on the obnoxious.

As an afterthought, she swiped on some mascara and lip gloss before leaving, and she was rewarded for her half-assed effort when he smiled in appreciation.

"You look pretty," he said, jiggling his car keys in his hand.

"Why do you sound surprised?"

While Ian chuckled, Marta slid into the car and tried to squelch the flashbacks of the last time she'd sat in the seat.

She hadn't properly mourned Coach Wesley—she couldn't believe he was gone. He'd been such a large part of her life; he knew more about her than she ever thought possible.

"You're quiet," Ian said.

"Thinking about the coach."

"Any word about that?"

"Spaulding still hasn't reached out, and I don't know if I should be worried or happy I don't have to deal with him. I guess I'll have to talk to him at the funeral later this evening."

"I'll be there. And Dane and Brett will be there, too, won't they?"

"They haven't said for sure, but I doubt they'd miss it. Where are we shopping?" She didn't want to talk about the coach, or the school, or her position, anymore. It all felt out of her control.

"I have no idea. I was heading to the mall. Do you think they'll have what we need?"

"Babies are out of my element."

Though if things had been different, she would've been a pro.

Marta looked at Ian out of the corner of her eye. Whenever she looked at him, it was as if she were seeing him for the first time.

In school, she never thought of him as more than a friend, or a study buddy, like he accused her of.

Now when she looked at him, she noticed the way his hair glinted in the sun, his kind eyes, his mouth always pulling upward into a faint smile, even when he wasn't meaning to.

She'd broken his heart when she took off for California, but it also seemed as if he was in a better place than any of them.

Ian wrinkled his nose, making Marta laugh. "I'm not exactly an expert," he said, pulling into the large parking lot of the shopping center.

"Do you have a list?"

"Yeah, but I didn't print it out. I'll pull it up on my phone."

She walked with with through the mall, and he held her hand as he led her into a JC Penney.

What she wouldn't give to be spending a leisurely afternoon browsing then grabbing lunch. She'd never had that kind of normalcy with a man—after Brett she'd given a hundred and ten percent of herself to the sport.

"There should be something here," Ian said, helping her onto the escalator that would bring them to the second floor to the children's department.

As the escalator carried them upward, baby clothes came into view, and Marta's heart thumped painfully.

Her fingers grazed over tiny socks, onesies, and miniature sweaters. Pink hats and blue overalls.

A burn started behind her eyes, and she looked away before Ian could see her tears. She didn't want to have to explain why looking at baby clothes would make her cry.

She pulled her hand out of his grasp and pretended she needed to secure her purse onto her shoulder.

Ian didn't notice.

"It looks like we'll only be able to buy her some clothes here. We'll have to go to a Walmart or a Target for a crib. Maybe a furniture store for a rocker and a chest of drawers."

"What size is she?" Marta asked, admiring a white and pink dress decorated with pink elephants.

Ian checked his phone. "A 4T. Is that big for a two-year-old? Maybe she's tall or something."

Marta had no idea about sizes, but she wandered into the toddler section. They wouldn't find anything in Infants.

They browsed the mall buying Shyla dresses, leggings, and shirts.

After stopping briefly for lunch in the food court, they moved on to a toy store and Target. Ian's car was full to bursting by the time they were finished.

A crib and a few other pieces of furniture were scheduled to be delivered later in the day.

"It's too bad you had to pay extra for same-day delivery," Marta said over the head of a big cream-colored bear. There wasn't room for it anywhere else, and it sat in her lap on the drive to Ian's apartment.

"I know, but I'll feel better having it. Now that I said I would take Shyla, the social worker isn't wasting any time. They're flying out the day after tomorrow."

Navigating out of the furniture store's parking lot and narrowly missing a huge hole in the asphalt, Ian glanced at her. "I don't suppose tomorrow you'd help me paint my spare room? Shyla won't care, but it's painted ugly green now."

She wanted to tell him no. Putting together Shyla's nursery would be more than excruciating. The shopping alone had been a strain, her throat burned raw from the tears she forced herself to keep inside.

But she didn't want to disappoint him; she'd already done enough of that. "Sure, I wouldn't mind at all."

"And the funeral is early this evening."

Marta sighed. "Yeah."

"I'll keep the bar closed today and drive you there. I don't want you to go by yourself."

"You don't have to do that. Dane and Brett will be there. I don't want to take up any more of your time."

"Right," Ian muttered, parking in the small downtown lot behind the building that housed the bar and his apartment. "It's always Brett, isn't it? Is that why you really came back to Minnesota? It wasn't for the coaching job, at all, was it? It was to fix things with Brett, only, he didn't tell you he'd met Alyssa."

Marta's mouth dropped open.

Shoving the bear into the back seat, she snapped, "That's not it at all. I don't know what you're talking about."

Ian pushed the car door open.

Marta scrambled after him.

"Like hell you don't," he yelled at her over the hood of the car. "You get all misty-eyed, and your lips tremble when someone says his name. Whenever we're all together, you can't take your eyes off him. Tell me what that's all about if you're not still in love with him."

To finish his speech, Ian slammed his hands onto the hood of the car, the engine clicking as it cooled.

Marta's mind reeled. "That's not why I cry, you idiot, that's not why I can't talk about him or what happened. I'm not thinking about Brett. I'm thinking about our baby."

She didn't take any satisfaction when Ian's face turned ashen, or the way his throat worked even though he wasn't swallowing.

Head lowered, she turned on her heel and walked away.

IAN LET HER go, though there was nothing he wanted more

than to wrap his arms around her shaking shoulders and comfort her.

She and Brett had had a baby.

But that couldn't be, he thought as he began to unload Shyla's things from his car.

He'd gone to school, all four years, at the university with Marta, Brett, and Dane. He would have noticed if Marta had swelled with Brett's child. He wasn't sure what he would have done if he would have been forced to watch that. He wouldn't have been able to. It was that simple. Had she and Brett had a baby, he would have dropped out of school, or transferred his credits.

She hadn't actually said she'd gotten pregnant. Maybe she meant when she looked at Brett she could picture the family they could have had if they'd stayed together.

Full of resentment, he dumped the load onto the middle of his open-plan living room. Not only did Marta see in Brett a man she used to love, she saw the family she didn't have.

Great.

Ian finished hauling the rest of Shyla's toys and clothes from the car, and on his last trip Sadie met him in the hallway.

"What's all this shit?"

"Shyla's things. I have a crib and some furniture being delivered later today. Who knew babies needed so much stuff, huh?"

Sadie sneered at all the bags on his floor. Her face was free of bruises as were her arms and the parts of her calves he could see—her capris leggings stopped below her knee. Since the day he saw them, he hadn't brought up the marks on her back, but he couldn't let something like that go, either.

"I still don't know why you're doing it," Sadie said, flopping onto his couch.

"I took you in, didn't I?"

Sadie laughed, narrowing her eyes at him. "Yeah, and look where that got you."

Ian opened his fridge and pulled out a can of soda. "Sadie, sometimes you do the right thing because it's the right thing—not to get anything out of it."

Nope, he thought as his sister laughed herself to her own apartment, sometimes a person wasn't rewarded with anything but a headache and a broken heart.

Not able to do much with Shyla's things, Ian left the bags in a heap in the middle of his living room. He hoped the delivery men were ahead of schedule; he couldn't depend on Sadie to let them into the building.

Ian said he would take Marta to the funeral, and he planned to follow through.

He was in the middle of moving the old things out of the bedroom when the delivery men arrived. To keep the room clear to paint, he asked them to leave everything in his living room. He was going to hold Marta to her offer—there was no way he was going to decorate a nursery by himself, and he was sure as hell Sadie wouldn't help.

While he showered, Ian prodded the subject of Marta and Brett like he would a sore tooth.

Maybe she'd gotten pregnant and had a miscarriage. It would explain the tears and feelings she had for Brett. Miscarriages were emotional events for women—his mother had had two before Sadie was born. It was one of the reasons why there were so many years between them.

But it wasn't the baby that upset him. It was her obvious feelings for Brett that left him feeling angry and beaten down.

For the past ten years he'd been nothing but a shadow compared to Brett.

He dressed in black slacks, a grey shirt, and carried a black jacket. The temperature made it too warm to put on now, but he could slip it on inside the church. It had been many years since he'd attended a funeral, and his grandmother's had been a simple ceremony for family and friends.

Coach Wesley had been a well-liked member of the running community and a part of one of the biggest universities in the state. The funeral would be a large drawn-out affair.

He texted Marta to let her know he was on the way. Their afternoon fight didn't change the fact she would need him.

As Ian shoved his key into his car's ignition, his cell phone rang. He reached for it hoping it wasn't Marta telling him she was catching a ride with Dane and Nikki, though that would have been logical.

His father's number flashed on the screen, but he turned his phone off rather than answering it.

He hadn't touched based with his parents for quite some time because there was nothing new to report. His father might have heard he wasn't keeping regular hours at the bar anymore, but he couldn't help that.

The bar would have been open now if he hadn't wanted to go to the funeral with Marta. If his dad wanted to bust his chops about it, then he could come to Minnesota and run his own bar.

It irked him they hadn't called about Shyla. Their

silence about the little girl made it evident they hadn't thought about taking the baby or had even wanted to discuss options with him, though it would have pissed him off if they had.

They'd been so hell bent to get out of Minnesota, his parents hadn't even taken the time to finish raising their own kids.

Well, whatever, his dad could wait.

Ian buzzed Marta's apartment. When the security door clicked open, he trotted up the stairs. He tapped once on the door with his knuckles and let himself inside.

MARTA, DRESSED IN black, tried not to cry.

Coach Wesley had been a big part of her life while she'd been at school. Coaching track was only a small portion of what a coach did. They were nutritionists, cheerleaders, and counselors.

Brett had holed up with the coach for hours BSing and talking about his mom and dad. Coach Wesley had been a guest at Dane and Liz's wedding and had attended the ribbon cutting ceremony when Dane opened his store.

A coach was more than a coach. Along the way Coach Wesley become a friend, and she would miss working with him at the university.

When Ian buzzed to be let up, she was looking for her black pumps. She didn't know why he bothered when he could jimmy the lock open and let himself inside.

Butterflies flew around her stomach while she waited the few seconds it would take for him to reach her apartment. He would no doubt have questions, but she wanted to put off explaining for as long as possible.

"Hey," Ian said, opening her door.

Kneeling in front of her coat closet, she blinked at him. She'd probably go to hell for thinking the thoughts that bombarded her mind when he stepped into her apartment. Heat pooled in her belly, and a cold sweat covered her skin.

She wished they were going on a date instead of attending a funeral.

"What are you doing?" he asked, frowning.

"Looking for my shoes. I'm not completely unpacked yet."

"In case you decide to go back to California?"

Marta found the pair of black pumps at the bottom of a deep cardboard box. "No," she said, wiggling from out of the closet. "I'm lazy."

Ian held out a hand to help her stand.

She took it, his skin cool and smooth. "Thanks."

"You look nice."

"So do you. I wish we were doing something else."

"I was thinking about asking you out," Ian said, waiting while she grabbed her purse from the kitchen.

"You were?" Marta smoothed the wrinkles she'd made in her skirt from kneeling on the floor.

"Yeah. But now with Shyla, I guess I missed my chance."

Marta locked her door and followed Ian down the empty hallway.

"I wouldn't say that."

He paused it the middle of the hallway. "Yeah?"

"Yeah."

He stepped closer, and cupped her cheek in his palm. "Good."

Marta trailed her fingers over his jaw, his sexy whiskers scraping her skin. "I'm sorry for how things are going."

Ian rested his forehead against hers, and they stood in the middle of the hallway, not talking, trying to find a scrap of peace before the storm.

"You're here, Marta. It's enough for now."

But one day it wouldn't be, and then she'd have to decide how much she had to give him, and if it would be enough to make him happy.

The funeral was held in a nondenominational church located on the other side of Tower City. While they were early, the parking lot didn't have an available space, and they had to park several blocks away.

With an arm around her shoulders, Ian steadied her as they walked along the tree-lined street. They were joined by others walking the sidewalk to the church, and ahead, Dane and Nikki and Brett and Alyssa disappeared through the church's heavy front doors.

It stung they hadn't invited them to attend the funeral together, and if they were excluding her because of her history with Brett, Ian was also being left out through no fault of his own.

At first glance, there didn't seem to be room on any of the numerous pews inside the large church, and Marta resigned herself to having to stand in heels through the entire service.

"Miss Braddock!"

Spaulding's voice cut through the low murmurs of people waiting for the service to start.

Marta stiffened.

"Easy. He can't do anything to you."

Ian's gentle reminder did little to help her relax, and her heart beat frantically when Spaulding's stare locked onto hers as he pushed his way through the crowd.

"You'll sit at the front for the announcement."

"What announcement?" Marta muttered at Spaulding's back as he pushed aside mourners who were consoling each other.

Her cheeks flamed in embarrassment for Spaulding who didn't seem to either care or understand how his callous behavior made him look.

"Has he told you anything?" Ian asked when Spaulding stopped in front of the altar and pointed at the first bench in the row.

She and Ian could barely squeeze into the small space on the pew, but she sat like the obedient puppy Spaulding was treating her as, and Ian rubbed her back.

"I don't know what his game is," Marta mumbled.

He rested his arm along the back of the pew, and Marta leaned into his side.

"I guess we're about to find out."

The pastor began the service, and she let herself focus on the large mahogany casket decorated with a large spray of white roses.

She followed through the motions—praying when instructed, singing the hymns. Toward the end of the service, when it looked as if she were in the clear, she slumped into Ian's side in relief.

Ian nudged her, and Marta lifted her eyes from the dull brown carpeting.

Spaulding stood from his pew across the aisle from theirs and took a place behind the pulpit.

He cleared his throat and ran a hand down his blood-red tie. "I did not have the honor of working with John Wesley for long," Spaulding began, "but what I learned in that short amount of time was Coach Wesley cared about his students. He cared about the school, and he cared about the sport.

"I look around at this congregation and marvel at how many people cared about him in return. I want to do something special in memorandum of Coach Wesley, and as the Athletics Director at Minnesota State University, Tower City, I have decided to ask anyone and everyone who wishes, to make a pledge on Marta Braddock's race time at the Lady Slipper Marathon.

"The University will match every dollar and make a generous donation in Coach Wesley's name to the cardiac unit of Beacon Hospital where he was treated. Information about this, and the scholarship, will be made available on the school's website.

"Miss Braddock, please say a few words to honor the late Coach Wesley."

Marta's heart sank.

It was as if Spaulding had known she'd been thinking of backing out of the marathon. She couldn't withdraw now that both a hospital donation and a scholarship were contingent on her racing.

Ian jabbed her with his elbow, and she realized she'd been staring blankly into space.

Spaulding glared at her, though he tried to mask the dislike blazing in his icy blue eyes with a smile.

As though she were walking in a fog, she made her way to the altar. She was too short to stand behind the pulpit, and she stood next to it, resisted shaking Spaulding's hand off her shoulder when he grabbed her in what she believed was a show of faux support.

"Coach Wesley," Marta began, "meant a lot to me."

She focused on Ian and his kind grey eyes.

He gave her a discreet thumbs-up and she nodded, thanking him for being with her.

"Coach Wesley meant a lot to everyone who had the

honor of meeting him, working with him, running for him. He was more than a coach—he was a surrogate father to those of us far from home, many for the first time in our lives. He was therapist, cheerleader, and our biggest support out there on the road. I'm humbled to run in Coach Wesley's honor at the Lady Slipper Marathon, and I'll do my absolute best to make him proud—as I always have. Thank you."

The church was no place for applause, and she wasn't disappointed when she didn't receive any.

Spaulding, on the other hand, cursed under his breath when the pastor simply took his place behind the pulpit to conclude the service.

"You did good," Ian said, wrapping his arm around her as she sat.

She sank into his embrace but didn't lean her head on his shoulder the way she wanted. It wasn't the time for a display of affection, and she didn't want to give Ian the wrong impression besides. She should have been relieved Ian wouldn't have much time for her after Shyla's arrival, but the thought made her melancholy.

Spaulding had her pinned like a bug under a sheet of glass—she didn't have the right, or the time, to be sad.

She would need to train harder now that the race's outcome meant even more to the community of Tower City. The better her time during the marathon, the more money that would be raised for the hospital.

In the church basement, volunteers dished up casserole and dinner buns, and Marta sat through it because she wanted to be a part of the processional that would drive to the cemetery after the meal. She hoped Ian would stick with her through the evening.

She didn't want to be alone.

"Miss Braddock."

Spaulding's voice sent chills down her spine.

Under the table, Ian's hand resting on her thigh did little to calm her.

Marta looked over her shoulder and blinked in surprise. "Miss Layne."

The short, strawberry-blonde woman laughed. "You can call me Libbie, Marta. It's nice to see you again."

When Libbie embraced her, she tried not to pull away in distaste. While she and the other runner were friendly, they weren't friends.

"Libbie is here at my request," Spaulding said with obvious affection and pride. "She'll be filling in at the university while you train for the marathon. Coach Wesley, may he rest in peace, explained how difficult it would be for you to do both. Even on his deathbed he was thinking of others."

Marta flinched.

With a snap of Spaulding's fingers, her coaching position at the school had been taken away, and oh, so slyly, too.

Only until after the marathon, she reminded herself.

Coach Wesley had done her a favor giving her every opportunity to train for the race. But he'd also blocked her in—there was no way she could back out of the marathon claiming the track students needed her.

"I'm sorry for your loss," Libbie said, leaning into Spaulding.

Marta narrowed her eyes. There was something going on, but she couldn't quite put her finger on it.

"We'll let you get back to your meal," Spaulding said.

"Keep me updated on your training, Miss Braddock. You have much riding on your success."

Libbie held out her hand. "If you need advice or a running partner, let me know. I'd be happy to help."

Marta held the woman's hand limply in her own and dropped it as quickly as she dared without seeming rude. There was no way in hell she would ask the woman for help.

"What was that all about?" Brett asked when Spaulding and Libbie walked away, stopping to talk to other mourners and school staff as they made their way across the crowded basement to the exit.

"Spaulding replaced me. He said only until the marathon is over, but Coach isn't here to bat for me anymore."

Dane put his arm around her. "With the pledge money going to the hospital because of you, how would it look if he replaced you after the race? He has to keep you."

That sounded true enough, and Marta relaxed. "You're right. Are you going to the cemetery?"

"We're heading home, if that's okay," Nikki said, towering over her in heels matching her plain black dress.

"Yeah, that's fine," Ian said from behind her. "We'll go, then I'll take Marta home."

"Sounds good," Brett said, shaking Ian's hand.

Alyssa pinked, and Marta sighed. She thought she'd cleared the air with Alyssa at the park.

"Thank you for staying with me," Marta said as they sat in traffic.

The funeral procession stretched out in front of them, creeping along the road to a graveyard located near the outskirts of town.

"How do you feel about Spaulding's announcement?

He has a way of springing things on you in public." Ian asked, not taking his eyes off the road.

"I think he does that so I can't say no. If he would've asked me in private to run the marathon, I would have said hell no, and probably wouldn't have taken the job, either. But Spaulding couldn't force me out that way—Wesley wanted me to coach and had the school behind him. They're great ideas, the donation to the hospital and the scholarship, but I wouldn't have done it given the choice."

"He's a crafty one." Ian turned onto the narrow dirt road of the cemetery.

"There was something between him and Libbie Layne. Did you see it?"

"No." Ian pulled the key out of the ignition and rested his lips against her forehead. "Don't look for things that aren't there. Without the coach to keep an eye on you, you have enough to worry about."

Admitting that was true, she and Ian followed the other mourners who had taken the drive to the gravesite.

Marta allowed herself the tears then, and she cried into Ian's side.

After a final prayer the crowd dispersed, some throwing flowers onto the casket as the groundskeepers lowered it into the grave.

Marta wished would have asked Ian to stop—she wanted flowers too—but she was running the Lady Slipper Marathon in his name and that would have to do.

"Marta!"

Marta jerked her head.

Holly Carole tottered toward them, the heels of her pumps sinking into the grass.

"I'll let you two talk," Ian said, squeezing her hand. "I'll meet you at the car."

He was halfway to the small parking lot when Holly reached her.

"Hey," Holly said, watching Ian walk away. "I guess I know where his loyalties lay."

"I'm not sure what that was about," Marta said.

The cemetery was peaceful, a light wind blowing, the sun a buttery filter through wispy clouds. The grounds were kept in pristine condition with the grass mowed, and of course, flowers were colorful memorials on every grave.

The Ruby River ran along the border of the cemetery, slices of the water glistening through the trees in the sun.

Some of the mourners who had attended Coach Wesley's graveside service had moved on to other graves to pay their respects.

"Were you at the church? I didn't see you."

"I was there with some of the other faculty," Holly said. She slipped the heels off her feet and blew out a sigh. "I avoided you because I didn't feel like seeing Dane. At first I was surprised to see him there, but then I remembered he ran with Coach Wesley, he and Brett both."

Marta followed Holly's example and toed off her heels, grateful she hadn't worn nylons. The grass tickled her feet, and her spine cracked as she settled into her own height.

"We were all pretty close," Marta murmured, her mind drifting back to her college days—they felt far away, but she remembered them like they had just happened.

"Did you see the coach after he was taken to the hospital? Were you able to say goodbye?" Holly asked. She bent and picked up her shoes.

Marta began to walk toward the river, avoiding Coach Wesley's newly-dug grave.

She couldn't look at it anymore. Over her shoulder, she caught a glimpse of Ian leaning against his car checking his phone. He looked content enough. It would be okay to speak with Holly for a few more minutes.

"Yes. I visited him the day after the press conference, but I didn't know it would be the last time I would ever see him again. He looked weak, but he seemed to be on the mend."

"Messy business," Holly said, skirting around a large grave with a weeping stone angel atop the marker.

"You're not kidding," Marta muttered.

Spaulding's announcement at the press conference could have triggered the coach's heart attack.

"They didn't get along from the beginning," Holly said, confirming Marta's suspicions.

She paused when a doe walked from the tree line near the river.

"I find it hard to believe Spaulding would mesh with anyone," she said.

"He's very abrasive. In fact . . ." Holly tilted her head toward Marta and lowered her voice, though they were alone, ". . . Spaulding visited Coach Wesley in the hospital a few minutes before the coach passed away."

"How do you know that?"

"A friend in the Sociology department has a daughter who is a nurse there. Rumors were flying all over the hospital."

The hair on the nape of Marta's neck stood on end. "How did the coach die? Like I said, he seemed okay when I saw him. Not healthy, but he looked like he would be okay with more rest."

"That was the prognosis. Then Spaulding visited. Five minutes after that, Coach Wesley was dead."

"You're not insinuating Spaulding killed him, are you?" Marta asked, a chill running over her skin despite the heat.

Holly cast her a side-long glance. "Like pushing a pillow to his face or tampering with his IV? No."

She tucked a piece of brilliant red hair behind her ear revealing an emerald stud decorating her earlobe.

"But I'm not above speculating they had words that caused the coach to relapse. Spaulding was out the door by the time anyone thought to question him."

"Unless an autopsy report proves otherwise, Spaulding's off the hook," Marta said.

"There wasn't one. It was another heart attack, plain and simple. The cause of it doesn't matter. Besides, without family, there was no one around to press the issue."

"I don't like this," Marta said, meeting Ian's eyes across the cemetery.

"I don't either," Holly said, placing a hand on Marta's shoulder. "Be careful."

It was too late for that.

CHAPTER FIVE

MARTA WALKED TOWARD him, a frown puckering her face. Whatever Holly told her hadn't been good.

"What was that all about?" she asked, shielding her eyes from the sun with her hand.

"What?" Ian slid into his car. He'd turned it on to cool off the inside. The heat pressed down on him; he shouldn't have dressed in black.

Marta sat next to him and immediately aimed an air conditioner vent at her face. "Running off like that."

Maneuvering away from the cemetery, Ian said, "I didn't need to be in the middle of your girl talk. Besides, it's awkward seeing her again. She reminds me of a shark—gliding through the water uninterested until . . . bam!" Ian grabbed Marta's leg. "You're fish food."

"Jesus, Ian," Marta laughed, pushing his hand off her thigh. "You're going to give me a heart attack."

"Nicely done, and a bit too soon, if you care about that kind of thing."

"It's your fault, and I do care. I'm sorry he died the way he did. Where are we going, anyway?"

"How about food? The casserole at the church was disgusting."

Picturing the grey blob on his paper plate made his stomach churn. He'd only wanted to keep Marta company, not suffer from ptomaine poisoning.

"You're always feeding me," Marta said.

"You need it." Ian drove them to the bar and parked in the small lot.

"I thought you said we were eating."

"I didn't say where." Ian grinned.

"Nicely done," Marta echoed him, rolling her eyes.

"What did Holly have to say?" Ian asked.

The bar was closed, but it held as many people as it did open. He had to remember to call his father back. His dad hadn't left a message, and every now and then it worried Ian why he'd called in the first place.

Marta threw her purse onto his couch and kicked off her heels. "Wow, look at all this stuff," she said, eyeing the pile of Shyla's things and the new furniture that had been delivered. "The social worker is going to be impressed."

Ian hoped so. Anything to help make this go smoothly. "Yeah, and I'm holding you to helping me paint in the morning."

Marta sat at the kitchen table. "Wouldn't miss it."

Ian ran his hand over her hair. "Thanks. I'll make us a late dinner while you tell me what's going on."

While he chopped lettuce, tomatoes, and cucumbers for giant salads, Marta told him what Holly had said, and Ian frowned.

"Holly didn't want to make it sound like Spaulding was

responsible Coach Wesley had another heart attack," Marta said, picking up her fork.

"But he did."

"Maybe. I don't know if we can blame Spaulding for the first one."

Ian scoffed. "I was there—no one was more surprised about the marathon announcement than Coach Wesley. Plus, if they've been rubbing wrong this whole time, maybe the stress got to be too much."

He couldn't imagine anyone being able to put up with Gregory Spaulding for long—and that included Marta. "It wouldn't be a bad idea to back out."

"How would that look? You saw how many people at the funeral thanked me. Spaulding boxed me in to watch me squirm and make me quit. He already has a replacement when I fall flat on my face. I can't give him the satisfaction."

"But it isn't just the school, is it, that's making you feel stressed out? Because let's be honest here, if you're not ready to run, you're not ready. No one would fault you for backing out, even with the hospital donation and the scholarship riding on it. No, it's more than that. Is it Brett? Is it him and Alyssa getting engaged?"

The words popped out of his mouth, and he cursed under his breath.

Marta chewed a bite of lettuce and took a sip of the strawberry lemonade he'd poured them. "I've always struggled, Ian. Since school," she whispered, pushing her plate away. "I was just able to hide it better."

"I'm sorry. I have no excuse to pick on you." He ran a hand over his face. "But this afternoon what you said. I didn't want to ask because of the funeral . . ."

Marta stood and paced barefoot along the narrow strip of free space in his living room. She grabbed the large teddy bear off his couch and hugged it to her. "Junior year . . ." she started.

Ian's throat constricted.

Finally he was going to hear what happened between her and Brett. Finally he would know if he could compete with Brett's ghost, and all he'd left behind.

He pushed his plate away and rested his head in his hands, prepared for the worst.

". . . I got pregnant." She stared out the window into the narrow alley between the buildings. "You know Brett had a rough childhood."

Ian nodded. He knew all about how Brett grew up.

"I was trying to build a running career; a family was the last thing on my mind. Maybe if Brett had been in a better place . . . Well, he wasn't, so it doesn't matter. He pressured me to get an abortion, and I did."

He stood, the chair falling backward onto the hardwood floor.

Despite the clatter, Marta didn't turn around. "We both felt guilty. I mean, we should have tried, right? Tried to raise our baby, tried to be a family. Only, I knew Brett didn't know what family was. If I'd had the baby, he wouldn't have stuck around; I would've been high and dry. No husband, no career, and a baby I couldn't support."

Ian waited for the disgust to wash over him, waited for the disapproval and censure over what she'd done to consume him.

But it didn't.

All he felt was relief.

Relief Marta hadn't had another man's child.

If she wanted babies, he would be the man who gave them to her.

Disgust did wash over him then, but not toward Marta.

For himself.

He was as bad as Brett who wouldn't shoulder the responsibility of a baby like a man.

Ian drew her into his arms, her rigid back against his chest. "I'm sorry you went through that."

"It's why I can't stop. Do you see now? The sacrifices I've made? I have to make my baby's life worth it." She dropped the bear and turned in his arms.

He let her cry against his chest.

Ian wanted to say something, but there was nothing.

Nothing would make Marta or himself feel better.

Concerned about her, Ian wanted Marta to spend the night, but she begged off, claiming the need to sleep undisturbed.

She'd had such a long day what with shopping and the funeral, as soon as she made it upstairs, she changed into her pajamas and crawled into bed.

In a way, she was relieved Ian hadn't said anything about her abortion, but it worried her, too.

He hadn't said anything at all.

If actions spoke louder than words, then his hug while she cried should have meant more than a thousand platitudes. But it didn't ease Marta's worries, and it took her several hours to fall asleep, despite her fatigue.

The next morning she ran, the pledge Spaulding made on her behalf dogging her every step.

She ate a quick breakfast, and as she sipped her fourth mug of coffee texted Ian.

They hadn't made any arrangements for the day, though

she assumed he would want the room painted and put together as quickly as possible.

He replied with an *ASAP*.

Marta dressed in a pair of old faded black shorts and a Minnesota State University, Tower City, t-shirt she thought had belonged to Brett at some point.

Her clothes were old and grubby enough if she covered them in paint splotches, she wouldn't mourn their loss.

Ian already had the floor covered with plastic and had taped around the window when she let herself inside his apartment.

"I suppose you've been up for hours," Ian said, stirring paint with a thin wooden stick.

Colored a bright bubble-gum pink, the paint made Marta's eyes hurt. She had to agree with him, though; it would look a lot better than the split pea green that covered the walls now.

"Sure have." She smothered a yawn. "I don't know how long I'm going to last before I need a nap."

"Then it's good Spaulding replaced you, right?" Ian asked, handing her a foam paint roller. "You couldn't have started coaching if you're training for the race all the time."

"That's true, but I'm still put out by it. I shouldn't even be running the stupid thing."

They worked in silence until the quiet stifled her, and she couldn't breathe.

"Ian," she said, dipping her roller into the pan of paint.

"Huh?" Ian grunted, standing on a ladder, reaching to the ceiling.

Already the room looked cheerier.

"You didn't have much to say yester-day . . . about . . . what I did."

Ian leaned his forearms against the top of the ladder and

fixed his stare on her. His flinty grey eyes held a storm of emotion, and she was sorry she asked.

He could be morally, ethically, and religiously against abortion and didn't want to tell her. What she'd done could have completely changed the way he felt about her.

But it was better for her to know the truth than pretend it didn't matter because it did.

She cared what Ian thought of her. Too much.

"You don't want to hear what I was thinking."

Marta's heart sank.

It was bad.

So bad he didn't want to tell her.

She couldn't stay there knowing that's what he thought of her. "I'm sorry," she murmured. "If you feel like that, I should go." Resting her sponge in the paint pan, she tried to hold back her tears.

"You don't know what I'm feeling," Ian snapped, jumping from the ladder. The plastic crackled under his tennis shoes.

"Well it can't be that great if you don't want me to know."

"No, no it's not, but not in the way you're thinking."

"Then why won't you tell me?" Marta asked, shoving her hands onto her hips.

"Because I'm afraid you won't like me after I do."

Marta softened.

She took a step toward him and ran her fingers over his arm.

He'd dressed much like she was in an old Butler's Bar tank top and basketball shorts already speckled with white paint.

"There's nothing you could say that's worse than what I told you yesterday."

She was damn sure of that.

Ian sighed. "Don't be too sure."

She opened her mouth to speak, but Ian stopped her from saying anything when he dropped to his knees and cradled her hips in his hands.

"You know I've been in love with you for a long time, don't you?"

Marta nodded, her heart in her throat.

"A long time," he repeated. "Since we met in college. Seeing you with Brett on campus all the time was hard for me, hanging out with you while you and Brett were all over each other . . . But it was worse than not seeing you."

Marta smoothed her fingers through his dark blond hair. "I'm sorry."

He pressed his lips to the knuckles of one of her hands before he continued. "I can't lie. When you and Brett broke up, I was happy. I thought maybe after you got over him, I'd finally have a chance. Hell, I would've been happy being your rebound guy. Anything to have your attention, just for a little while. But instead, all you did was study, run, and after graduation, you left."

Marta searched his eyes wondering where he was going with this.

"I was devastated. It put me in a bad way, and when you came back, it was like I'd been given a second chance. But even what I felt for you then is just a shadow of what I feel for you now. When you told me you'd had an abortion?"

"What?" she whispered.

"I was glad." The grip he held on her hands tightened until Marta thought her bones would crack. "I was glad. Glad I didn't have to watch Brett's baby grow inside you. I was glad I didn't have to see what a baby between you and him would look like. I was glad because the only babies I want you to have are mine."

He buried his face in her shirt, and she hugged his head to her.

She'd had no idea men could feel that way. It was an emotion Marta could see women feeling easily enough, but a man admitting jealousy of another man's baby was something she'd never heard of before.

But before she could tell him she wouldn't be having any man's babies, a woman clearing her throat interrupted them, and Marta jerked her eyes toward the bedroom's doorway.

Sadie stood beside a tall black woman dressed in a grey suit holding a blonde toddler.

"This is Mrs. Gibson," Sadie said. "What's going on?"

"I asked Marta to marry me," Ian said from his kneeling position. "And she said yes."

IAN DIDN'T HAVE time to think about how pissed Marta would be about the announcement.

After she'd been polite to the social worker, had gone through the motions of being the joyful new fiancée, she'd bolted, offering the lame excuse she wanted to give Shyla time to adjust.

That had been two weeks ago.

Mrs. Gibson had stayed in Tower City for a week, studying him and Sadie and helping the little girl adapt to her new surroundings.

Worried how he'd look to Mrs. Gibson that he didn't have a plan in place for Shyla while he worked, he'd simply closed the bar until the social worker flew back to Colorado.

He'd figure things out when his and Sadie's every move weren't being scrutinized.

Ian hoped Marta would end up being right—having a baby around would give Sadie focus.

While that hadn't happened yet, he and Sadie had developed a tenuous arrangement of sorts, and he was grateful for the little bit of time she deigned to give him.

Nothing more was said about her bruises, and she always showed up to watch Shyla, though what she did when Ian didn't need her was anyone's guess.

He wished Marta would call or stop by. They hadn't talked about his confession, or the huge black lie he'd told the social worker.

While he scrambled eggs for breakfast for himself and Shyla, who was playing with a stack of blocks in the middle of his living room floor, he admitted the lie had certainly helped Mrs. Gibson leave Shyla in his care.

She hadn't any qualms with Ian acting as Shyla's father, she'd already known he was single, but shoving Marta into the picture had been good news and Ian had seen the relief written all over her face.

He'd only been speaking from his heart, not under any motivation to pull the wool over Mrs. Gibson's eyes, but while he was glad some good had come of it, now he was worried he'd scared Marta away.

His cell phone rang as he was sitting Shyla in her high chair to eat eggs and toast, and he grabbed it before the call went to voicemail.

"Hello, Ian," his dad's voice boomed from the phone. "It's been murder getting a hold of you. What have you been doing? Working the bar, I hope?"

"Hey, Dad," Ian muttered.

He paused at the silverware drawer. Did toddlers use forks?

Shyla took care of it, planting both her little hands into the pile of eggs.

"Things okay with you and your sister?"

"And Shyla," Ian said, wanting to make it clear he resented being the only family member who cared enough to take in the baby.

"Well, son, taking her was your choice," his father said, a Southern drawl seeping into his speech, softening his harsh Midwestern accent.

"Not much of a choice."

Shyla sprinkled egg onto his kitchen floor.

"There's always a choice, Ian," his father barked.

"Did you call for something, Dad? Sadie's not here, if you wanted to talk to her. You'll have to try her cell and hope she picks up."

He chewed on a piece of toast hoping if he showed Shyla where the food went, she would eat it.

"Yes, I did. You're not happy with the bar, and I know you've grown to resent taking it over—just the way in the next few years you'll resent your decision to take that little rugrat."

Ian could believe his father honestly thought that. If there had been a chance he would regret taking Shyla, he wouldn't have done it.

Now, announcing Marta was his fiancée, that was something else entirely.

"I don't resent taking over the bar, but it's not bringing in any money and I don't know how long you want me to run it."

"Not any longer. I sold it. The deal will go through by the end of the month. I've been trying to call you to warn you, but there must be other things more important than talking to your old man."

Ian's blood ran hot then cold, and Shyla's shrieks, as she used her piece of toast as a Frisbee, faded as the buzz in his ears grew stronger.

"You sold the bar? What about our apartments?"

He sank into a kitchen chair. Shyla eyed him warily, no doubt sensing the change in the room. The little girl probably had a gauge better than most adults. Ian tried to smile to reassure her, but he didn't succeed.

"I sold the whole building, lock, stock, and barrel. You have until the end of the month to move out."

"And Sadie?"

"Sadie's an adult and can take care of herself. You think your mother and I don't know what's been going on? She's not working and not going to school. You've coddled her and look where it got you. Your mother and I decided to split the money from the sale, and we're giving you half. Use it to get Sadie settled, find a place of your own, or do whatever the hell you want. The realtor will be in touch with you, and you better start packing."

"I just painted Shyla's room," Ian whispered.

"You'll paint another. Listen, Ian."

Ian focused on his father's voice.

"Shyla, she's a big responsibility. She's yours to take care of—for the next little while. If you're going to be her father, go all out. Buy a house, buy her a swing set and a puppy. Find a wife and give her a mother and a sibling. I know you think we weren't good parents, and maybe we weren't. You can't be all the time, but we loved you kids. Wait until you get older, and you've put fifteen years into raising Shyla. You'll want your life back, and that's not anything to feel guilty about. I need to go, your mother and I are meeting friends for an early lunch. Once the sale has been finalized, the check for your half will be delivered to you by the realtor. Stay in touch, son, let us know how things go."

His father didn't give him a chance to say goodbye.

With a trembling hand, Ian set the phone onto the table.

Shyla, sensing the bad news, burst into tears.

I have nothing for you, kid. Nothing for nobody.

MARTA DIDN'T MEAN to disappear on Ian, it just happened.

She started training harder which meant she slept more and ate more. She spent a lot of time soaking in the tub, dulling the monotony by propping an iPad on the toilet and watching Netflix while she numbed her body in icy baths.

She was closing in on the miles she needed, but her speed seriously lacked.

Libbie Layne called and offered again to be a running partner, but Marta declined. She'd rather not run at all than run with Libbie. Even if Libbie hadn't creeped her out at Coach Wesley's funeral, Marta had no interest in being the woman's friend.

Marta dodged calls from everyone, though she told herself if Ian would've called, she would've answered.

She didn't know if that was true, but she liked to think so.

Not that he'd given her the chance to find out.

Guilt gnawed at her.

Marta rolled on her foam roller trying to work a knot out of her leg when someone knocked on her door.

"Come in," Marta yelled, reluctant to pause her stretching. She felt lost without any training guidance. She had people she could ask for help and advice, but she didn't want to be told she couldn't do the one thing Spaulding promised everyone she could do.

"Hey," Nikki said walking through her kitchen into the living room. "It's so weird being in here when it used to be Dane's place. When are you going to buy a kitchen table?"

"I eat over the sink, I don't need one. Sorry about the texts. I've been training." Marta moved her legs through another stretch.

"Well, what are you doing right now?"

"I think that's clear." Marta inhaled to breathe through the stretch.

Nikki flopped onto Marta's couch, her blonde spirals bouncing around her shoulders. "If you're done, let's go shopping, Alyssa's free."

Dress shopping was the last thing Marta wanted to do, but she'd made a promise. First though, she wanted to ask Nikki about something that had been bothering her.

"How come you didn't ask me and Ian to go to the church with you for the coach's funeral?"

Nikki frowned. "What do you mean? Didn't you go together?"

Marta brushed the hair out of her face. "Yeah, but you and Dane and Alyssa and Brett went together. If Ian is being excluded because Alyssa is jealous of my history with Brett, that's not fair to him."

She stood and adjusted the crotch of her shorts. She'd have to change clothes before leaving. There was no way in hell she'd be caught in a bridal shop in her running clothes. Those places screamed sophistication, and she wanted to fit in.

She'd been doing such a horrible job of it lately.

"That's not why. Alyssa isn't jealous of you—she and

Brett are doing great. The thing is," Nikki paused, twirling her hair between her fingers, "it's Ian and Brett who haven't gotten along. They've been friends, but there's always been an animosity between them. Ian's blamed Brett for a lot of things, and after you came back, he believed there was still something between you and Brett. You're going to have to give them time to smooth things over."

Nikki stood and slid the straps of an icy blue dress farther up her shoulders. "This whole group thing is going to be different, you know?"

Marta shuffled into her bedroom, her legs like rubbery noodles. She started sorting through her closet, but before she could choose, Nikki shoved a maxi skirt and tank top combination at her. "Wear this, it's cute."

After falling backward onto Marta's bed, Nikki said, "Alyssa's acting off, I do admit that, but it doesn't have anything to do with you."

Stripping, not giving a crap about modesty, Marta shot Nikki a "yeah right" look.

"No, really. She's pregnant, but she doesn't want to tell me."

Regret tugged at Marta's heart. She was happy for Brett and Alyssa, she really was. Alyssa had been able to do for Brett what Marta herself had failed to do. She should be grateful to Alyssa.

And she was.

But.

Marta pulled on the white maxi skirt decorated with Japanese cherry blossoms and the matching white tank top she'd bought to pair with it. "Why wouldn't she tell you?"

"Because she knows Dane and I crunch numbers all the time. Unless we have another source of income, we can't get pregnant. That's it."

"And Dane doesn't want to direct the marathon."

"No. I can understand why, but anything else he does is going to take up time, too. I guess he's watched Brett deal with things for so long he doesn't want any part of it. I don't know what we'll do, but we have time. I mean, we wouldn't try until after the wedding. It would be silly to get knocked up when I've already spent a ton on my wedding dress."

"Then you and Dane don't have any kind of plan?"

Nikki rolled to her side and propped her head on her hand. "Not really. I can always go back to work. Seems like the easiest choice, though Dane doesn't want me to do that. What will happen will happen. That's my philosophy."

"At least Ian isn't being excluded because of me and Alyssa," Marta said with relief. "I didn't know all this was going on while I was in California. Brett never said anything, and I didn't think ask because I didn't know how Ian felt about me."

"Ian's blamed Brett for you leaving. He may have tried to hide it, but it was always there. That should go away now."

"Why is that?"

Nikki giggled. "Because Ian finally has what he wants."

But did he really? Marta wasn't so sure.

"I NEED TO talk to you," Ian said when Sadie appeared downstairs.

"I'm sorry I'm late," Sadie snapped, heading toward the playpen he'd set up for Shyla.

Dressed in a pink and white t-shirt, the edge of her diaper poking above the waistband of her pink shorts, Shyla was playing with a toy piano that lit up when she pressed the keys.

Ian had gathered as much hair as he could into a lopsided ponytail to keep it out of her face. He thought she needed a haircut, but he wasn't sure where he could take her to have that done. He would need to Google it or maybe call his mother.

"That's not what I want to talk to you about," Ian said, filling bowls of peanuts for tables no one would sit at. Well, at least not if Brett and Dane didn't stop in.

"Then what?"

Ian sighed. "Why does everything have to be a fight? Can't we ever have a normal conversation?"

Sadie slid onto a stool. "Can I have a beer then, if I have to listen to you bitch?"

"No. You don't need to be drinking, plus you're babysitting for me later." He pulled a can of Coke from the cooler. "I talked to Dad this morning."

"Oh, really? He finally took a break between rounds of golf to give you a call?"

"Yeah, but he had more to talk about than if the bar is in the black."

Sadie slurped her Coke, and Shyla laughed at the noise.

Ian smiled; it was nice to hear.

"I don't care what Dad has to say."

"You will," Ian said, shoving the bag of peanuts into a storage cabinet. "He sold the bar—the whole building. We have two weeks to pack and move out."

Sadie's eyes filled with tears. "Are you for fucking real?"

"You had to know this gravy train wasn't going to last forever. You haven't been working, you don't have any plans to go to school. You've been living off what the bar brings in, which isn't very much, and depending on free rent. I don't have it any better than you."

"I don't have a job, or a place to live," Sadie whispered, the blood draining from her face.

"You're not high and dry. I'll help you, but play time is over."

"Fuck you!" she screamed, swiping her can, making it shoot across the bar where it landed on the floor, the contents frothing from the small opening in the top.

Wailing, she ran out the door.

Shyla started to cry.

Resigned to the mess he would have to clean up, Ian hefted Shyla into his arms and let her cry hot tears into his neck.

He felt like doing the same. He didn't think things could get much worse.

On the drive to Ian's apartment, Marta gathered her courage. She didn't want to talk to him at the bar, and she timed it when he would still be home, maybe playing with Shyla or doing laundry.

They had a lot to talk about, and she hoped she'd given him enough time to get used to Shyla being around.

If Ian accused her of avoiding him, she could always say she was training. Which was true.

The marathon was six weeks away, and she'd gotten an email from a reporter at the Tower City Journal who wanted to interview her. She couldn't say no.

Marta had no way of knowing if Spaulding set up the interview, and if he had, saying no would travel back to him faster than she could sprint a mile.

She missed Ian and wanted to talk to him. Full of nerves, she pressed a hand to her racing heart as she trotted up the stairs to Ian's apartment.

It only took one knock before the door flew open and Ian, wild-eyed, pressed a finger over her lips.

Close to her ear he whispered, "Shyla's finally napping."

She suppressed a squeal when he took her arm and dragged her into his bedroom. Out of the corner of her eye, Marta caught the form of a sleeping toddler sprawled on Ian's massive black couch.

He closed his door, wincing when the doorknob clicked into place in the doorjamb.

"Sleeping hasn't been going well. She fell asleep after watching some weird show about a talking blue dog. Thank God."

Upon further inspection, it did seem as if Ian was more tired than usual, stress lines pulling at the corners of his mouth, purple bruises resting beneath his eyes, his hair mussed. She'd never seen him so disheveled.

"I'm sorry."

"No, I am." Ian whispered, pulling her into his arms. "I'm sorry for saying that to Mrs. Gibson. We were talking about babies and I wanted . . . it just came out. I'm sorry."

Relieved he wasn't angry at her for disappearing for the past two weeks, she rested her head on his chest. "It's okay. I wasn't avoiding you because of that. I've been training, and I wanted to give you and Shyla time to figure things out. I should have at least texted. Things aren't going well?"

Ian pulled away and pushed her toward the bed.

She sat on the edge of the mattress; her sundress rode up her thighs exposing the tan lines her running shorts made from running in the sun.

"Shyla has her moments," Ian said, tracing a line with his finger. "But she doesn't sleep well, which in turn, makes sleep impossible for me. Sadie's been helping off and on, but she can't persuade Shyla to sleep, either."

"Is she okay otherwise? How long did Mrs. Gibson stay?"

Goosebumps rose on her skin as Ian ran his finger up and down her leg.

Marta met his eyes, and she trembled with desire.

Ian gave to everyone without asking for anything in return.

She wanted to pay him back for all he'd done for her.

"She stayed longer than I would have liked, but she was a big help, too. It will take a while, but I'm afraid moving will set Shyla back again." Ian brought a hand to her cheek.

Marta stiffened, dread filling her stomach. "Moving? Moving where?"

"My dad sold the bar, the whole building. Sadie and I need to be out in a couple of weeks. If you hadn't come over, I was going to call and ask if you could look at houses with me. I've never bought a house before."

"Oh, my God, Ian. How could he do that to you and Sadie?"

Ian paced his bedroom. "In some weird way, I think he was trying to do me a favor—taking the bar off my hands. I broke the news to Sadie, and she ran off, freaked out because now she feels homeless. I haven't seen her since I told her yesterday afternoon, and she's supposed to help with Shyla at night. I'll have to bring her playpen down again. I guess it's not bad, but I don't like she's cooped up in one small space for such a long time. I appreciate the company, though. It can get lonely at night."

"You should have called me," Marta said, stung he hadn't reached out to ask her for help.

"And what? Risk you being pissed? You ran out of here, and I haven't heard from you since. What was I supposed to think?"

"I know. I'm sorry. All I've been doing lately is running and sleeping. The marathon is getting closer, and I haven't worked up to the speed I need. At this rate, I won't even make the top one hundred."

"You shouldn't run it at all." Ian sat next to her on the bed. "You're going to hurt yourself. Training like that can't be good for you."

"I'll be okay. I want my job at the school. One of us should be working," she said, trying to lighten the mood. "Sadie took it badly, huh?"

"Yeah, she did, but I don't blame her. I told her playtime was over, but she ran out before I could talk to her about any plans. She doesn't trust me not to make her fend for herself. I wouldn't do something like that, which is why I think buying a house would be a better option. We'll have the space we need to spread out. Living with her will be rough; living *near* her has been bad enough. All I can do is encourage her to go to school and get a job, maybe eventually she can live on her own."

"I'll do whatever I can to help."

"Then please don't disappear on me again," Ian murmured. "I was afraid you didn't want to see me anymore after what I said."

"I'm sorry," Marta whispered, hating the pain in his eyes.

She'd thought he'd be busy with Shyla and he wouldn't notice she wasn't around, much less miss her.

"I always think when you leave, you're gone for good,

like when you moved to California, and I'll never see you again."

"Oh, Ian."

Marta couldn't think of anything to say. Touched he'd been thinking of her like that, her heart melted, but she was horrified she'd wounded him that completely he still bled after all this time.

"Kiss me," Ian said, leaning toward her. "Kiss me and give me what I've been wanting from you for the past eleven years."

Marta obliged, pushing her lips to his, enjoying the groan he made in response to her kiss.

Flinging her leg over his lap, she pushed him into the bed and dove into his embrace, molding her body to his when he wrapped his arms around her.

So caught up was she in the moment the thump and wail didn't register until she was left alone in the bedroom, and a baby's cries filtered through her hazy desire.

Ian raced into his living room and scooped up Shyla who had rolled off the couch and sat in a heap of tears on the floor.

Luckily he didn't have a coffee table—she would have smacked her head on the way down.

Marta sprinted after him, huffing frantic breaths. "What happened?"

"She fell off the couch. I'm no good at this, Marta," Ian said, holding Shyla close, a band of stress tightening his chest. He suspected Shyla was crying more because she was disoriented than because she'd hurt herself, but that didn't make her tears any easier to handle. "My father accused me of being too soft with Sadie, and he's right. I'm not cut out for this. I—"

He thrust Shyla at Marta who took the little girl in an armful of elbows and knees. "I need some air. Do you mind?"

"Go. It's okay."

Ian didn't wait for Marta to change her mind, and shoving shoes on his feet, he gave her a nod of thanks.

Outside, feeling like a convict released from prison, he gulped a deep breath of air and willed himself to relax. His muscles loosened with every step he took away from the building—the building no longer a place he could call home.

Shoving his hands into the pockets of his cotton shorts, he squinted against the sun.

Maybe he'd take Shyla on vacation. That's what dads did, didn't they? Took their kids on vacation.

After the marathon, and Marta could go, too. They could fly to Savannah, and Marta could meet his parents. Then they could spend some time on the beach. Shyla would like that, chasing birds and collecting shells.

Florida wasn't far from Georgia. They could visit Disney World. Maybe the talking blue dog would be there.

Ian rolled his shoulders, the stress melting away.

He hoped Marta wanted to share his life with him, but she wasn't ready for talk like that. All she could think about was the goddamned marathon, like Brett had warned him.

Things would be different after she ran it. Marta could focus on other things then. Like him and family.

Ian frowned.

A lot of baggage came with loving him, though Marta wasn't ready for that kind of talk, either. He'd told her he loved her a couple times now, but she never responded the way he hoped.

He better head back.

Ian turned the corner to circle the block. He'd needed the small break, but Marta didn't know any more about kids than he did. Either he would need to rescue Marta from Shyla, or Shyla from Marta. The picture lifted the corners of his mouth.

A vehicle without a muffler pierced the silence, wiping the smile from his face.

Music blasting, a faded brown old car pulled to the curb beside him.

He recognized Trent, Sadie's deadbeat boyfriend, sitting behind the wheel, glaring at him.

The backseat door flung open, and a guy with pitch black hair and piercings in his face too numerous to count pushed his sister out of the car.

Sadie, crying, her body covered in bruises, landed on the sidewalk. She didn't even attempt to stand.

"Keep your fucking sister away from me. She won't be so lucky next time."

Ian knelt by his sister as the car, in a cloud of exhaust, squealed away.

CHAPTER SIX

"I'M SORRY WE didn't find anything last time," Nikki said, opening the door to the bridal boutique, Desiree's Designs, where she'd bought her wedding dress.

Nikki held the door for Marta who awkwardly navigated a huge baby stroller over the lip of the doorway.

"Sorry, sweetheart," she said, but Shyla giggled as the stroller bumped its way into the store. She'd been spending more time with the little girl hoping to give Ian a break.

"That's okay," Alyssa said, holding the other door allowing Marta to continue her way through. "There are a lot of choices out there. And you still haven't picked a color, either."

Nikki glared in frustration. "I'm lucky Peg and my mom aren't here. They wanted to come, but trying to decide among the three of us will be tough enough as it is. I'm glad my sister lives out of state; I don't need her opinion on top of everyone else's."

The last time they'd gone shopping, Nikki hadn't found anything she liked.

She wanted them to adore their dresses—maybe enough

to wear them other places, though Marta would never be able to think of another place besides a wedding to wear a bridesmaid's dress.

They'd tried on several, but what Alyssa loved, Marta disliked. The only saving grace was that she and Alyssa were the same height. Their coloring, though different, was at least similar enough they could wear the same shade.

Nikki's sister wasn't so lucky. Platinum blonde and tall like Nikki, Stacy had the opposite coloring of both Marta and Alyssa.

Marta sighed. Maybe she and Ian could elope.

No, never mind. She and Ian weren't going to be doing anything once he knew.

"Dane told me about Sadie," Nikki said, beginning to rifle through dresses.

Marta sat in a floral winged back chair and smiled at Shyla. "Want out, baby?" she asked.

Shyla nodded. Over the past few days the toddler had taken a liking to her making things much easier.

She hefted the girl out of the stroller and pulled some toys out of the baby bag.

Shyla would have none of that, and she began to explore the bridal salon. She'd be okay wandering around; the store was small and there weren't many places to hide.

"The whole thing is just sickening," Marta said, turning her attention back to Nikki.

She began to help the bride-to-be paw through the racks of dresses, though she had no idea what Nikki liked.

"She wasn't raped, but she's been sexually active with him in the past. Ian had to force her to press charges. Trent's in jail now, and with his priors, it looks like he'll be locked up for a while."

"Men are such slimeballs," Alyssa said.

"Some of them are," Nikki said, a shadow crossing her face.

Marta thought of Spaulding then. She would never be romantically involved with him—gross—but he was a slime-ball just the same. "You can't live with 'em, you can't live without 'em."

Nikki laughed. "That's what men say about women."

"It's probably a good thing we can't procreate without each other, there would never be any babies." Alyssa said, then fell silent.

The awkward quiet grew until Nikki burst out, "For God's sake, I know, okay? You don't have to keep it a secret on my account."

"How did you find out?" Alyssa asked, her voice trembling.

"Brett told Dane, and Dane told me, how do you think? It's not a big deal. I'm happy for you, I just wish you would have been the one to tell me. But now maybe you can decide on a dress. We can ask the seamstress if ordering up a size is a good idea." Nikki leaned over and gave Alyssa a hug. "You make me want a baby."

Marta's eyes darted around for Shyla. She found the toddler talking to a saleswoman. The woman dressed in a beige suit had bent to her knees and was nodding her head to whatever tale Shyla was weaving for her.

"Can you?" Alyssa asked, self-consciously rubbing her belly through her sundress.

"Well, I don't know," Nikki said, exasperated. "If I have the same problem Stacy's having, then no, probably not, but I won't know until we start trying."

"No, I meant, the ah, money." Alyssa turned away and leafed through a rack dresses, her cheeks on fire.

Marta stood back, too wary to insert her opinions.

They'd been friends a lot longer than she, and she didn't want to put herself in the middle.

Nikki deflated, crumpling to the floor amidst a pile of pink silk. "Not now. I would need to work somewhere else. Or Dane would. He refuses to even think about directing the marathon. Next year, the one before our wedding, is going to be Brett's last race."

"Ian is out of a job, too," Marta said contributing to a conversation that sounded like none of her business.

"What do you mean?" Alyssa asked, sinking into a chair next to her. A little table full of bridal magazines separated them.

"Ian's dad sold their bar—the entire building. I have Shyla today because Ian spent some time at the police station, but afterward, he was going to look at houses. They need to be out by the end of the month. Ian's been scrambling to secure a mortgage and find a house with everything he wants."

"Good Lord," Nikki murmured. Her eyes flicked to Shyla who was entertaining the saleswoman now with a game of patty-cake. "That on top of Sadie and taking Shyla. He's lucky to have you."

She'd been babysitting Shyla, but Marta hadn't felt like she'd been much help at all. "Well, lucky or not, he's going to need to find a job. He hasn't told me much, but I don't think he knows what he wants to do."

Nikki played with a bow on the dress she held in her lap. "No one does. The last thing I want to do is go back to HR. But HR is steady hours with weekends and holidays off. There are worse things I could do."

"Brett is writing the history of the Tower City Marathon—then he's done writing books. He's not inter-

ested in that, and he'll be looking for something else, too,"
Alyssa said.

"It's poor timing everyone needs work." Marta pulled
out a package of graham crackers, and like a retriever on
point to sniff out a duck in the marsh, Shyla darted to her
feet and ran to Marta's lap.

Shyla took the cracker and offered Marta her little pink
lips shaped for a kiss.

Marta obliged and hauled the little girl into her lap for
giggles and more kisses. She was growing attached to the
toddler, and giving her up to Ian at the end of the day was
turning harder and harder.

"There's a lot of skill in those men. They all have
degrees and years of experience."

"Yes, yes there is," Marta murmured as a plan began to
take form.

She hoped Ian would see it, too.

As Marta loaded Shyla into the car, her phone chimed
with a text, and she dug into her purse.

Speak of the devil, she thought, swiping her finger to
accept the call from Ian.

"Are you ladies done with your girls' day?"

"Yeah, for today, anyway. It took a little longer
because Nikki came up with the idea to have Shyla be a
flower girl. I hope that's okay. Shyla loved trying on the
dresses."

"Oh. I didn't think of that. I guess that's all right. She's a
little young, isn't she?"

Marta crawled behind the steering wheel and waved at
Nikki who was driving away. "She'll be almost a year older

by then. Half the fun of having a flower girl and ring bearer is watching them toddle down the aisle."

"Or burst into tears," Ian said with a laugh.

"Or that, but I don't think Shyla will have a problem. She either loved the dresses or all the attention, but probably both. She's been an angel all afternoon. So, what's up?"

"It's good timing you're done then. Can you meet me? I want to show you a house. It's in my price range, it's big enough, and it has a decent yard. If it passes inspection, and I think it will, I want it. But I want your input."

"Oh." Why did he care what she thought? She wouldn't be living there. "Okay. Text me the address, and I'll listen to the directions through Maps."

"Sounds good, see you in a few."

Ian hung up but two seconds later a text came through with the address. "Wanna go see your daddy?" Marta asked Shyla, looking at the baby in the rearview mirror.

"Daddy!" Shyla shrieked.

Marta laughed, but her laugh faded as the implication of what she said took hold.

Ian was Shyla's daddy now, but he would never father her children.

She couldn't keep thinking like that, she chided herself as she navigated the streets of an older residential section of Tower City. The past was the past, and no amount of moaning would change that.

Marta parked behind Ian's car and pulled Shyla's stroller out of the trunk. Massive, the stroller barely fit.

In time, Ian would need to buy a minivan or an SUV, but it wasn't feasible for him to think of something like that right now, as busy as he was. She, on the other hand, needed a new vehicle . . .

Don't be ridiculous. She wasn't Shyla's mother, and

besides rare occasions like today, she wouldn't be driving the little girl anywhere. Lifting the sleeping toddler from her car seat, Marta ignored the pull to her heart.

She pushed the car door closed as gently as she could, hoping the noise wouldn't wake the baby.

Ian met her at the door and said, "The realtor had an appointment to show a house across town and left to make it on time. She gave me the key to lock up, and I'll drop it by the office on my way back to the bar. Come in and tell me what you think."

After Ian helped her carry the stroller up the porch steps, Marta pushed the sleeping toddler into the entry way.

"This is the front door—we wouldn't use it much. We'd be using the other door near the garage—it opens into a mudroom, I can show it to you," he said.

Ian moved aside, and Marta stepped into the house that would never be her home.

Ian felt complete for the first time in his life.

Marta stood by the stroller, Shyla sleeping in a reclining position inside it, her mouth hanging open.

This could be their house; the home they would live in together. He hoped she would fall in love with it as he had.

"How can you afford something like this?" Marta asked, then colored, looking away. "Sorry, that's none of my business. This house looks huge, and the kitchen smells like it's been renovated."

"It has. It's one of the reasons I like it so much. Houses in this part of town are older, and this house isn't as expensive as you would think. The couple only put it on the market today, this afternoon. The guy's mother was diagnosed with an aggressive cancer, and they have to move out of state to take care of her. They've put a lot of money into the house, the realtor said, but moving is more important than recouping their losses, and they're looking to dump it as fast as they can."

"You don't have much time to decide then. People will swarm all over this house once word gets out it's for sale."

"Leave Shyla here, she'll be okay," he said, tugging on her hand. "You're right. A house like this, I need to make an offer today, right now, or it'll be gone by morning. Let me take you through the rest of it."

Ian tried to look at the house through Marta's eyes, praying she could picture herself living there. The family room fit two couches, bookshelves, fireplace, and an entertainment center.

A little hallway led to a bathroom and storage closets, a study, and a bedroom.

"There are more bedrooms upstairs," Ian said, pushing her up the carpeted stairs.

"This is incredible," Marta said, poking her head into a bedroom. Not all of them were furnished; some were used for storage with boxes and unneeded furniture.

"Wait until you see the yard." Ian tugged her back downstairs.

"Oh, my God."

Ian opened the sliding glass doors and nudged her outside.

The people living there had set up wicker furniture and a grill. A wooden swing, swaying on rusty chains, sat to the side in the overgrown grass against a weathered fence. Flowers bordered the yard.

"Shyla would love to play out here," she said.

"I don't guess I would love to mow it much, but yeah,

this is a great house for a kid, right? And with the fence, if we decide to get a dog, we wouldn't have to worry about putting one up."

"Ian, this house is fantastic, and if you can afford it . . . why did you want me to see it? This house is too good of a deal to let go because you waited for me. Call your realtor right now and tell her you'll take it."

Ian led her to the padded loveseat. "I wanted you to see it because I need to know if you would want to live here." He ran his finger along her jaw. "I've made it no secret I love you, and I want us to be a family. You, me, Shyla, and . . ."

He was putting his heart on the line, sharing his dreams.

". . . Our kids. Moving sucks, and this would be it for me. This would be home. Our home."

Marta looked down at her hands.

Heart in his throat, Ian resisted shaking her, demanding she answer him.

"I'm in a lease," she whispered.

Ian's breath swooshed out of him. "Is that all that's worrying you? God, Marta, you had me worried for a second. Come here."

Capturing her mouth with his, he pushed away a feeling of doubt and tried to convince himself the tears in her eyes were from happiness.

She hadn't said yes, but she hadn't said no, and he would take that, for now.

Running his hand up her bare thigh, past the hem of her dress she'd worn, he murmured against her mouth, "Let me make love to you."

She pulled away. "Here? What about Shyla? You need to call your realtor. She's probably setting up another showing for this place right now."

Ian bit back a groan of irritation.

She was right.

He pulled his phone from his pocket and dialed the realtor. "Melanie, it's Ian. I want the house. My fiancée thinks it's perfect."

He winked at her when she glared.

The more he said it, the better it sounded.

"Yes, yes, I'll stop by tomorrow, yes, goodnight."

He turned off his phone and peered through the glass. Shyla still slept in her stroller. It didn't look like she'd even moved. Trying on dresses was hard work.

"There," Ian said, reclaiming his seat on the loveseat which squeaked in protest under his weight. "Now, where were we?"

"My lease," Marta whispered, staring across the grass.

"We'll worry about it later," Ian said, tugging her into his lap.

When she laughed, the tension in his gut loosened.

Lacing his fingers through her hair, he tugged her down for a kiss. He lapped at her like a dehydrated cat, ignoring the strange sense of déjà vu clouding over him.

Shyla couldn't hurt herself in her stroller. She could start crying, but that wasn't the same as rolling off the couch.

The little girl would always being in the back of his mind. He already loved her, and nothing would tear at his heart more than if Shyla were ever hurt.

Just as much as he loved the woman sitting in his lap, her breath fluttering over his skin in ragged little breaths.

He ran his hands over her thighs, up to her panties. "We've put this off long enough," he murmured, tugging at the lace waistband.

"Okay," she whispered, and when she peeked through

the glass, double-checking on Shyla, Ian knew he could never live without her.

Marta pulled her panties from her legs, and Ian freed himself from his denim shorts, unbuttoning and unzipping them in record speed.

"I'm clean, sweetheart. I don't remember the last time I slept with anyone. Do we need protection?" he asked.

He wanted babies with her, but not until she was ready.

Marta was still scarred from what happened between her and Brett, and he didn't want them to have an accident.

It may take a while to convince her having a baby would be okay, that she deserved to be a mother despite the past, but for now, he would take it slow.

Her eyes blanked, but before Ian could question her, they cleared, and she smiled. "No. I'm clean, and I can't get pregnant."

Good, she was on birth control.

"Then come here," he said.

His hands encircled her waist, and he positioned her over him. "Slow now, slow," he hissed as she sheathed herself around him.

"Ian," she whimpered, burying her face in his neck.

"Sh, sh, it's okay," he said, wrapping his arms around her, bringing them heart to heart.

He encouraged her to move, and she grinded against him to take him deeper, holding onto his shoulders for support, her head tipped back.

The curve of her neck was too much to resist, and he nibbled her skin from her earlobe down to her shoulder, the thin straps of her sundress giving him all the access he could want.

He wished he could touch her breasts, cover them in

kisses, but they were outside and he didn't want her completely naked.

Instead, he reached between their bodies and rubbed at her slick center. Engorged, her nub quivered under the tip of his finger.

"Come for me."

"Yeah," she cried, and she took his mouth with hers in the moment she began to contract around him.

He let himself go, pulsing inside her. "Marry me," he gasped, "spend the rest of your life with me."

Marta sagged into him, and he clutched the material of her sundress in his fists, pulling her closer.

She rested her head on his shoulder.

Trying to swallow his fear, Ian hid his face in her hair. A simple yes was all he needed, all he wanted. They could work out the details later. Much later, if she needed the time.

But she didn't say anything.

Nothing at all.

"HE ASKED ME to marry him," Marta murmured, peering out Holly Carole's small office window that looked over the campus.

Marta hated the university.

Over the past few weeks, Spaulding had been quiet as a mouse, Libbie's offer to be a running buddy the only communication she'd had between her and the school since she'd been replaced.

Classes had begun, and if Spaulding hadn't benched her, she would have been coaching.

Coaching while training would have been too much,

but it didn't take the sting away knowing Libbie was across campus working on plans and running with the track students.

They should have been *her* students, dammit.

When Holly asked to get together, Marta thought it would be better for them to meet at the school; she didn't need Holly bumping into Dane and Nikki in the hallway of her apartment building.

She'd stopped by the student exchange and grabbed them coffees before meeting the tall redhead in her office.

"And you don't want to?" Holly asked from her desk.

"There's nothing I want more, but he's already got enough troubling him without thinking about me right now. I'm not without baggage."

"I think you not saying yes is probably worrying him a lot more than anything you would tell him after accepting," Holly said.

"Maybe, but do I want to find out? Engagements are broken all the time. Saying yes doesn't mean we would make it down the aisle. How are you after Dane?" Marta asked.

She couldn't put her foot in her mouth any more than she already had, so she went ahead and asked because she wanted to know.

"I'm all right, trying to get back into the dating groove. I thought I wanted to marry him, and maybe I'd have been happy with a big fat ring on my finger. But it's hard to say now, because I've had time to think about it. His whole life is running, and I don't want any part of that. It was different when we were dating, but being married to it? He's with someone now who fits him much better than I ever could."

That made Marta think of Ian always telling her to quit. Was he annoyed by it, or honestly concerned about her welfare? There was no doubt running was a huge strain on her.

"The sport is a huge time commitment," Marta said, sinking into a chair in front of Holly's desk.

"I don't know how you do it." Holly wrinkled her nose.

"I gave up a lot to be where I am. I would be throwing it all away if I stopped now."

Holly laughed. "That's the silliest thing I've ever heard. What have you given up? It's not like you're sixty and don't have any do-overs. You're what, thirty-three? Thirty-two? Same age as Dane, right? What have you given up you can't get back? You have plenty of time to go back to school, find something you like to do. Get married, raise a family. Go on vacation, see some of the world. Start living your life."

"I gave up a baby," Marta said.

Holly choked on her coffee, and she grabbed a tissue to cough into it. "I'm sorry. I didn't know."

"It was Brett's, but he wasn't ready to be a dad. He convinced me it was for the best if I . . . so I did."

"I see."

"I have to keep running. I owe it to my baby to continue my career."

Leaning back in her chair, Holly laced her hands behind her head. "So, you're going to run until you're ninety? How much will you sacrifice to the sport before you consider yourself 'paid up'?"

Marta jumped to her feet. "I don't know. I never thought of it like that."

"Well, you better start, or one day your life will be gone, and you'll wonder what happened. Look, Marta," Holly said, leaning forward, her elbows resting on the blotter, "we all do things we regret or feel the need to atone for. Some people go to church and step out guilt-free because they've asked God to shoulder their sin. Some give to charities, some volunteer. When I was in high school, I went to a party and drove home drunk. I hit someone—"

Marta gasped and covered her mouth with her hand.

"—but he was okay. It scared the living hell out of me because I could have killed that man. I was ordered by the judge to do a billion hours of community service, but I never stopped driving. I never thought to give up my driver's license. Otherwise, even now, I could still be walking everywhere and taking the bus. Don't call giving up your baby a mistake because it was the right choice for you at the time. You did the best you could, so why can't you forgive yourself and move on?"

"It's not just moving on."

"How's Brett?" Holly asked.

"Good, he's good. Engaged. Alyssa's pregnant."

"Ah huh. And how did he manage that?"

"I talked—"

"Oh, you did?" Holly stood from her desk and scuffed the worn utility carpet with the toe of her high-heeled sandal.

"You tricked me." Marta frowned.

"Yeah, I guess I did. What's good for the goose is good for the gander, and all that, right?"

Marta let out a dramatic sigh.

"Come on, fuck this coffee. Let's go get a drink."

"Is that a good idea after what you told me?"

"I think so. I'll order an Uber to take us there and home, okay? I don't drive drunk anymore. I learned my lesson a long time ago."

"And what lesson am I supposed to have learned from my abortion?" Marta asked.

"I don't know. What do you think?" Holly put her arm

around Marta's shoulders and led her out of the office, turning the light out behind them.

Sitting next to Holly in the cab, Marta thought about what Holly said.

The only thing she'd learned from her abortion was she wasn't fit to be a mother, and she'd made sure she'd never be one.

"How's it going, kiddo?" Ian asked as Sadie slid into his car.

"Fine, I guess," she mumbled, securing her seatbelt.

She looked better, Ian thought, pulling out of the parking lot of Safe Harbor, a family service center where Sadie was seeing a therapist twice a week.

After bringing Sadie back to his apartment, he'd had to call the cops.

The officer who answered the call had ordered him to bring her to the clinic for a checkup and rape kit.

The doctor who looked her over told him she hadn't any broken bones and she hadn't had any recent sexual activity, but her mind might be more messed up than her body.

Ian agreed and set up counseling for his sister.

Sadie, either broken down by what had happened, or finally seeing the light of day, agreed without a fight.

He brought her there twice a week, dropped her off, staying until she went inside, and an hour later, picked her up.

"Where are we going?" she asked, looking around the residential section of the city where he'd driven them.

He wished she would tell him what she talked about with the therapist, though he could be patient.

The therapist had reached out to him after Sadie's first session and recommended he sometimes attend. He'd been practically raising her for years, and she thought having him there would help Sadie's recovery.

"We're here," Ian said, parking in front of the house he'd bought.

He'd waited to show Sadie the house—he'd wanted to wait until she was situated with the therapist, reluctant to spring too much on her at once. But time was running out, and they had to start clearing their things out of the building downtown.

"What's this place? Are we visiting someone?"

"No, I bought this house—the white one. I didn't have a choice; Mom and Dad left us in a bad spot without much time. It'll be close, but we'll be able to move in by the time the sale goes through on the bar."

"I guess that means I'm going to have to find some-where, huh?" Sadie said, her eyes welling with tears. "And get a job."

"This house has four bedrooms and a big yard." Ian tapped her shoulder. "Look at me."

He waited until Sadie met his eyes. "I told you I wouldn't abandon you, and I won't. But after what happened, you can't deny it's time to grow up."

Sadie swallowed and tucked her hands between her knees. "I know."

"You're lucky Trent didn't do worse, and you're lucky he didn't rape you."

She opened her mouth to interrupt.

"I know you were sleeping with him anyway, but rape is different—you didn't need to live with that. It's bad enough you'll always have this in the back of your mind, and I hope with therapy you can put it behind you and start on a better path. If you want to live with me, there're going to be rules."

Her shoulders stiffened, and Ian bit back a sigh. "See? You can't get defensive like that. The ball isn't in your court —not anymore. I want to help you, and you need the help, so stop it."

"Fine," Sadie muttered.

Ian didn't like it, but it would take more than a couple therapy sessions for her to change.

"You'll be home every night by ten. You'll start classes, either full-time or part-time, I don't care, but you need to start taking an interest in your own future. You can get a job, if you go part-time. If you go full-time, I want you to concentrate on classes. I think that's fair, Sadie."

"Why do you want me here? You and Shyla . . . where is she anyway?"

"Marta's keeping her at the apartment. I asked her to babysit so we could talk. We're taking Shyla to the zoo after her nap, if you want to come along. But anyway, those are my terms."

"How did you afford this place? You have no money."

"I have money, I saved what I made from the bar. It wasn't much, but better than nothing. And Dad said he's giving us, me, half the money from the sale. I can put some of it toward your tuition. Come on, we can take a look around if you want to check it out. The closing hasn't gone through yet, but there's no reason why it shouldn't. I asked the realtor if I could bring you by today, and she gave me a key."

"What are you going to do now?"

"What do you mean?" Ian asked, leading Sadie up the white front porch. He pushed the wooden swing, making it sway, the chains creaking.

"For work? You need to get a job, right?"

"Yeah, I'll need to find a job. I'll try to keep the bar open as long as possible until the businessmen who bought it take over, but yeah, after the bar is completely out of my hands, I'll need to find something, too."

"This sucks," Sadie mumbled, stepping into the spacious kitchen Marta had admired days before.

"You can think like that, or you can consider this a new beginning—for all of us."

"All of us? Is Marta going to live here, too?"

"Would you mind?" Ian asked, jiggling the keys in the pocket of his khaki slacks. The weather had cooled, and he wore slacks and a dress shirt.

"You love her a lot, don't you?" she asked, walking into the large living room still furnished but devoid of any personal effects of the family who had left.

"Yeah. But she's running a marathon next month, and she's got the coaching job at the school. She's thinking about a lot right now, and we don't have any concrete plans."

"I guess it wouldn't be so bad, I mean, the more time you spend with her, the less time you'll have to harass me."

"Kid, I'll always have time to harass you." He pinned her to him, thankful she didn't fear being touched after what happened, and tickled her ribs.

Instead of running away, she hugged him.

Surprised at the uncommon display of affection, Ian hugged her in return, hoping this meant a fresh start for both of them.

"What's going on here?" Ian asked, throwing his keys onto the table.

Kneeling on the kitchen floor of Ian's apartment, Marta was packing pots and pans when Ian brought Sadie home from her appointment.

"I started packing for you. I hope you don't mind," she said, suddenly self-conscious she was taking liberties in Ian's life.

Shyla struggled to her feet, chubby legs pumping, a grin lighting her face. She'd been playing drums with the pans Marta was packing into cardboard boxes.

"Daddy!"

It made Marta's throat burn when Ian beamed at the little girl whenever she called him that.

"No, that's great, I appreciate it. Has this munchkin napped?" Ian asked, sweeping Shyla into his arms.

Marta hefted herself off the floor as well and brushed at the thighs of her running leggings. She'd dressed for the zoo and the cooler weather in her regular running clothes. "Yeah, she's all set to go—maybe change her diaper. That's it. I have the bag packed."

"Pigs!" Shyla giggled, capturing Ian's face between her two little hands forcing him to look at her instead of Marta. "Bears!"

Sadie stood awkwardly by the door, and Marta wanted to try to make her relax.

It was a shame the girl wasn't comfortable in her own home, and Marta hoped it wasn't because of her. "Did Ian show you the house? Did you like it?"

"It'll be different—I've never lived in a house before, with a yard. We've always lived up here. Ian mentioned a dog." Sadie squinted at her, and Marta felt like she was being tested.

"Dogs are nice to have around," Marta replied mildly, unwilling to fight.

She wasn't going to be part of the household dynamic. She hoped when Ian talked to his sister about the future he hadn't included her.

There was no reason for Sadie to be jealous.

"Are you coming to the zoo with us? You're welcome, of course. In fact, if the three of you want—"

"No, you're coming. Shyla wants you there," Ian interrupted, frowning at Sadie.

"It's okay. I should probably start packing up my apartment. The house isn't going to fit all our stuff, is it?"

"Yeah, actually, I think it will, but I'll check into renting a storage unit, just in case."

Without a word, Sadie grabbed an armful of flattened cardboard boxes and disappeared into the hall.

"Sorry about that," Ian said, tugging on Shyla's droopy ponytail. "She's still a bit prickly. I hope the therapist will smooth her over. I'll be attending a few sessions with her, see if I can find out what's going through her head. Nothing good, I'm sure."

"It's okay. Change is scary. Let's go, before Shyla explodes from excitement. All she's been talking about is the zoo. She was a 'bear' to put down for her nap. I had to lie with her in your bed."

"That's not true, is it? You're not a bear, are you?"

"Bears go rawr!" Shyla growled, making claws with her hands.

Ian set Shyla to her feet and growled. "Rawr!"

Shyla shrieked and ran into Ian's bedroom. She scrambled onto the bed, his comforter clutched in her little fists, and hid under the sheets of his unmade bed. "No, no, no!" she laughed with glee.

Watching the exchange, Marta's heart broke.

She should get out now before it was too late.

CHAPTER SEVEN

"You're quiet."

Ian's words roused Marta out of her daydreams. "Sorry, I don't mean to be. How did Sadie like the house?"

Shyla's nose was glued to the aquarium's glass as she watched the brightly colored fish swim by.

Marta sat with Ian on a sticky bench waiting; they still had plenty of zoo to see, and she was grateful she'd already taken her run for the day.

"She didn't like the rules. There're going to be rules—I can't let her make us miserable."

Marta's skin prickled.

He could have meant him and Shyla, but with the proposal, she was sure he meant her, too.

"She asked about me getting a job, and I guess I'm going to have to start looking. I only need to keep the bar open a few more days."

"I was thinking about that," Marta said, watching Shyla try to give the fish kisses through the glass.

"Aren't you the slave driver," Ian said, nudging her with his shoulder.

Marta blushed. She hadn't meant to nag. "I didn't mean it like that."

"I know, I'm kidding. What were you thinking?"

"Well, you know Brett doesn't want to do the marathon anymore, right?"

"You want me to take over the marathon?" He lifted his eyebrows.

"No, stop it." Marta laughed. "Let me finish."

She explained what the other girls told her at the bridal salon. "Dane doesn't want to take over the marathon, and Brett doesn't want to do it anymore, so he needs something else to do. Nikki told me if she and Dane want to have a baby next year after the wedding, they would need to figure out another source of income."

"What does that have to do with me?" Ian asked, standing. Shyla had finally unglued herself from the aquarium.

"Frogs!" Shyla hollered, stamping her feet.

"I guess we're going to the amphibian and reptile building." She grabbed the stroller they'd parked behind the bench. Keeping an eagle eye on Shyla, she continued, "I was thinking all three of you need something."

Ian pulled the door open to the building where immediately a large turtle swimming in its tank mesmerized Shyla.

"You think we should go into business together? Doing what?"

Marta shrugged. "I have no idea. What did you want to do with your business degree? Why did you choose that for a major?"

"I chose it because I didn't know what I wanted to do with my life, and it seemed a generic enough degree I could get a job after graduation without too much trouble."

"That's true. You can do whatever you want. Brett and Dane are your friends, you can trust them to pull their weight if you go in on something. You all have experience; there has to be something the three of you could do together."

"I don't know, Marta. Brett and I haven't been on good terms for a long time."

"I know. I asked Nikki about that when we went dress shopping. I was offended on your behalf when the four of them went to the funeral without us."

"I didn't expect to be included in much after Brett and Alyssa got engaged. They're a natural foursome. You know, best friends and best friends? It happens."

Shyla ran on to the Snake Pit and approached a zoo worker holding a snake for people to touch. Several children were running their hands along the snake's skin.

"She's a brave one."

"That's good. I hope she's always like that. Life is too short to be scared all the time." Ian pinned her with a stare. "Anyway, I would have to think about it. I don't know if I would want to work with them, see them all the time. If our business tanked, that could be the end of our friendship, too."

"I know, but if it worked out, you would at least be working with people you liked and trusted. It wasn't Brett's fault I ran away, and I'm here now. You should bury the hatchet. What happened is in the past—we should leave it there."

"You can't," Ian said, making her flinch, "so why do you expect me to? It's easy to say, but not so easy to do, is it?"

"What do you mean?" Marta asked, though she knew exactly what he meant. "Come on, Shyla's on the move."

"Don't think I didn't notice you didn't answer me when I asked you to marry me."

Ian grabbed the stroller and followed Shyla into the

sunshine of the open zoo. She began to follow a roaming peacock, its brilliant tail feathers gleaming in the sun.

"I need to think about it, that's all. It's not like we don't have time, and with Dane and Nikki being married next summer, and Brett and Alyssa engaged, the queue is full."

"I wasn't suggesting we run to City Hall tomorrow, though I would happily do that, too. But a simple yes or no would've been nice. Anyway, speaking of Brett and Alyssa getting engaged, and me not having access to the bar for much longer, I was thinking of throwing another party. It could be an engagement party for Brett and Alyssa and kind of a farewell party for the bar. What do you think?"

"You won't announce our engagement, will you?" Marta asked.

Shyla had found her way into the petting zoo and to a pen of goats.

Marta dug into her purse for quarters to buy pellets to feed them.

"Is there an engagement to announce?" Ian asked, holding his hand out for the treats as Marta twisted another quarter in the dispenser's slot.

Marta sighed and looked over the small corral.

One goat looked uncomfortably pregnant, its huge belly swaying with every step.

"I need to figure things out."

"Not much to figure out." Ian knelt and handed Shyla the pellets, helping her feed an aggressive goat who stuck its head between the slats for first dibs at the food in her little hands.

"Ewwww!" Shyla squealed as the goat's tongue lapped at her palm. "Again, again!"

Marta was already putting another quarter in the slot.

"You do it, okay, baby?" Ian said, handing Shyla the

rest of the pellets. "Either you love me, or you don't. I think that's the bottom line." He wiped his hands on his jeans.

He'd changed before they'd gone to the zoo, and he looked fine in a tight-fitting pair of dark jeans and a white button-down dress shirt. He'd brushed his blond hair away from his face, his skin pinking from standing in the sun all afternoon.

With a hand to his arm, the muscles in his bicep tensing with her touch, she said, "I love you, Ian, don't think I don't."

The first time she'd said it, in the middle of a zoo, the smell of manure drifting around them, babies crying, the fall sun beating down on them.

How romantic.

And how sad he practically had to force it out of her.

When had it happened? The afternoon in the park when he first kissed her? The morning of the press conference when she offered herself to him and he'd turned her down out of respect for her shock and grief? In Shyla's room, when he told her he didn't want her to have any man's babies but his? Maybe the day at the house, when he waved the future at her, bright and sparkly, everything she wanted, everything she dared take.

It had been all of those times, little by little, falling so softly she hadn't known she had. Until right now, if she didn't say something, he'd lose patience with her and walk away.

Ian pulled her to him and pressed a kiss to the top of her head. "If that's true, if you do, then I can wait forever if I have to."

"Kiss more, kiss more!" Shyla yelled.

Marta looked down at the little girl. She'd finished

feeding the goats and was watching them intently. "Kiss! Mommy and Daddy!"

The words clogged her throat with emotion.

She would never tell Ian that he may very well need to.

IAN WANTED TO wipe at the sweat running into his eyes, but his hands were full.

Dane held one end of the box spring while Ian held the other, maneuvering the light but bulky part of Sadie's bed up the stairs. It had been a blessing Dane and Brett volunteered to help Ian and Sadie move.

They set Sadie's box spring in the bedroom she'd chosen for herself, upstairs across from what would be Shyla's nursery and down the hall from the master bedroom Ian had taken for himself.

That she'd chosen a bedroom upstairs and not the lone bedroom downstairs and to the back of the house both worried and relieved him.

It worried him because he didn't want her to change her mind only two nights into sleeping there, and he didn't want to put up with her music.

On the other hand, it relieved him because he hoped it meant Sadie was willing to become a bigger part of the family rather than hiding while she was home.

"That dresser for Sadie's room is going to be a bitch to bring up," Dane said, huffing, using the hem of his tank top to wipe at his forehead.

"We'll take the drawers out of it, that will help. I can't thank you enough for doing this." Ian leaned against the window and caught his breath.

Sadie and Shyla were playing in the backyard. They

were throwing a ball around, the little girl's screaming in delight. Hunter, Brett and Alyssa's dog, watched from the sidelines in case he needed to make a quick escape.

Dane joined him at the window and gazed over the landscaped yard. "God, you lucked out with this place. What I wouldn't give to be able to buy a house like this for Nikki."

"You'll get there, one day. I'm not sure how quickly I would have taken the plunge if my dad wouldn't have pushed me out the door."

"You would have realized soon enough Shyla needed more space."

Ian's dad's words came back to him. Get married, buy Shyla a dog and a house. Well, he was a third of the way there and working on the rest.

His dad had a point, especially after seeing how happy it made Shyla to run around in the grass.

"We'll eventually be thinking about something like this, too," Brett said, hauling a box of Sadie's things into the room. "Alyssa doesn't want to leave the loft, but if she wants more than one kid, she's going to have to. The park out back will work instead of a yard, for now, but we don't have the space inside, not for a baby and a dog. The loft only has two bedrooms and we filled it up fast," he said, setting the box down in a corner.

Ian had never been to Alyssa's loft.

"You okay with that? Moving?" he asked Brett as they trotted downstairs.

It turned out the people he'd bought the house from needed more of their furniture than they'd realized, which had been fine with Ian, and he'd given in without the fight the previous owners had anticipated.

Between him and his sister, they would fill up the kitchen with pots, pans, plates, and silverware.

He wouldn't need to look for a storage unit after all. In fact, the basement would need to go unfurnished for a while.

Ian didn't mind—it would give Shyla a place to work off her energy on the rainy days she couldn't play outside.

"I'm still trying to get used to the idea of having a kid. I don't care if we move. Anywhere is better than where I was without Alyssa," Brett said, jumping into the trailer. "I'm not wrangling with that thing. It looks crazy heavy, and I have a bad back." He nudged the corner of Sadie's massive dresser with his toe.

"The hell you do."

"We'll all grab it," Ian said. "Once the baby is born, you'll fall in love quick. It doesn't take much to give your heart away to a child. I fell head over heels for Shyla pretty damn fast. I'm looking forward to having kids of my own."

"Making any progress with that?" Dane asked. He bent down, shoved his fingers under the dresser, and prepared to lift.

"Hold on, Hercules, we need to take the drawers out first." Brett pulled out the top drawer. "Ian shoved them back in to make room for other crap."

"Right, I forgot."

"Not really," Ian said, picking up the original thread of the conversation. He eyed Brett while he spoke. "I asked Marta to marry me. She didn't say yes."

"Did she say no?" Brett asked, pulling out the last drawer. "You can't make her do anything she doesn't want to do."

"You were able to," Ian muttered.

"What do you mean by that?" Brett rose from his haunches and glared.

"Nothing."

"Are you talking about Marta's abortion? Because I didn't talk her into that. We both decided."

"I'm not talking about anything." Ian shouldn't have mentioned it, though it was true he thought Brett had had more of a say in Marta's choice than Brett wanted to believe.

"I had a lot more going on than only Marta being pregnant," Brett said.

"I know. It's between the two of you, and you managed to work it out and stay friends, so it's none of my business."

"You've always made it your business, hating me for making Marta leave. A while back she told me even if she wouldn't have gotten pregnant, we wouldn't have worked, and she's right. Eventually, she would have gone back home to California. She went *home*. And sometimes I think that doesn't have anything to do with me at all."

"I want Marta to feel like she's home here, in Minnesota."

"She's not going to feel like that unless she can relax," Dane said, bending down again.

Ian followed suit, and the three of them picked up Sadie's heavier-than-shit antique dresser. He better not have to move it ever again. "What do you mean?"

"The school is giving Marta a hard time, this marathon situation sucks. She should walk away from the whole thing. It puts a bad taste in my mouth, that's for sure."

Ian focused to keep his fingers from slipping and concentrated as they walked the piece up the porch steps. "I've told her that, but she said Spaulding pushed her into a corner, and she would look bad if she backed out now."

"I know, and that's my point. She's going to be working

with Spaulding? That's some fucked up thing right there. You've got to learn when to walk away, when what you're fighting for isn't worth it."

They carried the dresser through the kitchen, and Ian prepared for the long haul up the stairs, his jaw clenched.

It helped that the three of them were moving it together, but there wasn't much room between the wall and the handrail. Navigating the stairs would be tricky.

"And what do you mean, you're still sweating bullets? I thought you were past that?" Dane asked Brett.

"I'm trying. My parents were assholes my whole life, I'm not going to get over that in a couple days. What happened between me and Marta sucked, and it didn't help my frame of mind. I didn't make her get an abortion, but she told me what put the final nail in the coffin was even if I would have supported her, I would've bailed after it was born. She's right. I was twenty-three and scared shitless. After she popped out that baby, I would've run like hell. Marta knew me well enough to look out for herself."

Ian flinched under Brett's stare.

"But that's not all my fault," Brett said. "My mental health wasn't my fault."

"Sorry," Ian muttered, but Brett could have done a lot more for himself a lot sooner than he had.

"Let's put this bitch down. Careful now, we don't want Brett hurting his *bad* back."

"Fuck you." Brett laughed.

After the dresser was where Sadie assured him she wanted it, because holy hell, Ian wouldn't be able to move it himself if she changed her mind, he stretched his hands over his head, working the kinks out of his spine.

They still had other furniture to move and he needed to put Shyla's nursery together, though he had a sneaking suspicion she would end up in his bed just like every other night since the first day Mrs. Gibson had dropped her off.

It was a horrible habit to fall into, but he didn't have the heart to kick her out.

Dane slid the mattress leaning against the wall onto the box spring and flopped onto Sadie's bare bed.

Brett perched in the window seat and rested his head against the glass.

Now that they'd cleared the air somewhat, he wanted to broach the subject that had been rolling around in his brain since Marta brought it up. "So, we all need some cash—"

"Ya think?" Dane asked, speaking to the ceiling, his hands laced under his head.

"Well, I know *I* need a job. By this time next week, I'm unemployed."

"It all went through then, officially?" Brett asked.

"I still haven't been paid my share, but it should happen any day. My dad called to warn me to get my ass in gear, move the hell out, and hire a cleaning crew to go through the building. We still have stuff in there, obviously, but we'll start sleeping in the house tonight."

Ian had closed on the house with little fanfare.

Most couples went out to eat or popped champagne.

Marta had been doing whatever the hell it was she did and hadn't even answered his text until the next day.

He'd taken Shyla to McDonald's for chicken nuggets. A chocolate shake had been his celebratory drink. Sadie hadn't wanted to tag along, saying she needed to pack, which had been, and still was, true.

But something wasn't right with her, and her secrets made him nervous.

"Anyway, Dane you need another stream of income, I'm

out of a job, and Brett doesn't want to do the marathon anymore, right? Is that all the gossip?"

"The women need to stop talking to each other," Brett said shaking his head.

"Pfft. Like that'll happen. Nikki wants me to do the marathon, it would be an easy fix to our money troubles, but I want no part in it. Helping you over the years has been enough. I wouldn't want to do it alone."

Ian sat on the floor.

Sadie would need another piece of furniture in here. A desk, maybe. If he had it his way, she'd have homework.

Soon.

"I'll be sad to let it go, though, even if it is a pain in the ass. I wish there was someone in our group who would do it. Nikki doesn't want to, does she? She's already got the women's race going on."

"The whole point of more money is so Nikki can have a baby. She's going to be hurting watching Alyssa, I know that already, and it makes me feel like shit. She doesn't want to leave the store, she's more committed to the place than I am, now. Asking her to do both wouldn't be fair, and I then wouldn't have anything to do. Besides, I think if whoever took it over wanted to direct the women's race, too, Nikki would dump it. When she volunteered to direct it, we weren't in a relationship, and she had more time."

"I can't take credit for the idea, but what do you think about going into business together?" Ian asked.

Brett frowned and shifted on the thin padding of the window seat's cushion. "Like what?"

Ian scooted backward, leaned against the dresser, and crossed his ankles. "I don't know. We all have business degrees, we'll think of something."

"It would have to interest all of us, because we'll be in it for the long haul. Among the three of us, we have experience to spare, but we don't want to jump into anything and regret it later. We'll need start-up money." Dane swung his legs from the bed.

"Yeah, there's a lot to think about."

"We can talk more about it at the party," Ian said.

"What party?" Dane asked, leading the others out the door.

Dane had the right idea. They'd had their rest, but they still had a couple more trips to make between the apartments and the house.

He was grateful Sadie was keeping Shyla occupied, but they would want to eat lunch soon and Shyla couldn't skip a nap.

"I was thinking of throwing another party, you know, like Dane and Nikki's engagement party, except for Brett and Alyssa. And it would be a goodbye party for the bar. I won't miss working there, but it's been a part of our family since I was a kid. It'll be weird not managing it anymore."

"Hey, thanks," Brett said.

"Don't sound so surprised. If we're going into business together, we're going to have to set the past aside. You didn't mean to hurt Marta, she might have gone back to California, anyway. All that matters is that she's back, and I'm going to do my best to make sure she stays here this time."

"We all want her to stay. I missed that little goofball," Brett said.

"Let's grab another load," Dane said, pulling his keys out of his pocket. "I'm thinking burgers and beer for dinner tonight, let's all of us go out."

Warmed by his friendship with Dane and Brett, Ian nodded. "Sounds like a plan. My treat."

Marta parked her car across the street from Ian's new house.

She'd taken a run and a nap. Becoming harsher, her training was taking a lot out of her, and after her early morning run, she'd slept for three hours. She'd missed a couple texts from Ian asking her if she was going to stop by or help, but rather than answer, she decided to surprise him at the house instead.

Her heart plummeted when only Ian's and Brett's cars were parked under a tree that took up most of the front yard, dripping with what looked like Spanish moss. She'd missed them; they were probably at the apartment for another load.

Rather than drive to meet them and risk passing Dane's truck on the highway, she slid out of her car and walked down the sidewalk of the quiet residential neighborhood.

Ian wanted her to live there, but she hadn't made up her mind.

That kind of decision took more commitment than she was willing to give at the moment.

Everything with her life was so up in the air, she didn't dare give Ian hope they had a future.

Telling him she loved him had been a huge step for her, and not that she regretted it, she did think she'd done it too soon.

It wasn't anything she could take back.

A child's shriek pierced the air, and rather than go inside, Marta found her way around the side of the house and looked for an opening in the fence. She found the door ajar, and she pushed it open.

Marta caught Shyla's eye, and with a joyous scream, Shyla shot toward her. "Mommy!"

She caught Shyla in a hug full of body and dress, and she laughed when the little girl planted kisses all over her face.

"Do you care she calls you that?"

The voice came from out of nowhere, and Marta looked around the yard over Shyla's shoulder, her skinny arms gripping Marta's neck.

Sadie sat on a wooden swing petting Hunter, whose head was in her lap.

They hadn't spent much time alone, not without Ian there to act as a buffer. Though, if she and Ian were to ever get married, and if this was indeed going to be her home, she'd need to learn to get along with Sadie, otherwise their living conditions would grow uncomfortable. Fast.

"I feel bad for her real mom, but I'd like to think she'd be happy Shyla's cared for and loved. Otherwise no, I'm kind of humbled she thinks of me like that. The first time she did it, I thought she was trying to say my name."

She tried to set Shyla to her feet, but the little girl hung on tight.

"Do you mind if I sit?" Marta asked.

The swing, besides the patio furniture nearer the house, was the only thing to sit on, and Shyla weighed heavy in Marta's arms.

Despite her nap, her body dragged in exhaustion, and sitting on the ground wasn't an appealing idea. She might not ever get back up again.

Sadie scooted over, though the swing was long enough it wasn't necessary. "So, you're going to live with us, huh?" she asked.

Marta didn't hear any derision in Sadie's voice, only

curiosity and a hint of resignation.

"I don't know. Would it bother you if I did?" Marta asked.

She didn't know what was going to happen; it was best to be clear anything was possible.

"You make my brother happy, and if you were around, I wouldn't have to be alone with squirt, here, so much." Sadie poked Shyla with obvious affection, but Shyla had fallen asleep, her little body dead weight in Marta's lap.

Marta kissed Shyla's temple. "She's sleeping. Yeah, I guess I would be around to help, but Ian's probably going to look into daycare or preschool soon. Little kids like to play with other kids, and it will prepare her for kindergarten."

"Oh."

"I'm sorry about what happened between you and your boyfriend. I'm around if you ever want to talk, girl to girl, or whatever." Marta hadn't spoken to Sadie alone since her attack, and she wanted Sadie to know she had her support.

"I should have known better. I don't know what was going through my mind, hanging out with Trent all the time. Ian warned me off him, told me he was trouble, but I wouldn't listen. Sometimes I feel . . . lost, you know?"

"Yeah. It can't be easy doing all this without your mom."

"That's part of it, I guess," Sadie said, running her hand along Hunter's snout and earning her a lick in return. She bit her lip. "What were you doing at my age?"

"Oh, what was I doing at twenty-one," Marta said, shifting Shyla into a more comfortable position on her lap. "I was here in Tower City, at the university, running track and majoring in business. It's where I met Ian, you know. I went to school with him, Dane, and Brett."

"How long have you been running?"

"Since junior high school. It started as a lark, but I

found I was good at it. It's been a long time."

"You must love it a lot."

Sadie was growing the dye out of her hair. The golden blonde would look a lot better with Sadie's fair complexion. She was filling out too, and a rosy glow flushed her cheeks. It could have been from health or the heat of the summer afternoon, but either way, her sallow look was disappearing.

"I guess." Marta's voice lacked conviction. She *had* loved it.

Now she wasn't quite so sure.

"I wish there was something I loved that much."

"You have plenty of time to find your passion. Do you have any interests that would maybe carry over into a career? Have you been thinking about classes, what you want to do?"

"Ian wants me to get a job and go to school, but I have no idea what I want to do for the rest of my life. It sounds bleak as fuck."

Marta laughed. "You have time, there's no rush. Most schools make you take general courses first, and that will give you a couple years to choose a major. You're lucky Ian is so supportive."

"I know," Sadie murmured.

"What's the matter, sweetheart?"

The tone of their conversation had changed. More somber, more serious. They weren't talking college classes anymore.

"Do you want babies?"

"I didn't think much about it, not when I was your age," Marta said, her mind drifting back to her first years at the university. "I was homesick for California, and I missed my mom and dad. I had big dreams for my running, you know. A lot of people said I could make it, go all the way."

"You didn't though. I heard Ian talking about it once."

"Nope." Marta smiled, but the heavy weight in her heart filled her smile with wistfulness and regret. "Nope, I never did. I gave up a lot to try, too. Sometimes you can have too much passion for something, so much it becomes an obsession, blinding you to everything else that matters."

Her passion for Brett and her obsession for the sport had blinded her to how Ian felt about her.

It wouldn't have made a difference if she would've known how much Ian loved her all those years ago. She'd been in love with Brett then.

She hadn't had room in her life for another man.

And she'd only made room for Brett because they shared running.

That was something she hadn't thought of until that moment.

Running hadn't been the only thing that had kept them together, but when the hard times came, it hadn't been enough to save them.

"What would you have done if you would've gotten pregnant?"

The worry in Sadie's voice made Marta study the girl. There was no way in hell Marta was going to tell Sadie she *had* gotten pregnant, and what she'd done to take care of it.

"What is this all about?" she asked, touching Sadie's leg.

"I haven't told Ian. I haven't told anybody."

"You haven't told us what? It's okay, Sadie, you have a lot of good people in your corner. We're all here to help you."

Looking over the yard, Hunter's head resting in her lap, tears filling her eyes, Sadie whispered, "I'm pregnant."

"Shouldn't you be moving furniture?"

Ian carried two bottles of beer and walked barefoot across the grass, his shirt stained with sweat.

"All the heavy stuff is done. I'll have to make a few more trips, but I can do that later. We still have some odds and ends in the apartments, but I have to keep the bar open a few more nights, anyway. After the last night, I need to let the cleaning crew in, and then that's it."

The burn seared the back of his throat, but it faded quickly when Shyla ran from the corner of the yard where she'd been throwing a stick for Hunter. The little girl hadn't wanted to give up her new pet, and Brett and Alyssa agreed to let Shyla play with the dog for a few more days to make the transition from the apartment to the house easier on her.

"Dog!"

"I know. Hunter is a nice doggie."

But Shyla was already running back to Hunter again, whose chocolatey brown eyes were wistfully watching the stick Shyla held in her tiny hand.

"You're talking to her like she's two." Marta said.

"She is." Ian laughed. "But you can't help it. She's so cute, it's like the baby-talk starts on its own. Here."

"I shouldn't be drinking while I'm training." Marta said, taking the bottle of beer he held out to her.

"It's a good day for it. We're all going to eat soon. Dane and Brett went to clean up and they're going to meet us at Grill with Nikki and Alyssa. Did you want to go with me and Shyla?" Ian hoped she would; he hadn't spent much time with her lately.

He missed her.

"Sadie isn't going?"

"Nah. She said she might go back and forth from the building a few times with her car; most of her clothes are still in her apartment. I'm not going to say no if she wants to help. Everything she does, I won't have to."

Ian took a sip of beer and sat next to Marta on the swing.

"I'm glad to see you two are getting along. I hate to say it, but what that asshole Trent did to her, it helped her grow up, see things a little more seriously. Her therapist can't talk to me about much, but she said she's making real progress."

"That's good, and you're getting along with Dane and Brett?"

"Yeah, today went well. We did a little gossiping of our own for a change," Ian said and winked.

"Oh, anything juicy to share?"

"Not much. Ah, I talked to them about going into business. I thought about it, and it really isn't a bad idea if we can make it work. They were intrigued, I think. I still have no fucking clue—"

"Sh! Shyla's at the age where she's starting to repeat everything. She doesn't need to be going around saying the F word every chance she gets."

"Sorry, sorry. This parenting thing is new to me." He yelled to Shyla, "You're not going to start swearing, are you baby?"

"Baby!" Shyla shrieked, her blond lopsided ponytail shining in the setting sun. She tapped Hunter's head with the stick.

The dog took it like a champ, but he pleaded with a whine she throw it instead.

"See?" Marta poked his shoulder.

"Hush, woman, and drink your beer. Anyway, I don't know what we're going to do, but they didn't say no. That's a start. I think Brett and I said our piece, and now we don't have that hanging over our heads anymore."

"Good, there's no reason for it. We were kids, and it was a long time ago."

"He said you might have gone back to California anyway."

"It's funny you say that." She started peeling the label off the amber bottle. "Sadie and I were talking about what she wanted to do, what she was passionate about. And it made me think, I was passionate about running, obsessed, really."

"You still are," Ian said, placing the cool palm of his hand on the nape of her neck. He loved sitting here in his backyard, having a conversation with her while Shyla played. He could easily fall into a routine like this, the simple joy of it outshining anything else he could be doing.

"Yeah, I guess so, but back then, I was possessed, I wanted to make a name for myself in the sport."

"You've done that."

"I have. I didn't get as big as some of the others, maybe even Libbie Layne, but I did okay. But talking to Sadie today made me see, maybe, maybe, Brett fit into my life because we both ran. Would I have made time for him if he hadn't been a runner? If we hadn't had some of the same goals?"

"Speaking as someone who saw you two from the outside, you loved each other, you loved him a lot. Don't sell Brett short because of how things ended."

"Wow, you did put things aside," Marta said.

He rubbed her jawline with his thumb, and she leaned in to his touch. "He had the, broody, hurt look about him. Still does. I know women like that fixer-upper quality; it didn't take him long to hook Alyssa."

"Well, he changed for Alyssa. He never changed for me. He didn't love me enough to try to change for me."

She gulped her beer.

"He probably couldn't. He wasn't old enough to have a strong enough handle on his feelings to change. I don't think it means he loved you any less than he loves Alyssa now."

"That's very astute, Doctor Freud."

Ian dipped his head. "I try," he whispered, searching her deep brown eyes. "Besides, his loss is definitely my gain. Brett could have surprised you—you could have been married with a passel of kids running around, and then you wouldn't be here with me, letting me kiss you."

"Is that what you want to do?"

Ian dropped his beer onto the ground where the contents fizzed into the grass, and threaded his hands into her hair. "Yes, I want to kiss you, kiss you for the rest of my life."

He took her lips then, and she tasted of beer, the chocolate she must have shared with Shyla after lunch, and all his hopes and dreams.

She tasted of his future, of their lives together, and nothing had tasted sweeter.

She didn't relinquish her drink, holding it as she snaked her arms around him, and he felt the cold glass through the t-shirt he'd worn to move furniture.

He should be cleaning up too, squeeze in a shower, but he didn't want to waste the time he could be spending with Marta.

"Marta. I love you."

She drew away. "I love you too, but—"

He placed a finger over her lips. "That you love me is enough for now. I know you have things to take care of, but all I ask is you don't block me out while you do them. Please."

"I won't. I promise."

"Good." Ian kissed the tip of her nose. "Don't think I won't hold you to that."

He'd gotten off lucky bringing up the topic, and he changed the subject shouting to Shyla, "Shy, baby, you want some food?"

"French fries!"

Marta laughed. "That girl has a bottomless pit for a stomach."

"She's growing. Me, too. Let's go get a big steak."

"French fries!"

"Yes, and French fries. Are you coming?" Ian picked up Shyla who dove into Marta's arms instead.

"French fries," she whispered into Marta's face.

Marta caught Ian's eye.

"I'm in."

Following Marta to the house, Ian hoped Marta meant for life.

MARTA GROANED, THE steak and loaded baked potato from the night before still sitting in her stomach.

She wouldn't have eaten her whole meal had she known the reporter was going to reschedule their interview.

Trying to loosen up, she jogged a few paces. Last night she'd texted him the directions, and she waited on the trail behind her apartment.

He hadn't wanted to meet at the university's track, which surprised her, but she was glad, too. The less chance of running, literally or figuratively, into Spaulding, or Libbie Layne, the better.

"Miss Braddock!"

A middle-aged reporter, well, Marta assumed he was the reporter, shuffled to her, his gut straining his dress shirt.

Even in the rising heat of the morning, he wore a jacket. His only concession to the temperature was that he lacked a tie.

His dress pants were already rumpled, as if he'd chosen his clothes from the floor when he dressed. He held a small notepad and carried a pencil in his fist.

She scowled. It would be too much to ask for that he recorded the interview. There was nothing worse than being misquoted because the reporter thought he could remember everything she said.

"I'm Marta Braddock," she said when he was close enough to hear. "I assume you're Mr. Warner, from the Tower City Journal?"

"Yes, ma'am, I am," he said, panting. "Whew! I overslept this morning."

That ticked her off; he'd been the one who changed the time. But she didn't want to start the interview on the wrong foot, and realizing he was alone, she asked with exaggerated politeness, "I thought you were going to take pictures of me running?"

"Dammit! I forgot to tell the photographer I changed the time."

She bit back a sigh.

Warner brightened. "I'll take a snap of you with my phone. That should be good enough."

"Sounds fine. Would you like to walk the path while we talk?"

There wasn't any place to sit; they wouldn't find a bench for half a mile.

"Yeah, okay. I wrote down some questions here, let me

look." He rifled through the pages of his notebook. "Here they are. How are you dealing with Coach Wesley's death?"

He wasn't going to make this easy.

Lifting her eyes from the pond, she checked to see if he was ready to write down her answer.

His eyes had narrowed, and his lips were curled into a sneer. "You could use him right about now, couldn't you, Miss Braddock?"

Heart fluttering, Marta tamped down her fear.

She refused to be scared of a man she could out run in five seconds.

If he already had a hold of her, now, that would be a different story.

"What do you mean?"

"He's not around to pull for you at the school anymore, is he, Miss Braddock? I have it on good authority he was the only one who wanted you there. After his heart attack, Gregory Spaulding didn't waste any time replacing you. Can you tell the paper your official stance on that?"

"Mr. Spaulding hasn't replaced me. He's giving me a chance to train for the Lady Slipper without interference. I'm grateful he had the foresight to see both training and coaching would have been a struggle for me."

The words tasted bitter in her mouth; replacing her wouldn't have been necessary if Spaulding hadn't volunteered her participation in the marathon in the first place.

"You're confident your position at Minnesota State University, Tower City, is secure?"

"There's no reason for me to believe otherwise," she said, though the look in the reporter's eyes gave her that very reason.

"How's training going?"

"As fine as it can be with the little notice I was given to prepare," Marta said, shifting her gaze to her building.

From where she stood, she could see Dane climbing into his truck, and she recognized his TCRC gear.

He must be going to work, or maybe he was going to marathon headquarters to help Brett or Nikki for a while.

October was fast approaching, which meant Nikki's inaugural women's run was coming up. At dinner last night, the race and the related activities were all Nikki could talk about.

Ian had been a good sport about it, though.

"I understand Libbie Layne offered to train you, and you turned her down. Do you want to explain why?"

Marta thinned her lips. There was no way he could have known that had he not been in contact with Spaulding.

During interviews like this, all her answers were on the record. Even if she asked not to be quoted, she would find her words in the paper. She had to be impartial and sound like she was grateful for Libbie's offer.

"I prefer to run alone."

"But the advice from a runner of Miss Layne's caliber must be extremely valuable, do you disagree?"

He was trying to bait her, but it wasn't going to work.

"I agree her advice is valuable, why else would she have been given my coaching position for the *interim*? Besides, I can call any running coach anywhere in the world for advice; I'm not without my resources."

The reporter made a note, though Marta couldn't see what he was writing. He could have been drawing stick figures for all she knew.

"You are well-connected," he said, squinting at her. "What do you feel your chances of winning the race are? In case any of our readers would like to place a little wager on the outcome?"

"I'm not privy to the race roster. There are several talented runners I could be up against. It's impossible for me to say either way."

"It's a simple matter of deduction, wouldn't you say? Couldn't you accurately guess who will share the elite starting line with you?"

Marta couldn't admit to this slimeball she hadn't cared enough to go that far. She should have.

She'd slacked on her preparation, letting Ian distract her with kisses and promises.

Dammit.

Finally she said, "Knowing wouldn't make a difference. I can only make my body do what it can do. Who runs with beside me, behind me, or in front of me, is irrelevant."

"There's a rumor going around the local running community that Brett Sommers, director of the Tower City Marathon, and *close* friend of yours, is stepping down, and that you're going to take over the race. Do you have anything to add?"

"I can't add to a statement that isn't true," Marta said. "How would I have time to direct a marathon of that size along with my coaching duties? Directing the marathon takes Brett, Mr. Sommers, so much time he rarely runs his own race. What are you implying, Mr. Warner?"

"Nothing. It seems to me you would be the natural choice to direct the Tower City Marathon—you have the experience."

Marta lifted her chin. "I'll be coaching at the university. But I'll make an announcement, since you seem to want one. After the Lady Slipper, I'm retiring from professional racing."

CHAPTER EIGHT

"HE MADE ME so mad, and then he took my picture with his stupid cell phone and the way he squinted at me, it made my skin crawl. Blech." Marta grimaced.

"How did he know about Brett?" Nikki asked, running alongside her.

Marta had needed to work an easy run into her training schedule, and Nikki offered to keep her company.

She took her up on it since they rarely saw each other, and Marta liked her. Dane was a lucky guy.

"It could have been anyone. Brett's a complainer, and if he whined to the wrong person, or the wrong person overheard . . . It wouldn't be hard to come to the conclusion he was done. Besides, he's been running it for a long time. It's natural to get sick of doing something."

"Well, if the guys go into business together, they better not get sick of it."

"Dane talked to you? That was fast. Is he considering it?"

Marta took a moment to look around the trail.

The leaves were starting to lose their green, some of them falling and littering the paths.

Fall was her favorite season, and she'd missed it fiercely when she'd moved to California.

Cali claimed the ocean, but Minnesota owned the glorious seasons. The air held a hint of the upcoming crispness, and she breathed in, detecting the scent of wood smoke.

"Yeah, but I'm a little worried. He'd need startup money, and well, the loan for the store isn't paid off. Brett has his advance from the book, and Ian, I don't know about his finances to make any assumptions." Nikki looked at her from the corners of her eyes.

"I have no idea where Ian gets his cash. We're not close enough for me to ask. All he said, without me prying, was his dad sold the bar, and he decided Ian should have half. Besides that, I don't know anything."

Marta picked up speed. Nikki was taller than she was, and it didn't take much for her to run faster.

Nikki would have been a wonderful long-distance runner if she'd had the proper training and the will to go pro.

"But I'm sorry if you're uncomfortable with it. It was my idea they do that, and if I would have known . . ."

"Dane can do what he likes. The store brings in money now, that's not the issue. But don't most startups lose money in the first years?"

"I have no idea, but look, whatever they go into, they won't have to pay many employees. We would help where we could right? So, if you, Alyssa and Sadie . . ." She stumbled over Sadie's name.

Pregnant, Sadie wouldn't want to throw what little

energy she had into Ian's business, and he might not let her, anyway.

He wanted her to go to school, and that was all the more important now. ". . . Work for," Marta motioned air quotes, "free, then that would help, right?"

"Pfft. Marta, get real. I'm the manager of Dane's store. His full-timer doesn't want to do it, he offered it to her before he hired me. I *have* to go in. Someone needs to be around in case it burns to the ground, or some moron decides he wants to rob it—again."

"Alyssa could—"

"Alyssa's a writer. She wants to keep writing her books, not help Brett start a business. Yeah, he already asked her, and she doesn't want to do anything but write. You don't have to listen to her piss and moan over the time she lost while running and writing that manual with Brett."

"Jeez, thanks a lot."

Nikki laughed. "I'm just giving you a heads up. Besides, you're going to be coaching. Even if you do retire, coaching takes a lot out of you, and sometimes you'll be out of town and stuff, right? What time are you volunteering?"

"Grrr."

"And don't volunteer Sadie's time. She's going to be watching Shyla while Ian works and probably going to school, right? We're all spoken for. Hey, I'm not against the guys doing it, I mean, Dane's been pretty happy lately hanging out with Ian and Brett and not having to worry about them fighting over you. If he could work with them and enjoy it, I'm all for it. But I'll be thirty-four next year, and I want a baby. I don't know if I can get pregnant. Stacy's been trying for a long time. Waiting is only going to make it worse for me."

"Oh, my God, if you want to get pregnant, get pregnant.

You aren't homeless, and you'll have plenty of free daycare —Alyssa told me Dane's parents and your parents are champing at the bit to babysit. *Just do it already*. You and Dane are blowing the whole thing way out of proportion. Babies don't cost *that* much. Besides, I'll throw you the biggest baby shower you've ever seen, you won't need to buy diapers for a whole year. Dane can handle it. The store in the mall did nothing to his sales like he thought—their grand opening barely dented his profits that week. I'll even loan my face for a new ad campaign if that will make him feel better. You accused Alyssa of pissing and moaning," Marta muttered. "It must be catching."

Nikki stopped dead in her tracks. Her skin glowed in the sun, sweat giving her cheeks a glittering sheen. Her ponytail elastic was falling out, and her hair sat in thick spirals on her shoulder.

Marta could see why Dane had fallen hard and fast. If she played for the other team, she would have, too.

"You would do that for us?"

"As long as the contract I signed with the school lets me, yes. Yes, I will."

Marta gasped when Nikki captured her in a bear hug. "That is fantastic! I never thought of it that way, *at all*."

"Dane wants to put you in a house first, but you don't need to live in a house to have a baby. Half of Tower City would be childless if that were the case."

"He's sweet, isn't he?" Nikki asked, picking up the pace again. They still needed to make the loop that would take them back to their apartment building.

"He's always been a worry wart, and his ex-wife made him worse. You've been good for him. It will be nice to watch him be a dad. He'll be a fantastic father."

Nikki beamed. "Yeah, he will. It'll work out, I know it.

Speaking of the wedding, how about another round of dress shopping?"

"I CAN'T BELIEVE your dad sold this place," Dane said, then took a long pull of his beer.

Ian sat at a high-top table with his friends. After tomorrow, the bar would no longer belong to the Butler's.

He didn't feel right behind the bar now, and he'd opened it up for the party. Two of their friends stood behind it mixing martinis, trying recipes they were finding on their phones.

"Yeah, but I won't miss it. Maybe the new owners can turn it into something. It's a good spot, my dad just wasn't invested, and I didn't care if it made money or not."

"Remember when you'd sneak booze to us out the back, and we'd get shit-faced in the parking lot?" Brett asked.

"I remember," Dane said, laughing. "That one night—we had an Economics test the next morning. When we showed up, Marta was pissed because she hadn't been invited."

"She never drank as much as we did," Ian said.

He remembered that morning in class, his head spinning out of control, and his stomach churning so badly he could barely focus.

He'd aced the test—Marta had fed him all the answers.

"I think I sat here for three days straight thinking about divorcing Liz. It was the hardest decision of my life."

"That was tough. But it worked out in the end. You have the store instead of a harpy. It seems like a fair trade to me," Brett said, opening a new beer.

"Yeah, I would take it any day. And I wouldn't have met Nikki if I hadn't thrown in the towel. I think everything will work out now; we're all pretty settled."

"Marta isn't," Brett said, and Ian barely heard him over the people hooting over a game of pool and a Def Leppard song screaming from the jukebox.

"I'm doing my best." Ian couldn't keep the bitterness out of his voice.

He'd been trying like hell to help Marta.

He supported her running; he'd rub her down after long runs. He was there for her when she needed to talk.

Nothing he did took away the feeling something wasn't quite right.

It wasn't that she still slept at her apartment and didn't talk about breaking her lease. It wasn't that she still hadn't given him any indication she would one day accept his proposal.

And it sure as hell wasn't that she only said she loved him when he said it to her first.

"At least she's retiring. She's too old for all that bullshit."

"Do you believe it?" Ian asked.

When Marta told him she'd given that creepy reporter the okay to announce her retirement, it had given him hope she was finally thinking about their future.

So far it hadn't done anything. She trained harder than ever; the Lady Slipper was three weeks away.

"Professionals go in and out of retirement all the time, but Marta, once she says she'll do something, she'll do it. This whole mess has given her a bad feeling. I'm surprised she hasn't told the school to shove it." Brett popped a peanut into his mouth.

Ian sought out Marta in the crowded bar and spotted

her chatting with a few others who used to run track at the university. He hadn't known them from school, but he'd met them at Dane's and Nikki's engagement party.

Ian encouraged her to make friends.

Anything to keep her in Minnesota.

He didn't like thinking it, but sometimes he felt like she could disappear at any moment.

"She won't let Spaulding make her look like a fool. All those promises he made on her behalf . . . she'll do her best to keep them, He really twisted the knife in her back at Coach Wesley's funeral."

He couldn't stand feeling helpless, and Ian changed the subject. "Anyway, what about our business? Should I start looking through the Journal's classifieds? Call an employment agency?"

"Nikki was reluctant at first, and she was right to be. We already run a business, but when I told my dad about the opportunity, he said he would give me my share of the start-up costs." Dane shrugged.

"That's great. You have to look at this as an investment —if we go through with it, you'll be able to pay it back, with interest. You guys have any plans if we decide not to bother?" Brett asked.

Ian hadn't thought that far ahead. Keeping track of Shyla and Sadie filled up his time. "I suppose I'll be looking sooner or later. I've been taking a break, situating Shyla and getting my sister on track, and I didn't want to jump into looking for work. Besides, even though the bar was a pain in my ass, being your own boss has a certain appeal I don't want to lose."

"I hear you there," Dane muttered.

"None of us wants to work for someone else. That

doesn't sound like it gives us much choice," Brett said, thrumming his fingers on the tabletop.

"Alyssa okay with it?" Ian asked.

Being that Marta had been the one to give him the idea, he wasn't worried about what she thought, but it would be important for their fiancées to have their backs.

Starting a business from the ground up was no easy task; it would require a lot of time and work.

"She doesn't care. Morning sickness is making her miserable. She feels like she's going to throw up all the time, and she's just waiting for these next few weeks to pass. Her doctor says to let the first trimester go, and if she's still feeling ill, they'll put her on anti-nausea medication. She probably wants me out of the house—I can't help but hover over her. She's got my baby inside her, and I want to do it right this time."

Ian wanted to jab at him, but Brett was trying and Ian had to respect him for it. "Women get pregnant every day, she'll be fine."

"Wait until you knock up Marta. We'll see how you feel then."

A little zing shot through Ian's heart.

She was terrific with Shyla; she was a natural mother.

First she would have to work through some of the things Brett had been forced to face before she'd be willing to carry his child.

And she hadn't accepted his proposal yet.

"I can't knock her up without a job."

"Then let's figure out what the fuck we want to do," Brett said, leaning in.

Ian listened to Dane and Brett bicker about what kind of business they should open. An idea began to form, and he raised his hands to hush his friends.

Meeting Dane's and Brett's eyes, he explained.

"WHERE'S THAT CUTIE-pie Shyla?" Nikki asked between sips of a Cosmopolitan martini.

"She's at home with Sadie. Sadie's been feeling sick to her stomach," Marta said.

At first, she thought it was morning sickness, the same thing making Alyssa green, but after prying, Marta realized it was guilt.

Sadie hadn't confessed to Ian she was pregnant, scared of what he would say, and what the legalities would entail. Trent was in lock-up awaiting trial; his parents couldn't afford, or didn't want to pay, bail.

Before the party, Marta warned her that if she didn't tell Ian soon, she would. It wasn't fair to keep him in the dark, and keeping Sadie's secret made her feel guilty, too.

"I know how she feels," Alyssa said.

"You should go home and rest," Nikki said, rubbing Alyssa's back. "You look tired."

"I want to, but I can't. Brett would come home with me, and the guys look like they're in a pretty deep conversation over there."

"They're probably talking about their business," Nikki said.

"Have they been meeting about it?" Marta asked.

She'd been busy training for the marathon—she hadn't kept in the loop when it came to gossip.

When she did surface from training, she spent time with Shyla while Ian did last minute things for the bar. The cleaning crew would come tomorrow, and that would be the last Ian would see of BB's.

"Yeah. Actually, Dane told his parents what they were thinking of doing, and his dad said they would give him the money. I guess it's some kind of guilt-gift for the way they treated him after he divorced Liz. It pissed Dane off, but I told him to get over it and take it. You were right, Marta, this is probably the best way for us to have another source of income. I have more good news, too," she said, her eyes sparkling.

Alyssa said, "Oh, yeah?" at the same time Marta said, "Let's hear it."

"After I told my parents Dane's were giving us some start-up cash, they didn't want to be outdone, and they said they would give us the down payment for a house!" She shrieked into her hands.

"Oh, that's great," Marta said, gripping Nikki's arm. "That must mean a lot to you."

"It does. They didn't want to tell me, but they've been paying for my sister's IVF treatments. This was a good way for them to help me out the way they've been helping my sister and her husband."

"Things are looking up," Alyssa said. Turning to Marta she asked, "How is your training going?"

Marta winced. "It's going okay, but someone from the paper emailed me, and my interview is going to be in the Journal tomorrow. Be prepared for some backlash from marathon runners. The reporter was very blunt in saying he knew Brett didn't want to direct it anymore. There might be some unhappy people, and maybe some worried ones, too."

"For a sports reporter, he wasn't very supportive. It sounds like he wants to cause problems in the running community here in the city," Nikki said.

"He wants to cause problems for *me*, that's for sure. But I already have enough; his profile of me won't to hurt me any. But I'm afraid Nikki's right. I don't want him making trouble for Brett and Dane just because they're my friends."

"We'll keep the marathon together," Alyssa said firmly. "Even if Brett doesn't want to direct it anymore, it's ours."

"How do we plan to do that?" Maybe Alyssa had baby-brain. "And what's gotten into you, anyway? Since when do you care about helping the running community?"

It was callous of her to ask, but Marta didn't need more two-faced people in her life.

The running community, or The Running Community, used to treat her with respect and professionalism. Since being over-powered by Spaulding, and with Coach Wesley's death, she was feeling more like an outsider than she ever had before.

"We all turned to running in some way, shape, or form. We're going to keep the marathon in our family, and you're going to kick butt at the Lady Slipper. Then you're going to tell Spaulding to kiss ass. We'll help our men with the business they're starting, and our kids will grow up together."

"If only it were that easy." Marta didn't know what else to say. Alyssa's rosy view of the future was one that Marta couldn't share.

"Nothing that comes easy is worth it," Nikki said.

Marta huffed a laugh. "Did you make that up?"

Nikki giggled. "No, it's a motivational poster at the store."

Groaning, Marta slid off her chair. "And with that, I'm going home."

But Marta didn't go home. After the bar emptied, she helped Ian throw garbage away and wash glasses.

They didn't want the cleaning crew to find a job they weren't prepared for.

Ian also counted the bottles of liquor they'd used—technically the booze didn't belong to him any longer, and he would have to reimburse the owners for what they drank.

Reluctantly, she agreed to go home with him when he asked.

She wanted to give more to their relationship, but she didn't feel as if she could, not now. For her, it was enough she'd told him she loved him, though he made it clear he wanted more.

They drove down the quiet streets of the residential area, and Marta's eyelids fluttered with exhaustion.

One of the lamps in the living room shone gold through the curtains, inviting her in. There was nothing more she wanted than to call this house her home.

Her hopes of going immediately to bed were dashed when they opened the door and found Sadie sitting on the couch crying.

"What is it?" Ian asked, rushing to her and kneeling on the carpet in front of his sister. "Are you okay? Is Shyla okay?"

Calmly, Marta took off her shoes and started making coffee. It was going to be a long night.

"Shyla's okay," Sadie sobbed, throwing herself into Ian's arms.

As the coffee dripped, Marta sat in a chair near the couch.

It would figure that after a pleasant night of being with friends, Sadie would choose tonight to tell Ian her secret.

Marta knew guilt would eventually eat at the girl until she could no longer stand it, and tonight the pressure had broken her.

She was thankful she hadn't done anything drastic, like run away, and she could only think it was because Shyla had been left in her care. Sadie didn't want to admit it, but she'd fallen for that little girl, just as Marta had.

Alyssa said running brought them together, and she agreed, but Shyla had changed Ian's family for the better, and that included Marta as well.

"But you're not? Is that what you're saying?" Ian asked, pushing Sadie away to look into her face.

Sadie shook her head and started crying again.

"What do you know about this?" Ian asked Marta.

Instead of answering, because it wasn't her story to tell, she poured them cups of coffee. "Here," she said, handing Sadie a mug, "I made decaf."

Ian frowned. "Why would you do that?"

Sadie took a deep breath. "Because I'm pregnant."

"Did you know about this?" Ian asked, swinging his angry glare to Marta.

"Yeah, for a few days. She was scared to tell you."

Ian sighed and sat on the couch next to his sister.

Sadie sipped her coffee, the aftermath of her crying still running down her face.

"Do you know whose it is?" Ian asked.

"I've only slept with Trent."

"That's something, at least. How are you feeling? We need to make you an appointment to see a doctor."

Sadie caught her eye, and Marta flinched.

"Let me guess."

"Well, I just couldn't—"

Maybe taking Sadie to the ob/gyn behind Ian's back hadn't been the best idea, but Sadie had begged. Marta couldn't say no, and she'd paid the price.

Realization dawned in Ian's grey eyes. "Marta . . ."

He knew then, what a visit like that would cost her.

She'd never be able to describe the heart-wrenching pain of holding Sadie's hand during her exam, or what Marta had felt hearing the baby's heartbeat.

While standing next to Sadie, the onslaught of memories almost drowned her. At least she'd been able to wait until after she'd dropped Sadie off before she'd broken down. She'd parked around the corner in front of a house for sale, and she'd cried long and hard. For over an hour.

She didn't say anything, and Ian looked away. "There's not a lot we can do tonight. I'm tired. Did you get Shyla down to sleep okay?" he asked Sadie, pressing a kiss to the top of her head.

"I left her playing in her crib, like you told me to," she said, staring at the floor, holding her coffee mug close to her chest.

"Okay, we'll talk more in the morning. Are you coming up?" Ian asked Marta.

She stood from the chair, debating on if she should go home. "Maybe I should—"

"Do what you want." With a dejected slump to his shoulders, he trudged up the stairs leaving her alone with Sadie.

Running her fingers through her hair, Marta sat on the couch, not knowing what to do. "That wasn't terrible, huh?"

Sadie shrugged.

"Well, I know Ian, and it could have been a lot worse. You know it too, but you also know he'll help you. He's always been there for you. He won't stop now." Marta tried to console her. If there was anything she knew, it was a damn scary thing to be pregnant and feel like you were all alone.

"What if I don't want help?" Sadie asked, finally lifting her eyes from the beige carpet.

Chilled by the despair on the girl's face, Marta shivered. "What do you mean?"

"I mean, Trent is an asshole—he'll never be a father. I'll be doing this by myself. My baby will never have a mom and a dad together. That's not fair."

"You don't know you won't meet someone and get married. Have more kids. And until then, Ian will be a wonderful role model."

"But he expects me to go to school and get a job. How can I do that and have a baby?" More tears started to drip down Sadie's face. They landed in her coffee cup.

"That will be something you'll have to talk about with him," Marta said.

She couldn't speak for Ian. She was already afraid she'd overstepped her bounds in the family.

"Besides, you're going to be pregnant for months. Plenty of time to figure out the details before the baby is born."

"I don't want to."

Marta's mouth dried up, and the memory of Brett's horrible confession the day she told him she was pregnant hit her like a sucker punch to the gut. "I don't understand."

"What if I don't want to? Have it?" Sadie met Marta's eyes. "I can get an abortion. Pretend it never happened. Put all of this behind me."

"Sadie, you'll never be able to put it behind you. Maybe some women can, or they think they have." She placed a hand on Sadie's belly. "You have a baby in there. You've heard its heart beating. You may think an abortion is the answer, and it could be. But it may also be the biggest mistake of your life. You have to do what's best for you.

Don't do it because you hate Trent, or you think you're too young, or you think a baby will get in the way of what you want. A baby can bring your life a lot of joy, too, if you let it."

"I guess," Sadie mumbled.

"Maybe talk to your therapist about it, huh?" Marta smothered a yawn.

She'd been close to telling Sadie decisions had a way of haunting you, but it was closing in on four in the morning, and this was no time for a conversation like that.

"Thanks," Sadie whispered.

"You're welcome. I'm here to talk whenever you need to. But for now, get some sleep. You need it."

Marta left Sadie curled on the couch staring into space, the scent of coffee lingering in the darkened room.

She plodded up the stairs, her footsteps heavy with the weight of her problems, and, now, Sadie's.

The nursery glowed orange from a butterfly nightlight plugged into the wall near the floor, highlighting the empty crib.

The hallway that led to Ian's room was also lit with a nightlight. Maybe Ian made several trips to Shyla's nursery every night. That brought a faint smile to her lips, picturing Ian trying to persuade Shyla to go to sleep.

She found them both in Ian's bedroom, Shyla snuggled into his side. The baby must not have been sleeping like Ian had hoped, or they'd woken her when they came home.

Marta leaned against the doorjamb wishing like hell she felt free enough to take off her clothes and slip between the sheets, maybe snuggle Shyla like the baby was hers. And they'd wake in the morning to Shyla's giggles and a leaky diaper.

She backed away before Shyla felt her presence and

woke up. She was already on Ian's bad side of his dark mood, she couldn't imagine his reaction if she woke Shyla now.

Sadie slept on the couch where Marta had left her, and she didn't stir when Marta let herself out the door and into the cool fall night.

IAN EYED THE building before he stepped out of his car.

It sat in the perfect area—across the street from the main shopping center in Tower City. The prime location would ensure they always had customers. The previous owners decided running their own business wasn't for them and closed only a year after opening.

Their loss, our gain. Ian stepped out of the car when Dane pulled up next to him in the empty parking lot.

The lot would need to be paved, and he wished he'd brought a notebook to start a list. But this was their first walk-through, and if they liked the look of the building, he would have plenty of time to make a million lists.

"Nice location," Dane said, slamming his truck's door. "Are you lucky in real estate or what?"

Ian would have preferred his luck be in other areas of his life, like, say, his love life, but he'd take any luck he could get. "Maybe. I think it's just good timing."

Brett parked next to Dane's truck and the three were walking toward the entrance when the realtor opened the frosted glass door for them.

The restaurant was done in greens and golds, and Ian curled his upper lip in distaste. "We'd need to redecorate, ASAP."

Brett made a beeline toward the bar. "Lots of space back here."

Dane followed Ian into the kitchen. "We'd need to figure out the food thing."

"Yeah." The idea held little appeal, but if they didn't offer food, appetizers at the very least, their customers would drop off. "In a place this size, and in a location this close to the mall, no one would stop in just to drink."

"Well, I can't deny this could work," Brett said, pushing the kitchen door open. "The location is perfect. The price is right. Cheap, really, for where the building's at. We're lucky that they want to unload this place."

"How long do we have until we need to decide?" Dane asked.

Ian shrugged. "The real estate agent said there isn't anyone interested right now, but the price is right, yeah, so that may not hold true forever."

"This is just a walk-through. We need to bring the women here, let them see it, tell us what they think. This would be our lives for months, years, until it got off the ground. We'd need their help, or, at the very least, their patience."

Ian took Dane's advice seriously. BB's had already been running when Ian took over, but Dane had built his running shoe store from the ground up.

"You two can show Nikki and Alyssa. I don't know where Marta is at with me, and I'm giving up."

The fact that she'd kept Sadie's pregnancy from him and didn't stay the night of the farewell party hurt like hell.

The fact that she hadn't spoken to him since that night broke his heart.

He knew she was busy training—the marathon was

Saturday, but a text, a phone call, would only take a few moments of her time.

But she didn't see fit to do either of those things.

Shyla asked where Marta was all the time.

Sadie acted like she didn't care, but whenever someone mentioned Marta's name, it was as if a set of antennae on her head perked up and she would tense, waiting for news.

Marta was letting down more than only him, and he wanted to damn her to hell.

Brett rested a hand on Ian's shoulder. "Don't. Alyssa didn't give up on me, and she could have, easily. Marta needs you. I hurt her so much she won't ask anyone for help. She'd drown before she would beg for a rope. Don't give up on her because of what I did."

Ian appreciated what Brett was saying, but it didn't change anything as far as Ian was concerned. Tired, he lowered himself into a chair at a table in the middle of the restaurant. His arm stuck on the sticky tabletop.

"I don't have any choice. The race is only a few days away. That's all she's thinking about. I don't have time for that. Sadie's pregnant—"

"She is? When did that happen?" Dane asked, perching on the table, one of his feet resting on a chair.

"Gee, I don't know. Two or three months ago? Do you need me to explain how, too?" Ian asked sarcastically.

Dane kicked him. "No, smartass. I mean, when did you find out?"

"The night of the party."

"Then that explains it," Brett said, running his hands over a row of booths.

They would need to be reupholstered, the Naugahyde already cracking in places. It wasn't any wonder the owners wanted out.

The building looked like they hadn't put a penny into it the whole time they'd ran the place.

"What?" Ian asked, raising his eyes from the oak booths.

"Marta wouldn't want to be around Sadie, not if she's pregnant. She's close to the age Marta was. It would make sense that Marta wouldn't want to see Sadie like that."

Ian blew out a breath. That had to explain it. He had to stop being a selfish asshole and start thinking about Marta and how she was taking this whole mess.

Sagging in relief he said, "I thought it was me."

"Nope. She's got a lot on her mind. Sadie made it worse. Are you going to watch her race?"

"Yeah, of course."

"No," Brett said, sinking into a chair across from Dane. "Are you traveling with her?"

"I can't. I'd love to, but with Shyla . . . and well, my sister's in a delicate frame of mind. I need to be around for her. I don't want her to do anything stupid. She misses Marta, even if she won't say anything."

"I wish someone could go with her," Brett said.

"Then you go. I have people who need me here. It'd be different if we were a couple, and as much as I'd love us to be, I have to get it into my head we're not. If she needed my help, I hope she'd ask, but she hasn't. If that puts her in a tough spot, well, I'm in one, too. I can't force myself on her, and I don't have time to coddle her."

"I can go. Calm down, both of you. We all want to be there for her, but women think they can handle things on their own and it probably didn't occur to Marta to ask. Alyssa's still not feeling well, and I don't think she'd like you running off with Marta anyway," Dane said, glaring at Brett.

"That's not what I'd be doing, and you know it."

"Alyssa wouldn't see it that way," Dane said.

Brett ran a hand over his face. "You're right. Her pregnancy makes her moody, and that wouldn't look good to her at all."

"Then it's settled. I agree she shouldn't go alone. Now, what about this place?" Dane asked.

Ian didn't have the mental energy to think about that now.

He didn't want to admit all he could think about was Marta.

Not when this business stuff had been his idea. He didn't have a good feeling about it—but nothing was gained without taking risks. The sports bar could very easily work out, turn into a Tower City hot spot.

If they played their cards right.

Something Ian hadn't been doing very well lately.

"Why don't you bring Alyssa and Nikki to look around, then we'll talk more. If someone steals it out from under us, then it wasn't meant to be."

"I agree. Let's not rush into anything. I need to get going. Alyssa has an appointment, and I don't want to miss it," Brett said, pulling his keys from his pocket.

Ian gave Brett a half-hearted wave as he slipped out the door, and after he was gone told Dane, "Thanks for going with her. I feel better knowing someone has her back."

"It's fine. I haven't been to a big race like that in a long time—they're fun to watch. If Nikki wasn't busy with the women's race, she'd probably go with us. I'll watch out for Marta the best I can, but once she's on the route, she's on her own."

"I know. I need to get back. I've been saddling Sadie with Shyla a lot more than I should, and Sadie's not very stable right now."

"That's a hell of a thing," Dane said, following Ian to the door.

"Tell me about it. What Brett said makes sense, though. I never would have put two and two together. It helps, not much, but it helps. I thought we were making progress with what happened between her and Brett, but maybe she'll never be okay."

Ian nodded at the agent climbing out of his car to lock the building.

"If you stick by her long enough, she'll get past it, or maybe, at least, she'll learn to live with it. The past, the way people treat us, how we respond to it, it becomes a part of us. I'll let you know about Marta."

"Yeah, thanks."

As Ian drove home, he'd thought when Marta finished the marathon it would be a turning point for them.

They could get on with their lives.

But now he knew that was only wishful thinking.

———

MARTA SHOVED THE Tower City Journal aside in disgust.

The reporter had done a hatchet job of their interview, just as she'd known he would.

He was clearly team Spaulding, and his bias gleamed brighter than a pair of running shoes caught in the headlights of an oncoming car.

Not that it mattered.

Didn't matter if she came across bitchy and insensitive toward Coach Wesley.

Didn't matter if he portrayed her as someone who wouldn't do the best she could during the race.

Didn't matter he painted Brett as a rat abandoning a sinking ship.

They'd keep the marathon together, just like Alyssa said they would.

She wasn't sure how, though.

When a knock sounded on her door, she frowned.

She wasn't expecting visitors, and she needed to finish packing.

Dane's offer, no, more of a command, that he go with her, had pissed her off.

She'd raced more than her share of races alone—she didn't need a babysitter.

But it would be welcome, too. Conversation with Dane would take her mind of things during the long drive.

Plus, he would give her a shoulder to cry on if things didn't go well.

When Marta opened the door, expecting to find Dane, Nikki, or even Ian, she was stunned to see Sadie shifting from foot to foot. The girl was dressed in ripped jeans and a ragged tank top, black circles rested beneath her eyes, and her lips were pinched into a scowl.

"Sadie, what's wrong?" Marta moved aside to let her into the apartment, and she paused for a few moments before stepping over the threshold.

She didn't speak, only shuffled into the kitchen.

"Is everything okay?" Marta tried again. "Come sit in the living room."

When Sadie was sitting on the edge of a couch cushion, Marta said, "Tell me what's up."

Sadie had to have stopped by for a reason. The shadows on her face were plain enough evidence things weren't going well.

"Why did you stop coming over?" Sadie blurted, tears

starting to trail down her cheeks. "Ian misses you, and Shyla says your name all the time."

Shock rippled through Marta's body. She'd had no idea the few days she'd taken to herself to mentally prepare for the race were hurting anyone.

"Is it because of me? Because if it is, I can move out. I'm too much trouble now that I'm pregnant, right? I can get an abortion, or run away, or, or—"

Overcome with weeping, Sadie threw herself into Marta's arms.

In equal measure, guilt and shame crowded Marta's heart. She'd been selfish, so selfish.

She'd had valid reasons for staying away, but those reasons weren't any more important than Ian's missing her, or poor little Shyla who probably felt like she'd lost her mother all over again.

Her reasons weren't any more important than the girl in her arms taking the blame for Marta's faults and failures as a human being.

As a girlfriend. As a maybe-fiancée.

If she would accept Ian's proposal . . . If there still was one.

"Sadie, look at me, honey," Marta said firmly, drawing the sobbing girl away from her. "Look at me."

Sadie lifted her head, her face splotchy from crying, her nose bright red. Her eyeliner had smeared under her eyes, and it looked as if she'd chewed off her lipstick long ago.

"It has nothing to do with you."

After drawing a shuddery, watery breath, Sadie asked, "How can I believe that? You disappeared the night I told Ian I'm knocked up. He blamed you for helping me, and you never came back. It's all my fault."

Before Sadie could start crying again, Marta said, "No,

it's not. Ian and I . . . we've been on shaky ground since I came back from California."

Deciding she needed to be clear, banish Sadie's fears once and for all, she took Sadie's hands and whispered, "It doesn't have anything to do with you, or you being knocked up. It doesn't have anything to do with you deciding to get an abortion. It has to do with *my* pregnancy and *my* abortion."

Sadie blinked. "I don't understand."

Marta stood and leaned against the French doors. The trees were losing their leaves, and one blew across the grass.

"When I was your age, a little older, I was in college, running track, and I got knocked up. I was going to lose my running scholarship, and my baby's daddy didn't want to be a dad. I was in the same situation you are, I guess. I felt lost, my parents were in California. I wanted to keep running, make a name for myself, and I had an abortion. Not a big deal, really. Women do it every day. And I got the life I wanted. I may not have made it to the big time, but I've had a good career."

"Then you don't regret it?"

A smile ghosted Marta's lips.

"Regret? Sometimes I wonder where I would be now, had I kept it. Could I have still ran? Made a name for myself? Would I have been offered the coaching job at the school? I don't know. I think about my baby, yeah. But you know the clichés—don't cry over spilt milk, everything happens for a reason. There are a million platitudes for a situation like that."

"That's why you told me not to make a decision too fast," Sadie said.

"Yeah. It's one of those things you can't take back, and it's one of those things you'll never forget."

"If you weren't avoiding Ian and Shyla because of me, what were you doing?"

"I didn't stop visiting because of you. If anything, I want you to feel like you can come see me, talk to me, whenever you need to." She paused. "You know I'm training for a big race."

"Yeah, a race you're not ready for."

Marta laughed. "You've been listening to Ian. Yeah, a race I'm probably not ready for. But I have a lot riding on it, and I needed a few days to myself. Took some quiet time. I hadn't realized anyone would miss me."

"Shyla does, and Ian. Though he won't say anything. He's just in a bad mood all the time."

"Then maybe I should stop by the house and say good-bye. I'll be spending a couple days down there before I run, so I can rest, do some interviews, that kind of thing."

"When you get back, will you move in with us?"

"I don't know, Sadie. Ian . . . he's going to want a family someday. After what I did, I don't feel like I would be a very good mother."

"That's how I feel. What do I know about babies?"

Marta took her place on the couch and put her arm around Sadie's shoulders. "The fact that you'll try will put you ahead of me in that respect. But Ian will help, and your baby will grow up with Shyla. There are worse situations."

"And you, right?" Sadie asked, relaxing into Marta's embrace. "You'll help, too?"

Flattered Sadie wanted to include Marta in her family, she said, "Let me race, and we'll figure it out from there."

"Don't leave us," Sadie pleaded, turning her face into Marta's neck. "Ian loves you, Shyla loves you, and . . . I love you."

Marta could barely speak. "I love you too, Sadie. I love you, too."

BEFORE SHE STOPPED by Ian's house, Marta finished packing and confirmed with Dane when they would leave. Dane's truck was just as crappy as her car, and they would be driving Nikki's vehicle to avoid breaking down on the interstate.

The race was hosted in Springfield, Minnesota, five hours away, and Marta had made reservations at a Holiday Inn the minute Spaulding made his announcement.

Well, the minute the shock had worn off, and she could feel her fingers enough to dial the numbers.

It as her responsibility to take what Ian would throw at her. She straightened her spine and followed the sound of a lawnmower to the backyard.

Anger blazing, Ian's eyes flicked to her and away.

Shyla held no grudges, however, and ran across the grass from where Ian had built a sandbox. She looked adorable in jeans and a pink t-shirt. Her bangs were an even line above her eyebrows, the rest of her hair, shining ringlets around her face.

Marta's heart sank. Ian had taken Shyla to the salon.

What else had she missed?

She sat with Shyla on the wooden swing while the toddler babbled about taking Hunter for a walk, ice cream, and her new sandbox.

While Shyla regaled her with tales of what she'd missed, Ian concentrated on mowing the grass, and he didn't glance her way after he cut the engine and stored the mower in the shed near the house.

He looked good, his dark blond hair plastered to his head with sweat, and his muscle t-shirt clung to his flat stomach. Without acknowledging her, he disappeared inside the house.

Twenty minutes later, when Ian came out in fresh clothes, a beer dangling from his hand, Shyla was showing Marta the new sandbox.

He still trusted her enough to watch the toddler. She didn't know what she would have done if he'd chosen to let Shyla play in a playpen instead of leaving the baby with her.

That's probably what he had to do if Sadie wasn't around. Her cheeks flushed. Marta had promised to help, and she'd done anything but.

"Hey," she whispered as he approached.

Shyla handed him a shovel, and Ian sat on the side of the box, his beer wedged between his knees. Slowly, he ran the bright yellow shovel through the sand.

Shyla's eyes darted between them.

That made Marta feel worse, if that were possible.

The little girl already had enough trouble in her short life. Ian adopting her was supposed to be a fresh start.

"So, you deign to bless us with your presence," Ian said, his voice clipped.

"I was ah, getting ready for the race," Marta murmured.

"Shyla's missed you," Ian said, implying he had not, and Marta's mouth dried in fear.

"I know. Sadie came by to see me."

Ian's eyes widened in surprise. "She did, huh?"

"Yeah. This morning."

"She's at therapy now. Said she's going to ask them about parenting classes."

"Oh, good for her."

"What'd you say to her? I know she was thinking about not keeping it. Did you spook her? Because you know as well as I do, parents who keep kids they don't want do more harm than good. Look at Brett."

"We talked about my experience, yes," Marta said, stung he could accuse her of using scare tactics. "You may not believe it, but even with my experience, I'm pro-choice. I only told her a choice like that can't be undone. She said she didn't feel fit to be a mother. I told her after what I did, I didn't especially feel like mother material either."

Bitter, she looked away.

"If she decides she doesn't want it after all, she can put it up for adoption, or make arrangements with Trent's family. But that's none of my business," she said.

She smoothed her hand over Shyla's curls and stood, brushing sand off her running capris.

She'd taken to wearing her running clothes again.

A runner was all she'd ever be.

"The fact is, she probably won't get over that, either."

Shoulders hunched, she walked across the freshly mowed grass. She'd been a fool to think she could be part of a relationship.

Not with her past.

Her baggage.

Her scars.

If she'd spared Sadie some of that, then she'd do it all over again, no matter how angry it made Ian.

"Marta, wait."

She stopped but didn't turn around.

"You'll call me when you get back?"

Over her shoulder, Marta looked at him. He'd changed after his shower into jeans and a light blue button-down shirt, similar to what he'd wear at the bar. It made her wonder if he'd talked to Dane and Brett any more about their business.

She guessed she'd hear about it from Dane on the drive to Springfield.

That made her think of Nikki's and Dane's wedding.

Walking down the aisle, she and Ian would be a poor match after all.

"What's the point, Ian? What the fuck's the point?"

CHAPTER NINE

Ian leaned against the rail of Alyssa's balcony while his friends chatted inside.

Brett was in the kitchen baking take-and-bake pizzas, which seemed a bit ironic to Ian, since in a few minutes they were going to watch more than a thousand people run over twenty-six miles, but his stomach rumbled with hunger and unease.

He hadn't been able to eat since he watched Marta walk away from him in his backyard.

Shyla had chased after her, and he'd had to pull the crying toddler from Marta's arms.

They belonged together, probably more than Marta and he did. He could see on Marta's face Shyla's tantrum had carved a jagged hole into her heart, but before he could say anything, she'd run out of his yard, and he hadn't seen her again.

Grateful Dane was with her, because he didn't trust Marta's frame of mind for her to be alone, Ian took a pull of his beer.

"Are you okay out here?" Brett asked, sliding the door open to step onto the balcony.

Ian shrugged.

What was the definition of okay?

He was healthy, excited about the prospect of The Finish Line, the name they'd decided on for their sports bar. Shyla was fine, Sadie, more upbeat than he'd seen her in a long time.

But it was all about Marta, and it always had been. He was broken, bruised, and when it came to her, he didn't think he'd be able to feel anything besides that.

"She's going to be okay, you know," Brett said, leaning against the rail, sipping on something that looked like a rum and Coke. "She's done this a million times."

"I know," Ian said, staring across the park. "But I just don't see this making any difference, you know? She's been telling me, wait until after the race, let her put it behind her, but I don't think that's what this is any more. Has she said anything else?"

Ian hated bringing this up with Brett. The subject always made Brett defensive, whether Ian meant it that way or not.

Inwardly, Ian grimaced when Brett narrowed his eyes.

"What do you mean?"

Dane wasn't there to play referee, and Ian tried to suppress his temper.

"I don't know, I get a feeling she's not telling me everything, like she's keeping something from me that's going to blow up our whole relationship."

"She's already told you what happened between us," Brett said, peering through his reflection on the glass toward the living room where Nikki and Alyssa sat watching the elite runners' interviews during the pre-race show.

The sportscasters, race participants from back in the day, were speculating on who would be the male and female winners of the Lady Slipper.

Brett could maybe give him a realistic idea of Marta's chances, but all he cared about was Marta coming home in one piece, ready to finally give their relationship a go.

None of this one step forward, five steps back garbage.

There was more at stake than just their relationship—his whole family depended on her getting her shit together.

It was why he'd been so pissed when she'd finally shown up.

When people loved someone, that someone owed them back.

Marta owed Sadie and Shyla.

Goddammit.

"Yeah, she did," Ian said.

He couldn't argue that, and he'd been grateful for so many things on so many different levels it still made him feel sick inside.

"Then there isn't anything else I can tell you." Brett swished the rum and Coke in his glass. "Let's go inside. The race will be starting soon. The handcyclists are starting to cross the finish line. The elite male runners go first, then the women, then everyone else. We'll know in a couple of hours which way the race will go for Marta."

"She's not going to win."

Brett shook his head. "Nope. But she'll try."

Ian wished she'd work at their relationship half as hard as she'd been training to win this race.

MARTA PACED, KEEPING her muscles warm. Her little bikini running bottoms and sports bra top felt foreign to her.

The bib attached to the bra crinkled when she moved her arms, arms that were encased in running sleeves.

How long had it been since she'd worn serious gear? Other races weren't as important as this, and she relaxed her running clothes for the more casual races.

But this race, this was going to be either her ascend into heaven, or her descend into hell, only, she couldn't decide which was which any more.

Winning the race would secure her job at the school.

She'd have a future there; she'd be able to tell Libbie Layne to fuck off, and it would sound glorious coming out of her mouth.

Marta would have the recognition from Spaulding, that, well, she hadn't craved it, but God, it would be great to thumb her nose at him once and for all.

And the scholarship money would be a coup as well, just as the donation to the hospital.

The thought of the hospital brought tears to her eyes.

Coach Wesley was the real reason why she was racing the Lady Slipper. It was in his memory, after all, she was running, and she couldn't forget that.

"Miss Braddock, it's time to line up," a race volunteer said, touching her arm.

"Of course, I'm sorry," Marta murmured, taking her place.

She recognized many of the runners, but she'd never met them in person.

The elites who ran on a regular basis were younger than she was, and they raced more often.

They couldn't spare the time to speak at her retreats, or run at events like Brett's marathon. She'd lost touch with the running community more than she thought she had, and she tried to care, but she didn't.

Her stomach rumbled.

When she and Dane had come into town, she fell right into her race routine. Sleep, eat, light runs. Interviews.

Ian was the only thing she could blame the butterflies on.

She wanted, more than anything, to put all this behind her.

The starting shot surprised her, and she sprang too fast.

She corrected, grateful she hadn't stumbled. A fall would have upset her rhythm, and she wouldn't have gotten it back.

Marta joined a group of runners and ran with them for quite a few miles at an easy pace. Her mantra for the first half was not to burn out. She couldn't burn out. She'd made peace with the face she wouldn't win, but she needed a decent time.

Luckily, the weather held. The sun was shining, and there wasn't a breeze to create resistance. She'd tried to train in all kinds of weather, but she hadn't come to Springfield to run the route and familiarize herself with the hills and turns.

Another failure.

Marta was glad the prick reporter hadn't called her out on that, too.

It'd been enough he accused her of not caring who would be sharing the starting line with her, but it wouldn't have made a difference, even if she'd taken the time to find out.

Maybe that had seemed like an excuse to the reporter, but it was the truth. She couldn't compete with youth, with better training, with the time they'd had to prepare.

Running by a station, she grabbed her bottle filled with electrolytes and sucked a few swallows as she ran.

She wondered if Ian was watching her race—what he thought of the whole thing. He probably thought it was dumb, stupid, and pointless. Well, maybe it was, but she'd given up a lot to be here.

Shyla's face flashed through her mind as she flung her bottle onto the side of the road for a volunteer to pick up.

Which baby had she given up to run this race?

IAN BREATHED A sigh of relief.

What the hell had Marta been thinking about that she'd stumbled like that?

The pizza sat in a greasy lump in his stomach, and he rested his elbows on his knees, staring at the TV. He jiggled his leg, his nerves at the snapping point.

"Calm down. She's doing good. A lot better than I thought, and the weather's in her favor."

Ian ignored him.

It frustrated him that the cameras cut back and forth between the male runners and the women who had started half an hour after the male elites.

They'd be hitting the half-marathon marker soon. Another hour of this mess, and it would be all over.

The next time he saw Gregory Spaulding, he was going to punch the jerk with as much force as he could muster.

The fucking asshole, making Marta go through this.

The marathon coverage cut to a commercial, and Ian went into the kitchen and took a couple shots of Jack to soothe his frayed nerves.

MARTA RELAXED. THINGS were going to be okay. She wouldn't win, no, a tiny little girl from Nigeria seemed to have that in the bag, but she'd have a finish time she could be proud of.

Everything had aligned better than she'd ever dreamed.

Veering toward another water station, she kept her eye on her bright blue bottle. She concentrated, determined not to let the sweep of her hand put her stride off-kilter.

It was something Coach Wesley had drummed into all of them. Focus. Don't let anything distract you.

She cut from the pack.

With despair, Marta watched a black-haired volunteer pick up her bottle.

That wasn't the way it was supposed to go, but there wasn't time for Marta to indicate to the woman to put the bottle back onto the solid surface.

She would just have to take the bottle from the volunteer holding it out, a huge smile on her face, only wanting to be helpful.

Marta reached out.

The volunteer stepped in front of her, but Marta didn't have time to dodge her.

She slammed into the slim woman, their bodies colliding with a force that knocked the air out of Marta's lungs, and they fell to the pavement in a tangle of arms and legs.

Marta heard something no runner ever wants to hear.

Snap.

From then on, Marta was a mess of emotions.

At first, numb with the shock of the fall, she thought it hadn't been *her* leg that had sustained damage, but disoriented she tried to stand and discovered quickly it had been her ankle that had taken the brunt of the impact.

She collapsed onto the road, gravel biting into her palms, an unbelievable pain vibrating throughout her body, and paramedics allowed her only seconds before they pulled her off the course.

Clearing the road was for her safety, and for the other runners too, but it shamed her nonetheless.

Pulled off the street like an impostor, as if she hadn't belonged.

The pain in her ankle competed with her aching muscles which were beginning to realize she wasn't running anymore.

They jumped under her skin, rippling with strain.

She'd forgotten this part of it, forgotten that to come down from such euphoria took a high tolerance of pain and stress.

And to stop so abruptly.

She could have had a heart attack.

Zoning in and out of consciousness, she didn't pay attention to the emergency techs as they wrapped her ankle for the ride to the hospital. Her leg was swelling at an alarming rate, turning a sickly purple that made her stomach heave.

Unable to comprehend anything more, she let her mind blank, and mercifully, blackness took her.

Marta woke to Dane hovering over her.

"Hey, I don't think this is what you had in mind when you said you were retiring," he said, worry creasing his forehead.

"Be careful what you wish for, huh?" Her throat felt like it was on fire, and she wondered how long she'd been out. "Ian?" she asked.

"I called him. He knows you're okay. Well, as okay as someone can be who's had her ankle broken." He dragged a chair to the side of her bed.

"There was a woman . . ." Her mind was fuzzy—remembering what had happened seemed more like dregs of a nightmare than something real.

Dane fisted his hands together and rested his chin on his knuckles. "After you slammed into her, she disappeared into the crowd. They're looking for her. She didn't look familiar to any of the other volunteers. No one can say what she was doing there."

"Did you talk to a doctor?" She wanted to hear the news —wanted to hear the worst. Deep in her heart, she already knew, but she wanted to hear the words out loud.

"Yeah. You'll be setting off some metal detectors at the airport for a while."

Marta closed her eyes.

"But, he said you could probably still run again. It's going to take a lot of time, a lot of physical therapy."

"Better than nothing?" Marta couldn't see the point in trying to find the silver lining in this thunderstorm that was now her life.

"Of course it is. There's an older woman down the hall—she just had most of her right foot amputated because of diabetes complications. While you were in surgery I spoke with her, but you know what? She's upbeat, positive. Talking about spending time with her grandkids, a cruise she wants to take over Christmas. People live with all sorts of shit. Now, I can't say that I've been the poster child for not letting circumstances get you down, Liz did her best to fuck me up, and I let her, for a long time. But in the end, she didn't define me. Brett's parents, he didn't let them define him. Your injury won't define you."

Marta wasn't in the mood for Dane's pep talk. Her ankle throbbed; her painkillers were wearing off. She felt filthy, and with the thick white cast going up to her knee, a proper shower or bath would be impossible for weeks, maybe even months.

She wanted to go home, but God help her, she didn't know where that was anymore.

"When can we leave?"

Dane stood. "They didn't say. I extended our room at the hotel in case they want to keep you. You're dehydrated and low on some minerals or something," he said, nodding toward her IV. "I'll go tell a nurse you're awake. You can ask them, all right?"

Reminding herself that Dane was only trying to help, she muttered, "Sure," and with envy, she watched him step into the hallway.

Tired, hurting, she waited for the doctor to tell her that her life would never be the same.

IAN READIED THE downstairs bedroom for Marta. She would have to stay with him whether she liked it or not.

Her apartment was on the second floor, and the building wasn't equipped with an elevator. She'd need help, and with Sadie unemployed and only just beginning to look into classes for Spring semester, she'd be around to help Marta bathe.

They hadn't parted on good terms; he doubted she would let him do it.

Even if he could make it fun.

He worried this would be difficult for Shyla—Marta living there would encourage her to become even more attached than she already was.

But that could be a good thing.

A car pulling up to the curb in front of his house cut off further worry.

"They're here!" Sadie hollered from the top of the stairs.

Once again, Ian marveled at the change in Sadie, and it made him damn their mother to hell and back.

What a little womanly attention had done for the girl baffled him, but it also made him grateful. Sadie had needed someone in her life, and she'd chosen Marta, just as Shyla had.

Ian prayed to God that Marta didn't take something like that lightly.

Not like she'd taken him loving her.

"Take it easy. She'll be in a lot of pain."

"I know," Sadie said, hefting Shyla in her arms. "But it will be great to have her here. She can help me pick out classes, and play with Shyla, and . . ."

Ian tuned her out. Maybe all the activity would keep Marta from wallowing alone in her room. Something he could easily see her doing until she could take care of herself again.

Dane was helping Marta out of the car and settling her with a pair of crutches when he stepped out of the house, Sadie and Shyla at his heels.

"Mommy!" Shyla screamed, catching sight of Marta. She tried to fling herself out of Sadie's arms, but Ian glared.

"Don't let her go."

To Dane he said, "She doesn't need those. I can help her."

"You don't have to do this," Marta said, glowering. "I'll be just fine by myself."

"No, you won't," Ian said mildly, determined not to let her attitude get to him.

He had to take the advice he'd given Sadie. Marta would be in pain; she'd be feeling lost and confused.

Dane hadn't told him much of the prognosis, but doctors weren't always right, anyway. What would be would be—and a lot of it would depend on Marta and how much work she put into her recovery.

But he did know this much—whether she would have followed through on her threat to retire or not, she had no choice now.

He slid his arm around her, and she let him support her.

When she was steady, Sadie approached them, and Shyla leaned into Marta, pressing her face into Marta's neck. "Mommy," Ian heard the little girl sigh.

"Hi, baby," Marta said, kissing Shyla's cheek. "Missed you. Hi, Sadie. You're looking good. How are you feeling?"

As Ian shuffled Marta into the house, he relaxed.

Thankful Marta wasn't going to take her pain out on the girls, he helped her to the bedroom located under the stairs. He'd put a recliner in the room, along with a TV.

He'd have to ask Marta how she would want to sleep. It would be easier for her to keep her foot elevated in the recliner, though if she wanted to sleep in the bed, he could take the cushions off the couch to make a pile for her to prop her leg.

As Marta settled into the chair, Sadie and Shyla kept an eagle's eye on her while Ian walked Dane back to Nikki's car.

"How was it?" he asked. "I need the truth, Dane."

Dane leaned against the driver's side door. "Not as bad as it looked on TV."

Ian raised an eyebrow.

"No, really. I watched the replay on the Running-Channel—they couldn't get enough of it. But it looked far worse than it was. She might even have come out of it okay if she hadn't been running so fast. At that speed, it's like slamming into a brick wall. I think she passed out—she said she didn't remember the ride in the ambulance."

"She's never going to run again." Ian didn't make it a question.

"Not necessarily. Depends on how she heals—how cooperative she is with physical therapy. But they can never tell you for sure one way or the other."

"Right. Well, thanks for being there for her, for driving her back. I can't imagine the ride was pleasant."

"She's put up with me in the past; it's the least I could do. Let me know if you need anything. Nikki and I will do what we can, with the women's race next weekend. We'll be freer after that."

"Thanks, I appreciate it," Ian said.

Dane nodded and slid behind the steering wheel of his car.

As Dane drove away, Ian thought the next few weeks were going to be long ones.

The house was quiet when he went inside, and he peeked in at Marta to ask if she needed anything.

She lay in the recliner, leaning backward as far as the

chair would allow, and Shyla had wasted no time climbing into her lap.

They were both sleeping.

Ian blew out a breath and hoped that giving Marta a little taste of how it would feel to live with them would convince her to stay.

MARTA WOKE WITH a little girl sprawled on top of her bladder and an intense need to pee.

Her ankle shot pain up and down her leg, and she wished she could reach her purse for the pain pills she'd had filled at the hospital's pharmacy before she'd been released.

Thirsty and uncomfortable, she desperately tried to come up with ways to attract Ian's or Sadie's attention.

She was near tears when Ian poked his head into the room.

"Are you okay?" he asked.

"Oh, thank God. I have to go to the bathroom so bad, and Shyla's right on my bladder."

Ian smiled. "I'll take her. I have a feeling she won't leave you alone while you're here."

That was fine with Marta. If Shyla was around, maybe Ian wouldn't have any heart-to-hearts with her.

She could barely wrap her mind around what happened, much less what this meant for her future, with or without Ian.

Gently, Ian lifted Shyla from her lap, and Marta winced. Any movement at all made her feel like she was going to pee her pants. Depending on someone 24/7 was going to be a humbling experience.

She just had to remind herself she only needed to get

through the next few weeks until she could live by herself again. The doctors warned her to stay off her feet as much as possible, and that didn't mean she could run to the kitchen every five seconds for a cup of coffee.

Tears filled her eyes.

There would be no more running for her.

"You don't have to cry," Ian said.

He didn't know what she was crying over, and his rebuke pissed her off. "I've just been through a traumatic experience," she said, allowing him to push the footrest into the recliner and help her stand. "I think I earned the right to cry a little."

"You're right, I'm sorry," he muttered, helping her shuffle into the hallway. "Things must feel out of control for you right now."

"Yeah, they do." She hoped she could handle going to the bathroom; she didn't want him helping her off the toilet.

Fuck.

She'd need things from her apartment. Clothes. Maybe robes so she wouldn't have to fool will pulling pants over her cast. Shorts and tanks. The more she could do for herself, the better.

Who could she ask? Nikki was busy; the Tower City first annual women's race was approaching quickly. She'd be spending her days at marathon headquarters doing what Brett did before every marathon, though on a smaller scale.

No, she couldn't call Nikki, and she didn't want to bother Alyssa because she didn't know if Alyssa was feeling any better.

She didn't want to feel any more indebted to Ian than she already did. Maybe she could ask Sadie.

Or . . . tomorrow she could call Holly. She hadn't seen

Holly for a while, and maybe she would have some campus news.

But hearing what was going on at the school sounded just as bleak, or even worse, than having to depend on Ian, and him knowing it he was all she had.

God, she was not going to be a good patient.

"Are you okay in there?"

"Yeah, just moping."

"Well, come out and do that. I'll make you something to eat, and you can take more pain meds. I doubt you'll be up for doing anything more than eating and sleeping for the next few days."

Marta smiled; Ian sounded like he had his face pressed against the crack in the door.

She flushed, and leaning to steady herself against the sink, washed her hands. The warm water on her skin felt divine. She would need to figure out how to shower and wash her hair.

As he helped her down the short hallway, she allowed herself to relax into his side.

They found Shyla sitting on the bed, watching for them.

"She's still not sleeping well?" Marta asked, sinking into the recliner.

"Nope, but now that's my fault. She's used to sleeping with someone. Everyone told me to let her cry it out in her crib, but I couldn't. She's done enough crying in her short life."

"Hugs," Shyla demanded, lifting her hands. "Mommy."

"You need a new diaper and a snack, my girl," Ian said, lifting the toddler from the bed. "You're going to have to leave Marta alone."

Shyla shook her head. "Hugs."

Ian laughed into Shyla's hair. "Are you hungry? Can I make you something to eat?" he asked.

Marta's stomach slid queasily with the thought of food, but she wanted to take her pain meds.

The short innocent trip to the bathroom made her leg feel like it was going to fall off her body. "Not really, but I need another pain pill. I'll feel sicker if I try to take it on an empty stomach."

"Soup and grilled cheese would be an easy dinner, does that sound okay?"

"Yeah, it does, thanks. Can you hand me my purse? I need to grab my phone. I've been too out of it to look at any of my texts."

Ian grabbed the handles of the bag Sadie had looped over the post at the foot of the bed. "Are you sure you want to do that?"

"I can't hide forever. I can't pretend this isn't going to do anything to my career."

"I'll give you some privacy then, but I can't guarantee I can make Shyla leave you alone. I'm learning it's easier to lose a few battles and win the war."

Marta gazed out the window. It saddened her he thought he had to keep Shyla away from her, but that was her own doing. It wasn't like she'd been playing the role of willing mother since Mrs. Gibson dropped Shyla off all those weeks ago.

"It's fine, Ian, she can spend as much time with me as she wants."

"I don't want her getting any more attached to you than she already is."

With that, he disappeared into the hallway, Shyla wailing as he carried her away.

His words were like a slap in the face, but she deserved them.

She shifted in the recliner, fatigue weighing her down despite the long nap she'd already had. Marta brought her phone to life; her battery was almost dead.

She'd missed over fifty texts, and her mother had tried to call several times.

Spaulding had also tried to call, but the only voicemails were from her mother asking Marta to please call her back.

She returned her mother's phone call, ensured her that she was being taken care of and no, she didn't need to go home.

Marta wasn't thrilled with having Ian take care of her, but he wouldn't let her flounder. She could count on him for that.

Shyla peeked around the door frame, a cherubic smile lighting her face, a book clenched in her little hands, and a blanket pooling at her feet. "Read."

"Sure, baby, come here."

Marta settled the baby into her lap, Shyla's head tucked under her chin. A baby in her arms, her man in the kitchen preparing them a meal, Sadie, presumably upstairs, trying to hold on to the wisps of her own remaining childhood before she gave birth to her own baby.

A feeling of contentment swept over her, a feeling of belonging.

But Marta knew the feeling was temporary.

She didn't belong anywhere.

CHAPTER TEN

"TURN ON THE TV. Channel 6."

Ian didn't have time to crack his eyes open before the caller hung up.

Startled awake when he didn't feel Shyla's little body next to him, he bolted straight up, and his eyes darted around the room.

His pounding heart slowed when he spotted Shyla in Marta's lap.

Last night, it had taken all he could to convince Shyla it was bedtime, and the only way the girl would fall asleep was if she and Ian used the bed in Marta's room. She'd been gracious about it, understanding, but he couldn't help but think that as soon as she could live on her own, she'd leave.

He couldn't prevent that from happening, no more than he could prevent Shyla's heart from being broken when that time came.

Ian was torn between protecting Shyla from that, and taking care of Marta like he promised. He couldn't kick her out; she'd have nowhere to go, and she needed the help. But it stuck like a bitter lump in his throat that he couldn't trust her not to high-tail it out of there and not look back when she was well enough to do so.

"What is it?" Marta mumbled, her eyes slitted with sleep.

"I'm sorry the phone woke you. That was Dane. He said to turn the TV on."

Marta burrowed into the recliner, pulling Shyla closer to her. "It's bad news."

With a sinking heart, Ian fumbled for the remote.

He'd set up this room as a guest room, and he didn't remember where he put anything. He found it wedged between the wall and the lamp on the bedside table.

He hoped Marta was wrong. They've had enough bad news to last a lifetime.

Rubbing his eyes, he clicked the TV on and hurried to turn the sound down when a commercial for baking soda blasted from the speakers. "Sorry. No one's watched TV in here since we moved in."

"It's fine, she's sleeping like a rock. What did he want us to watch?"

"I don't know, he said Channel 6. Here."

The scene opened to a press conference, and a sense of déjà vu chilled Ian to the bone.

The camera centered on Spaulding.

"As you all know," Spaulding began, standing behind the same podium, the same dragon head mascot spewing fire, "Marta Braddock, involved in a horrible accident on the course, did not complete the Lady Slipper Marathon." He pointed his gaze directly at the TV camera, his eyes gleaming.

"Did you know about this?" Ian asked, his mouth dry. He wished he'd had time to make coffee.

Marta gripped Shyla and shook her head. "No, but he

called while I was in the hospital, and again while I was getting settled here. I didn't call him back, and he didn't leave a voicemail."

"A little warning would have been nice," Ian grumbled under his breath.

Marta opened her mouth to respond, no doubt to say he couldn't expect nice things from an asshole of a man, but Spaulding was still speaking, and she stayed quiet to hear what he said.

"This means many things—for us as a university and for Miss Braddock personally. The university, of course, will still donate a generous sum to Beacon Hospital in Coach Wesley's name. The hospital and staff extended his life and did what they could to make his final hours comfortable. That is not to be taken for granted, and the university is deeply grateful for the work the hospital does serving our community."

"Big of him." Ian didn't want to watch any more, but he couldn't tear his eyes away from the screen.

"In that vein," Spaulding continued, "despite Miss Braddock's lack of finishing time, we will also offer the track scholarship. The scholarship will enable a student to attend Minnesota State University, Tower City, for four years, food, lodging, and tuition fully covered, as long as that student maintains a 3.5 GPA and participates in track for those four years."

A smattering of applause made Spaulding pause, and he took the opportunity to take a sip of water from a bottle that had been hidden from view inside the podium.

"What happened to Miss Braddock was unfortunate, but as with any sport, there is risk of injury. Miss Braddock did not escape the collision with the water station volunteer unscathed, and it's with a heavy heart that I announce the contract the university had with Miss Braddock to coach our track team has been terminated."

Reporters started shouting questions, and Ian moved to turn the TV off, thinking they'd heard the worst.

"No, wait."

One reporter, louder than the others yelled, "Who will coach the track team now?"

Spaulding smoothed his silver and black tie. "Since stepping in to coach while Miss Braddock trained for the Lady Slipper, Libbie Layne has been doing a fantastic job. We have not spoken with her about continuing in the position, but that is a possibility."

"Bullshit. It's what the bastard wanted all along," Ian said.

"You can turn it off now. Can you help me to the bathroom?"

Ian clicked off the TV and scooped a still-sleeping Shyla into his arms and placed her where she should have been, in bed.

Without a word, he supported Marta down the hall to the bathroom.

He shut the door to give her privacy and leaned against the wall to wait.

The echo of her sobs slipped under the door, leaving an icy trail down his back.

AFTER A BREAKFAST of pancakes and pain pills, Marta called Holly, who was more than happy to pick up some things from her apartment.

That afternoon, Holly stopped by Ian's to grab Marta's

apartment keys and returned an hour later with a large suit-case filled to the brim with clothes.

"You do realize all you have is running clothes, right?" Holly asked, an eyebrow arched, setting the suitcase near the bed in the guest room.

Marta hadn't strayed far from the room, and Shyla popped her head in every five seconds asking for a story or a kiss. The little girl loved having her around, and it showed with the way her eyes sparkled and the giggles she heard throughout the house when Ian tried to distract the baby with a game of Hide and Go Seek.

"I guess I'll need to change that now," Marta said, trying to remain upbeat for Holly.

She'd been crying or trying to stave off tears since the press conference. The idea that Spaulding would outright fire her had never entered her mind, and now she cursed herself for her naivety.

Of course he would get rid of her the moment he could. He hadn't wanted her there to begin with.

"You didn't bump into Dane, did you? I'm sorry. I didn't think. I shouldn't have asked you to do that for me."

Holly lounged on the bed looking fresh in wide-legged pants and a tight-fitting russet brown sweater. "I saw him for a second, said hello. He wondered why I was picking up things for you when he or Nikki could have?"

"I didn't want to bother them, they have the women's race in a couple days—I know what goes into that. But I didn't consider that you'd be busy with class stuff, either."

"That doesn't matter, I'm not chained to my desk, in fact, this is a light semester for me. I'm transferring."

"Where are you going?" Marta asked in surprise.

"The University of New Hampshire needs a Sociology professor, and the head of the department is conducting a new study I would love to be involved with. My professional career has been stagnating, and since I'm not in a relationship, it'll be good for me. You always have to be moving forward in some way, right? Professionally or personally?"

"Yeah, I guess so," Marta mumbled.

"Now that your professional career has derailed, it's time for you to get a move on personally, don't you think? I haven't talked with you for a while. What's going on with you and Ian? You two must be close if you're living with him, and he's taking care of you. It's sweet, and kind of romantic."

A little giggle came from the hallway, Shyla peering at them from around the doorjamb.

"Shyla, I told you to leave them alone," Ian said, hefting her into his arms. "Sorry, ladies," he said, closing the door.

"And you have a ready-made family. Who could say no to a cutie like that?" Holly's smiled held a hint of mischief.

"Cutie? Ian or Shyla?" Marta said wryly.

"Touché," Holly said, lying on her side and propping her head on her hand.

Marta shifted in the recliner. Even with the pain pills, a dull ache accompanied her every movement. She itched to stand up, get some air, but at the same time, it sounded like too much work to bother with.

And she hadn't had a shower or bath yet. Now that she had fresh clothes, cleaning up was all she could think about.

"Ian's been really good to me."

"Then what's the hold up? It can't be your abortion, not any more. Your accident cancels that out, doesn't it? I mean, you gave up a baby to have your running career, but you don't have that anymore, not in the sense you were talking about before. You could use this accident as a clean slate.

Start over with Ian and Shyla. Have more children; give Shyla a sibling."

And that was why Marta couldn't stay there, couldn't be the person Ian needed, wanted her to be.

Holly sat up, the mattress springs squeaking under her. "I need to get going."

"When are you moving?" She was just getting to know Holly, and now the woman was moving away.

"Over Christmas break. They have a late start Spring semester. If everything goes smoothly, I'll have time to move, settle in, and even learn my way around campus. I'm excited. It's time for something new."

"Let me know if there's anything I can do for you," Marta offered, though laid-up, she wouldn't be able to do much.

"I will, thanks. After Dane, I need more. I haven't been able to get up any enthusiasm for dating. Maybe a change of scenery and meeting some new people will help."

"Stay in touch," Marta said, wishing she could walk Holly to the door.

"I'll see you again before I leave, at least to say goodbye in person. Concentrate on healing. There are people here who love you, Marta, and that isn't something to brush aside. Think about it."

Marta didn't need to be told to do that—she couldn't burnish thoughts like that from her mind, no matter how hard she tried.

OVER THE NEXT two weeks, Marta did nothing but keep her leg propped up, read to Shyla, and sleep. The forced break was both welcome and torture.

She'd always been a runner, always on the move. The sedentary lifestyle, while pleasant after many years of never having even a single vacation, began to wear on her nerves.

Sadie kept her company, sometimes sitting with her on the porch outside in the backyard while Shyla played in the grass.

The temperatures were cooling, but a light jacket sufficed in warding off the chill. The leaves were falling from the trees, the peak for seeing them turn to their golden yellows and oranges now past.

There was talk of Thanksgiving, and whether Shyla would like to go trick or treating for Halloween.

Nikki finally decided on a dress for her bridesmaids—a dress that Marta had fortunately tried on during a previous trip, and Nikki's and Dane's wedding plans were on track.

Brett and Alyssa had come to visit a couple times, and Ian and Brett squirreled away in the basement where Ian had set up an office of sorts.

The visits with Alyssa had been stilted, probably because her belly had popped, and Marta couldn't take her eyes off the baby bump. But both women tried, and she felt she'd finally gotten through Alyssa's defensiveness and could call Alyssa her friend.

Brett seemed like an improved version of the man he used to be: happy, confident, and so in love with Alyssa and their baby, Marta's throat clogged when she watched them together.

She was happy for them; she'd never deny Brett any joy, but she was bitter too, because she wanted some for herself, and damned if she could find any.

One lazy afternoon, Ian found Marta listlessly flipping through channels. The house was quiet; Sadie had taken Shyla to the playground to give Marta a break.

"Bored?" he asked, leaning against the doorjamb.

"Maybe. I guess. I'm not used to living in limbo like this. No job, no prospects. I'm glad I have some savings—I don't need to worry about how to pay for rent and the rest of my bills on top of everything else."

Ian pursed his lips.

He didn't need to say it. She didn't need to pay for rent if she'd move in with them. To his credit, he never mentioned it, but the invitation was always there under the surface, her indecision a layer of tension between them.

"Do you want to go for a drive? I want to show you something."

"Yes!" Marta said, already struggling to stand from the recliner.

After helping her go to the bathroom first, Ian steadied her on the way to the car. She was still in a lot of pain, but she was getting used to moving around a bit on her own.

Supported by the car door, she sat in the back, her legs propped on the seat. "I could get used to this," she said as he pulled out of the driveway. "Where are we going?"

"You'll see. We can swing through a drive-through on the way home for a quick bite if you're hungry."

After the intense marathon training and her strict diet, fast food sounded heavenly. "Sure, that sounds great."

Ian drove through Tower City, the parking lots for the mall and bookstore packed with cars.

"What day is it?" she asked, bewildered. She'd been hiding in Ian's house for so long she'd lost all concept of time.

"Sunday. I was thinking you and I could host Thanksgiving this year. You know, since I have the most space." Ian met her eyes in his rear-view mirror.

He didn't fool her; she heard the forced nonchalance in

his voice. It wasn't lost on her what that would look like—them hosting the holiday together as a couple. A couple with a child, because Shyla would be with them.

"If you want everyone together, it would have to be on the weekend before or afterward. Nikki and Dane's parents both live in town, and Brett and Alyssa might fly to Florida if her doctor gives her the okay, or her parents would maybe come up here if he doesn't."

Ian pulled into the parking lot of a restaurant that looked like it had been closed for months. She hoped this wasn't where he was trying to take them for lunch.

"That's okay. Better, actually. Then the four of us could have a small Thanksgiving on Thursday."

That sounded lovely to her, too, but she was reluctant to make plans.

Family plans.

This was the first large chunk of time they'd had alone in a while, and she decided after Ian showed her what he wanted her to see, she would tell him what she needed to say.

Get it out there once and for all. Take all the mystery away as to why she was hedging about their future. It wasn't fair to Ian, and all this holiday talk would be moot once he knew.

"What's this place?" she asked.

Ian parked and twisted in his seat to look at her. "It used to be a restaurant—it never received good reviews, and it tanked fast. The owners didn't know what they were doing and didn't have the cash to fix it even if they had. As of yesterday, this place belongs to Dane, Brett, and me. I wanted you to see it. Come on, I have the keys. You can put your leg up in there."

The inside smelled musty, of stale beer and grease. But

the potential hung in the air, rich in the walls, and anticipation stirred her blood.

"Oh, Ian, this is great! I could see this turning into something huge." Marta looked around the building that was similar to most restaurants she'd been in. A horseshoe-shaped bar sat in the middle, and high-top tables surrounded the gleaming wood. Booths lined the walls; large windows looked over the busy streets. "This is a great location."

"Yeah, it is, and all the owners could think about was getting it off their hands. We bought the place for cheaper than we deserved—but they let the place go to shit, so, it's an even trade in my opinion. We're going to have to sink a lot of money into refurbishing the inside. I didn't want to deal with food, but a sports bar wouldn't be the same without it. Welcome to The Finish Line, Marta. We're gonna make this work. We will."

With the determination shining in Ian's eyes, she was afraid he was talking about more than just the sports bar.

"I'm happy for you," Marta said, pulling away to rest on one of the benches inside the door where people would wait for a table.

He sat next to her, resting his elbows on his knees, cradling his head in his hands. He spoke to the floor. "Marta, you know I love you."

Marta touched his shoulder. "I know you do."

He continued as if she hadn't spoken. "But I'm concerned where all this is going. Shyla is getting used to you being around. Sadie says she has life talks with you in the middle of the night when you're too uncomfortable to sleep. They love you being there, and I can't blame them. You living in my house is a dream come true for me. It's what I've wanted—since school."

"You want to know why I won't commit."

"To put it mildly, yeah. I've proposed, you won't say yes, yet you say you love me. Don't you want a life with me? If all you're doing is leading me on because you don't want to tell me the truth, I'm a big boy, and I can handle it. I lived without you for ten years, longer if you count the years I had to watch you fawn over Brett. But I was okay then, and I'll be okay now. Just say it."

In her veins, Marta's blood chilled to ice. He may be able to live without her, but she doubted she would fare as well.

"I told you when I had that abortion, it was because I needed to keep my scholarship, to nurture my career, my Olympics prospects. All this time I've been trying to make my choice worth it. And even though I didn't make it to the Olympics, I feel like I've done an okay job. On good days I feel like maybe I gave up that baby for something. But I didn't give up just my baby, I gave up my entire future."

"What do you mean?" Ian asked, running a hand over her hair.

Marta studied his grey eyes, his pupils dilated in the dimly lit room.

"I saw a therapist for a while, tried to get a handle on what I'd done. Even though my intentions were pure, and Brett wouldn't have, couldn't have, helped me, I still had trouble processing it. I was in bad shape for a long time. Running helped. My goals. Therapy. Ultimately, I decided if I could make a choice like that, I wasn't fit to be a mother. So I made one last choice. With the support of my therapist, I had my tubes tied. Ian, I can't have children."

IN SILENCE, IAN drove them back to the house. He cast a quick glance at her in his rearview mirror. She lay propped against the door, her leg laying on the seat, her head resting against the seat's back, tears running down her cheeks.

Emotions he couldn't name swirled around his mind and heart, but Brett's car parked at the curb in front of his house stopped him from struggling to find something to say.

He wondered if Brett knew Marta had her tubes tied and had kept that from him. Not that it would have been Brett's place to tell him, no, that was on Marta, and she'd waited way too long.

"What do you think he wants?"

Marta lifted her head and blinked.

"What? Oh," she said, when Brett climbed out of the car and leaned against the driver's-side door, squinting against the late afternoon sun. "I have no idea. He didn't tell me he was stopping by."

Brett ambled up the driveway as Ian stepped out of the car. "What's up?" Ian asked.

"I need to talk to Marta. Where were you?"

Ian bristled. He wanted to say it wasn't any of his goddamned business where they'd been, but he was standing next to his business partner for the foreseeable future, and he couldn't shoot his mouth whenever he felt like it. "I took Marta to The Finish Line; she hadn't seen it yet."

Brett opened the car door and peered at Marta. "How'd you like— What's wrong with you?"

Marta wiped her eyes. "Nothing. My leg hurts. What's going on? Is Alyssa with you?"

"No. I drove over because Dane heard some people chatting at his store. Apparently, the director and the board of the Lady Slipper have been looking into your accident. Has anyone said anything to you?"

Ian rested his hip against his car, interested in Marta's response.

As far as he knew, Marta's fall had been chalked up as a freak accident.

That no one could verify who the volunteer had been, or where she'd gone after the collision, didn't seem to be on anyone's minds, even Marta's. She never spoke about it, and he'd forgotten, taking care of her and keeping Shyla away from her as much as he could.

"No, no one's contacted me, not even Spaulding. I heard about my termination on the TV—just like the rest of the world."

"That's bullshit," Brett snapped.

"What else were they going to do? A coach needs to be able to run, and they already have Libbie Layne there. Cutting me loose was obvious. I appreciate your concern, but I don't care about it anymore. I'm trying to focus on feeling better."

"Yeah, well, it's still bullshit. Can we talk?" he asked Ian. "I got a couple calls back from the contractors we contacted, and we need to hash out their estimates. I told Dane I would text him when you two got back."

Ian gritted his teeth in frustration. He wanted to talk to Marta about the bomb she dropped on him, but he needed to take care of business first.

Fuck.

If they were going to open in the spring, to coincide with marathon weekend, they were going to have to work on The Finish Line every second they could. "Yeah, it's cool. Let me get Marta settled in her room."

"Ian, I'm sorry," Marta whispered as he helped her down the hallway.

He could hear Sadie and Shyla upstairs playing, but his and Marta's time alone would last only seconds when they realized Marta was home.

Not that she considered this place her home.

He knew that now.

She'd been using his house to convalesce, a pit stop on the way to wherever she would go next.

Where that would be was anyone's guess.

California, probably.

"I'm not going to say it doesn't matter, because it does. You kept something from me, something that means something to our relationship. You—" He stopped.

He didn't know what else to say.

He settled her into the recliner, retrieved the remote from the bed, and pressed a kiss to her forehead. "I'll let Sadie know you're ho . . . here. If you need something, she'll get it for you. Get some sleep, I bet that little field trip wore you out."

It had him.

His muscles burned; his head throbbed. And now he still had to bicker with Dane and Brett about cost for the next several hours.

She was already sleeping when he softly closed the door.

THE RAGE HE'D been trying to suppress bubbled to the surface when Ian trotted downstairs and he found Brett sipping his good scotch.

That Brett had invited himself over, now making

himself at home, should have pleased Ian—they were close friends.

But all he could think of was what he'd made Marta do, and he hauled Brett off the couch and gave him a vicious left hook to the jaw.

"You fucking bastard," he growled, not caring one fucking bit that the impact made Brett fling his lowball glass across the room, spraying the amber liquid over the carpet.

"What the fuck was that for?" Brett gasped, holding his jaw, doubled over, wheezing.

"What's going on down there?" Dane asked from the stairs.

"I am never going to get away from you, am I?" Ian said, ignoring Dane, pacing the length of the room.

He was too much of a gentleman to kick a man while he was down, but God did he want to give Brett a kick to the balls.

"What the fuck did I do?"

"You know what Marta told me today, you asshole? When we were looking at the restaurant, she told me she got her tubes tied. You're just the gift the keeps on giving, huh? I cannot *get away from you.*"

Ian rested his forehead against the cool basement wall. He needed to calm down; he had too much going on to make himself this sick over something that happened more than ten years ago.

"She what?" Dane asked, grabbing a beer out of the mini-fridge he had moved into the study for evenings like this, when they would be working on books for the sports bar, or payroll, or whatever the hell else that went into running a place like that.

"She got her tubes tied, after the abortion," Ian muttered, taking the bottle from Dane with a nod.

He popped off the top and guzzled the ice-cold liquid. He was glad Sadie hadn't come down to see what was going on. Brett crying like a baby; Ian yelling. What a way for grown men to behave.

"That wasn't me. I didn't make her do that." Brett said, holding the beer bottle Dane gave him to his jaw.

"You always shake off the blame so easily, huh? You had the shitty childhood, you didn't make her have an abortion, you're not responsible for her getting her tubes tied. What about her? What about all that she's suffered since you two broke up? Have you ever, in your miserable fucking life, gave a thought to what she's been going through all this time?"

"She's been okay—"

"Fuck this," Ian spat. He hadn't gotten anywhere. "I need to cool off."

"Ian—" Dane started.

"Let him go," Ian heard Brett say as he stomped up the stairs. "We need to go over these estimates . . ."

Grateful Sadie wasn't around to badger him with questions, Ian let himself into the cool afternoon air.

As THE DAYS melted into weeks, Marta didn't try to speak with Ian again about her tubal ligation.

He was right, she'd been wrong.

She shouldn't have kept it from him. But she knew he would react this way, cut her off, and was it so wrong she'd needed that little bit of time with him keeping her secret had afforded her?

The Finish Line took up most of his time, and she spent as much time with Shyla and Sadie as she could, though it would hurt them all in the end.

Halloween passed with little fanfare; Ian had turned off the porch lights, saying he wasn't in the mood to hand out candy to the neighborhood kids.

Marta felt responsible for his lack of enthusiasm, but she didn't try to change his mind.

The Monday before Thanksgiving, the cast came off her foot, and while she still had to keep weight off her ankle, it gave her more mobility and she began thinking about moving back to her apartment.

Once she decided to leave, she wanted out as soon as she could, and though the timing was all wrong, full of guilt, she texted Brett the Wednesday before Thanksgiving.

Disappearing on Sadie and Shyla made her want to throw up, and just before the holiday no less, but God, if she wasn't going to be in their lives on a permanent basis, it didn't matter when she left.

Ian may think her a heartless bitch for not telling him she couldn't give him children, and well, she might as well make the point hit home.

"Are you sure you want to do this?" Brett asked, as she stuffed her toiletries into her bag. She'd chosen the perfect time to leave—Ian and the girls were doing a quick bit of shopping for the meal the next day.

Marta had already written a card for them; all she needed to do was put it on the kitchen table where Ian was sure to see it while they put the groceries away.

"Yes, I'm sure. He can't forgive me for I what I did, and I've felt like a stranger here for the past few weeks. I only stayed as long as I did for Sadie and Shyla, and I think I did more harm than good, there."

Tears pricked the back of her throat. She and Shyla had become closer than ever, maybe even closer than some mothers and their daughters, and the thought of leaving broke her heart to pieces.

She didn't have to go.

Marta shoved the thought away.

Of course she did.

Her relationship with Shyla meant nothing if she and Ian didn't have a strong foundation on which to build a family—any kind of family.

"I'm ready."

"All right," Brett said, hefting her bag, "but don't you dare tell him I gave you a ride. He'll still only talk to me when he absolutely has to. I was hoping that you two would work it out, and he would finally get over it. Keeping The Finish Line going won't be easy if two-thirds of its owners hate each other's guts."

"Ian doesn't hate you," Marta murmured, torn between needing to tidy the room and leaving before Ian and the girls came home.

"Yeah, he does, and after he punched me, I gave what he said a lot of thought." Brett turned the light off and held the door open, allowing Marta to fit through with her crutches.

She laid the butter yellow envelope against a potted poinsettia. The card said everything she couldn't say to his face.

If that made her a coward, so be it.

Minnesota, in a courteous gesture made by Mother Nature, hadn't yet been covered with snow, and Marta maneuvered her way to Brett's car without his help.

Brett threw her bag into the back seat while she did the same with her crutches. Uncomfortable in running shoes, but what the hell else was she going to wear, she hopped to the passenger door and fell into the seat.

While the heater spat cold air, Brett said, "Don't you want to hear what I've been thinking about?"

She didn't, not particularly, but she was trapped in the car with him and had no choice.

Her eyes darted along the road, watching for Ian's car. It would be just her luck to meet them at an intersection, his steely eyes witnessing her defection, her tail tucked between her legs.

Some things never changed.

"Sure."

"Ian was right."

That wasn't a revelation. Ian was right about a lot of things. About her, about their relationship. About where they were going, or weren't.

"About what?"

She met Brett's hazel eyes, the early setting sun shining through his cracked windshield. Alyssa should make him buy a better car.

"About me, how I never take responsibility for anything. I should have been there for you in college. I should have stepped up, told you I would help. I hid behind the way my parents treated me, used it like a shield not to let anything else hurt me. But you were right, that day when you told me to go after Alyssa. Hiding didn't help, blaming my parents didn't help. I *am* to blame for your abortion, for what you did after. We may not have made it, but plenty of people don't, even with little kids. At least we would have had that baby, tried our best."

He came to a stop in front of her apartment building. "I'm sorry. I'm sorry I didn't try. I'm sorry you went through that because I was weak."

He shifted into park and rested his forehead against the steering wheel.

"Brett, it wasn't you—"

"Yeah, it was," he spoke toward the dashboard, "but I'm telling you what you told me. We did what we thought we had to do at the time, and that's the best we can do. Don't let our past, your past with me, ruin your future with Ian. He doesn't care you can't have kids, Marta—"

She opened her mouth to protest.

"He doesn't. Listen to me. He's only wanted you. All this time, he's only wanted you. Now I've helped you run away from him. I am truly fucked."

Settling into her empty, dark apartment, Marta couldn't deny that she was, too.

HE KNEW THE minute he pulled into the driveway that she was gone. The house held no life without her in it.

But it wasn't until he boosted Shyla into her highchair for a snack and she said, "Daddy, cry," that he realized he was blinking back tears.

"What's this?" Sadie asked, holding a yellow envelope, a bag of groceries hanging forgotten in her hand. "Marta left, didn't she?" She pressed her lips into a thin line. "She left because of you. You made her go, how could you, Ian?"

Dropping the bag in a clatter of cans, she threw the envelope at him and ran up the stairs, her keening sounding throughout the house.

Ian sank into a chair, bent to pick up the envelope. He didn't open it. It didn't matter what it said, what it didn't say.

If she wanted to go, he was going to let her.

Simple as that.

The hell it was.

MARTA TURNED THE thermostat of her apartment up another two degrees. Winter finally decided to visit Minnesota, but instead of a nice hello, it kicked ass, and the temperature dropped to below zero overnight.

She hadn't given much thought to how she'd tolerate the Minnesota cold, brushing it off as just an inconvenience.

She'd forgotten just how frigid it could be.

It had only been a week since she'd walked out on Ian, but it felt like a lifetime.

Slowly, she was packing her things. When her cell phone rang, she was taping boxes together. In a lucky move, she'd kept the ones her landlady had used to ship her personal items to Minnesota. Marta had had no idea she'd need them again so soon.

"Hello?" she asked hesitantly, unfamiliar with the number.

"Vice President Bowen on the line for Miss Braddock," a professional-sounding voice intoned into the line.

The voice was replaced with holiday elevator music, and she frowned.

Vice President Bowen? The name didn't ring a bell. Maybe it was a prank, or a telemarketer attempting to keep her on the line. Maybe her cell phone bill was being charged a hundred dollars a minute because she didn't hang up.

Just as she was about to press Disconnect, a smooth male voice cut through an instrumental of "Rudolph the Red-Nosed Reindeer."

"Miss Braddock?"

"Speaking."

She stumbled through her apartment with her crutches, mentally taking note of how many more boxes she'd need.

"This is Vice President Bowen, at the university? Do you know who I am, and do you have a moment to speak with me?"

The name clicked with Marta then. Vice President Bowen was Athletic Director Spaulding's boss.

She'd never met the Vice President of the University of Minnesota, Tower City, but she knew who he was, at least. "Yes, sir, Mr. Bowen, how can I help you?"

"If you're free tomorrow, I'm asking that you come to my office. There are things we need to discuss."

"Getting around is diffic—"

"I understand, Miss Braddock, but I wouldn't ask, and in this weather no less, if it wasn't important."

"What time?" Marta asked, resigned.

At least she could say she tied up this loose end before she moved.

"I'm available before a lunchtime appointment, if that suits you. Eleven o'clock."

"That's fine, thank you," Marta said, but the line had already gone dead before the last syllable left her mouth.

———

BITING HER LIP in frustration, she found herself knocking on Dane's and Nikki's door the next morning. She needed a ride.

"Hey," Nikki said, peering around the door. "Want some breakfast?"

"Uh, no, I was wondering if you or Dane could take me to the university. I have a meeting with Vice President Bowen."

"Sure, let me warm up the car. Dane installed auto-start for my birthday. When do you need to be there? Come in and have some coffee."

"I don't have to be there for an hour, I wasn't sure if you or Dane were available, and I wanted to give myself time to order an Uber."

"Dane's at The Finish Line with Brett and Ian this morning." Nikki leaned against the kitchen counter and picked up a pink and white coffee mug. Cradling it to her chest, she squinted at Marta.

"Don't look at me like that," Marta said, letting her crutches drop in a metal clatter in the hallway. She limped into the kitchen and helped herself to a mug and the remaining half-pot of coffee. "I know what you're thinking. Don't."

"Don't what? Care about you? Care Ian is hurting? You left them right before Thanksgiving—"

"I know what I did," Marta snapped, slamming the carafe onto the hotplate. "Ian couldn't handle the truth, okay? After he found out I couldn't have kids, he shut me out. What was I supposed to do?"

"Is that why?"

"What do you mean, is that why? Of course it's why."

"Maybe it's not *what* you kept from him, just that you did it in the first place."

"Same difference."

She wasn't willing to talk about this with Nikki, or anyone. She'd already made her choice. Her taped-up boxes were proof of that.

"Anyway, let's go, if you're still willing to drive me. It will take me a while to walk across campus if we can't find a close parking spot."

"I'll take you," Nikki said, dumping her coffee into the sink. "Let me change, and then we can go."

They rode to campus in silence, Marta tongue-tied and unable to think of anything to talk to Nikki about that didn't have to do with Ian.

She couldn't bring up The Finish Line, because that would involve all three men, and she was so tired of talking about her history with Brett in relation to Ian she wanted to scream.

"I'm going to park in visitor's parking. Why don't you go ahead, and I'll wait for you," Nikki said, pulling in front of the academic building where Vice President Bowen's office was located.

"Thanks. Sorry you have to walk in the cold," Marta said. She pulled her crutches out of the back seat.

"No problem. I'll find you later."

Marta rode the elevator to the fourth floor of the building. Her winter jacket made her start sweating seconds after entering the warm waiting area.

"Can I help you?" A brunette receptionist asked, looking up from her computer screen.

"Marta Braddock to see Vice President Bowen," Marta said, and raised her eyebrows in surprise when the woman abruptly stood, flustered.

"Of course, Miss Braddock, right this way. Mr. Bowen is waiting for you."

The receptionist opened the door to Bowen's office and gestured for Marta to enter.

Bowen, dressed in a charcoal grey suit, sat behind a massive mahogany desk, a light blue file folder the only thing on his blotter. "Miss Braddock, thank you for coming. Susan will bring coffee in a moment. I apologize for asking you to come in the cold."

"That's fine," Marta said, sitting in a chair in front of Mr. Bowen's desk. It was a relief to sit; making her way to the office had made her ankle throb. "What can I do for you? I'm assuming this has something to do with the Lady Slipper?"

"Yes, actually it does. Has Spaulding told you anything?" Bowen leaned a hip against his desk.

Marta scoffed. She might as well be as honest and as forthcoming as she wanted; she had nothing to lose. "No. In fact, he didn't even tell me I was terminated from my coaching position. I heard about it when I watched the press conference—on TV."

"I see. Then you don't know that the Lady Slipper director, Babbs Dresden, began an investigation into your accident?"

"I'd heard that, yes. My friend, Dane Montgomery, owns the Tower City Running Company. He overheard a couple of his customers talking about it and passed the information along to me. Quite frankly, Mr. Bowen, I don't care. I'd already lost my job at the school; with my broken ankle, my running prospects aren't looking that great. The outcome of the investigation won't mean much to me."

Bowen smiled, a hint of humor warming his face. "I think you'll disagree."

Marta leaned forward. "Okay . . . ?"

"Babbs has always run a tight marathon, and the thought of a rogue volunteer pissed her off, to put it bluntly."

Babbs Dresden hadn't reached out in any way, not to apologize, not to ask how her recovery was going, nothing.

"She watched race footage, talked to the volunteers who saw the woman who'd gotten in your way. Worked with the

Springfield police. Race tampering is a criminal offense, and they were happy to help with the investigation."

Susan, Bowen's secretary, chose that moment to wheel in a coffee cart. "I'm sorry that took so long, Mr. B. I had to make fresh."

"It's fine, Susan. You should forward my calls to voice-mail and take your lunch."

"Thank you, I will."

After Susan shut the door, Bowen helped himself to a cup of coffee. Stirring in the sugar he'd liberally added, he said, "It didn't take long for them to identify her." He pulled a mugshot photo from the file laying on his desk. "Do you know who she is?"

Marta took the photo and studied the woman frowning into the camera. Her black hair was a mess, her makeup smudged. It was the same woman who had gotten in her way, but no, she didn't know who she was.

She shook her head and handed Bowen the picture.

"She's Libbie Layne's stepsister."

"What? What do you mean?" Marta asked.

"Spaulding hired her to make sure you didn't finish that race. He wanted Libbie Layne at the school so he could work with her—see her on a daily basis. They've been having an affair, and when he took the job here, he promised he would get her in."

Marta blanched. "That's why he despised me."

"When the Springfield police department identified her — she was in the system due to a shoplifting arrest a few years ago—a detective from Tower City questioned Miss Layne. It only took some light threatening to make her confess everything. Spaulding has been terminated. He's lawyered up, of course, but with Miss Layne's testimony, he won't get off."

"Thank you for telling me. It gives me a bit of closure to this mess." She reached for her crutches.

"Thank you, again, for coming in the cold. Maneuvering crutches over the snow can't be easy. But there was one other thing I want to ask before you go. Have a cup of coffee, this will only take a few more moments of your time."

IAN SLAMMED HIS car door shut, simmering with fury. If she thought he was going to let her walk out, she could think again.

Jimmying the lock—there was no way in hell he was going to give her the heads-up he was storming down the hallway—he tried to calm down. The rage had built up on the drive to her building.

How dare she think she could ruin his life again.

Running off with no explanation, no goodbye.

Just like last time.

She was running scared, and this would be the last time.

He would make sure of it.

Ian pounded on her door hoping Dane and Nikki weren't home. There would be yelling, oh yes, there would be, and he didn't need or want Marta's neighbors involved. This was between him and her.

The clatter of her crutches sounded through the door, and he unclenched his fists. At least she was home. He was good and mad, and if she wouldn't have been home, he'd have had nowhere to put it.

"Ian," she whispered when she opened the door.

"Marta. We need to talk."

He pushed his way into her apartment, and she stumbled against the closet door.

"Hey! You don't need to be—"

There were boxes everywhere. Her kitchen stripped.

She was moving.

"You're leaving."

He glared at her; couldn't take his eyes off her. She wore a fuzzy cream sweater and black leggings. Her feet were bare. He wanted to fold her into his arms and never let her go, but that wasn't the main objective here.

In fact, he felt off-kilter now. He hadn't expected her to be moving, thinking maybe she'd . . .

"Well, I'm packing," Marta said, using her crutches to shuffle to the couch.

"Then there's nothing left to say, is there?" Ian felt the finality of the situation now, the pressure of a billion gallons of water over his head, crushing him.

"I did get some news I wanted to talk to you about," she said, laying her crutches on the floor.

The echo of his heart pounding in his ears, Ian didn't hear her. He couldn't let Marta go. Maybe he couldn't convince her to stay for him, but maybe he could convince her to stay for someone else.

Slowly, never taking his eyes off hers, he walked across the floor and sank onto the couch next to her.

Taking her hands, he said, "Marta, I know you don't love me, you can't. Not with the way you've treated me since you came back."

Maybe that was harsh, but it was the truth. In all these months she'd never given him a straight answer about anything, always flirting along the outskirts of his life, too reluctant to make the commitment, to throw her chips all in.

She didn't speak, but tears did fill her eyes. Maybe he could get through to her, a little.

"But this isn't between you and me any longer. I have a little girl who asks for you all the time. She keeps running into the room you stayed in looking for you. Hoping one time, at last, when she pokes her head around the corner of the door, you'll be there. And Sadie. She won't stop crying. Hasn't talked to me since you left. She blames me for making you leave, won't listen to a thing I have to say. I came up with a compromise, I mean, it's more of a compromise on your end, but maybe we can make it work."

He swallowed.

If she flat-out refused, there was nothing else he could say, nothing else he could bargain with. This was his last Ace—her love for Sadie and Shyla.

"You won't live with us for me, so I'm asking if you would live with us for the girls. I know that's asking a lot," he hurried to say when her lips parted, "and I can't tell you how long I would ask that of you. But Sadie, she's changed since she's gotten to know you. She's looking forward to having her baby, she's reached out to Trent's parents. She's enrolled in school. You've been such a positive influence in her life, Marta.

"And Shyla, well, you know she loves you. It would mean a lot to me if you would do this—for the girls. I would stay out of your way as much as I could. You could have your old room back. Before you give me the no I see in your eyes, could you at least think about it? For the girls?"

MARTA HUNG HER head in shame.

She was lucky he was here—fortunate he loved Sadie

and Shyla so much he was willing to look past what she'd done to give her a fifth chance? Sixth?

No matter how many chances he'd given her, they were more than she deserved.

"Ian, can I ask you one question?"

What Nikki said to her the morning Marta had gone to Bowen's office stuck with her. Maybe it *hadn't* been what she'd told Ian about getting her tubes tied, maybe it had just been the fact she'd kept something else from him, and he was tired of the lies.

If she was going to make this work, then she was going to have to start being honest, and she was going to have to stop fearing what he had to say and how he felt about the choices she'd made.

"Anything."

"The day I told you I had my tubes tied, were you angry because I can't have children, or because I kept it from you?"

She held her breath.

Ian leaned his head against the cushion and closed his eyes. "Yeah, it hurt me when you told me you can't have kids. I know reversals don't always work, and I wouldn't ask you to put yourself through that for me. I was upset, but I was angrier that you kept it from me. This whole time since you've been back, I feel like you've never been truthful, like you've been afraid to tell me anything. At first I thought it was because you were still in love with Brett." He cracked his eyes open to look at her. "Now I just realize it's because you *didn't* love *me*, and you didn't want me close to you."

She could work with that.

Marta shifted to face him, sitting on a hip. Burrowing into the sofa she said, "Okay. I got some news yesterday. The Vice President of the university called me, and I met him at his office. The director of the Lady Slipper investigated my accident and found out that the woman who got in my way is Libbie Layne's stepsister. Spaulding hired her to trip me up, make sure I wouldn't win. Bowen said Spaulding has been in a relationship with Libbie for a long time and wanted her in the coaching position, so they could see each other."

"For God's sake," Ian snapped, swiping his hand through his hair. "They ruined your career for their relationship?"

"Yeah, well, racing is a risky business. Races have been tampered with for less. Doping for the money and glory is done all the time. But that wasn't all he wanted to talk to me about."

Ian traced a finger down her cheek, and Marta leaned in. "What else could there be?" he asked.

"Bowen offered me Spaulding's job."

"That's fantas—"

"I turned him down."

Ian bolted from the couch. "What the fuck? Oh, I see, you have no need for a job here anymore, is that it? Because you're leaving." He stared out the glass doors into the square covered in snow.

Marta hefted herself off the couch, but she didn't bother to grab her crutches. "I'm packing, Ian, but I didn't say I was leaving."

"What do you mean? Packing means moving. I'm stupid about a lot of things, but I know that."

"I turned down Bowen because my running days are over. Not because I broke my ankle, I think I'll still be able to run every now and then, and I could even coach, probably, if I wanted. He offered me that position too, after I turned down the Athletic Director's job. But I realized, while I was sitting in his office, that my running days are over because I want them to be."

"Then what are you going to do? Go back to planning retreats? In California?"

He still stared out the window. Marta wished he would look at her, but she was in no position to make demands.

"No. I'm packing to move. In. With you."

"What?" His grey eyes met hers.

"Coach Wesley told me there's more to life than running, and he's right. I gave up my baby to have a career, but in the end, it was too much. My career wasn't worth the sacrifice, but how could I have known that? I didn't feel I deserved you, and to punish myself for my abortion, I didn't let myself have you. But I'm not only punishing myself, I've been punishing you, and Sadie and Shyla. It needs to stop. I did what I needed to do at the time, and that's the best I can do." She took a chance and leaned into him, hoping he would support her.

He bore her weight against him, and she rested her cheek against his chest. "I turned down the Athletic Director's job, and the coaching job too, because they would take too much time. I don't want to work that hard, and I don't have to. I've spoken with Brett—I'm going to direct the Tower City Marathon . . . and be a mother to Shyla, if you'll let me."

"Marta, I want that, I really do . . ."

Marta's heart sank. She'd gone too far; what she'd done to Ian couldn't be repaired.

". . . But you have to be sure this time. You can't keep disappearing on them, on me. If you come home with me, it's forever."

He bent on one knee and took her hands, pressed them to his lips before he continued. "I've asked you a couple times now, but you've never answered me. Marta, I love you. Will you marry me?"

"I can't have babies, Ian."

"I know. But we already have Shyla, and Sadie is due in five months. If we decide we have room in the house, and in our hearts, for more, we can look into foster care. The family who took in Shyla was kind and treated her well. Maybe we can pay it forward?"

Relief flooded through her. They were going to make this work. Even after all the things she'd done to sabotage the love they'd found.

"That sounds perfect. I love you, Ian. Yes, I'll marry you. I'm sorry I kept running away."

Ian rose to his feet and kissed her.

She reveled in his soft touch, the love that radiated from him.

"That's okay, sweetheart. You were running toward the finish line the whole time. And we both won."

The Finish Line, a bonus ending novella, is coming soon! Catch up with Nikki, Dane, Brett, Alyssa, Ian, and Marta eighteen months later! Look for it summer of 2020!

HIS FROZEN HEART: A ROCKY POINT WEDDING BOOK 1

"You're here!"

Callie Carter tugged her suitcase into the Rocky Point Resort's lobby as Marnie Zimmerman, the bride-to-be and Callie's best friend, shrieked across the room making several people stare, a little old lady grin, and Callie laugh.

"I told you I would be, but my dad didn't make it easy," Callie said, easing her case to a stop in front of the registration desk and setting her purse on the counter next to a display of resort brochures.

Marnie frowned and shoved her fists onto her ample hips. "You deserve a break, you work too hard."

"No one knows that more than me. I had the time coming, and there wasn't anything he could do about it."

Her father didn't believe in taking a break. Horace "Ace" Carter didn't believe in downtime. Rest. Taking care of her emotional health, her physical health. He believed in getting the job done, no matter the cost. And for the past ten years, she had. But rubber bands, stretched too tightly, eventually snap, and Callie was almost there.

"I'll make sure you have fun . . ." Marnie said, linking

her arm through hers while the front desk agent ran her card and handed her a small stack of papers.

"Here's your key, Miss Carter," the agent—her nametag read Sophia—said, giving her an honest-to-goodness key attached to a maroon keychain with the gold Rocky Point Resort logo stamped into the plastic. "You're in room two-thirty-one, next door to Marnie and James."

". . . Starting tonight."

Callie untangled her arm from Marnie's and pulled her suitcase behind her. She'd left a few dresses hanging in her car, but she'd go to back for those later. "What's tonight?"

"I planned a get-to-know-you dinner. Jared is picking up Leah in Marengo, and she'll be here later this afternoon. I can't wait for you to meet her. Hell, I can't wait to meet her!"

"You are positively giddy," Callie said, laughing. She stopped at the base of the short set of stairs that would take them to the second floor. Purse hanging from the crook of her elbow, she hugged Marnie. "I'm happy for you."

Marnie hugged her back so hard her spine cracked. "I *am* happy, and I'm happy you could be here."

"I wouldn't have missed it."

She'd been honored when Marnie asked her to be a bridesmaid, and she hadn't thought for a second about saying no.

Standing outside Callie's door, Marnie said, "I know you want time for yourself after that long drive. Take a nap, order a bottle of champagne, whatever you want. We're meeting downstairs for dinner, and you'll meet everyone then. I'm so excited!"

Marnie's platinum blonde hair shimmered in the fluorescent lights, her pin curls, thick red lipstick, and clear skin giving her a Marilyn Monroe glow. She even had the curves to go with it, and Callie had always envied Marnie her softness.

Callie worked out seven days a week, three-hundred and sixty-five days a year. She had to. It was part of her job. Speaking of . . . she might be on vacation, but she still needed to workout. "You said the resort has a workout facility?"

"Yep," Marnie said. "It's downstairs by the pool. It's not as big as the set up in your basement, but it will work."

"Thanks. I'll see you tonight, then."

Callie didn't feel the need for a drink, but a light nap sounded divine.

She let herself into her room and tucked her suitcase into the closet. The room smelled like any hotel room she'd ever stayed in: air freshener and recycled air.

A huge gift basket sat on a table tucked under the window that overlooked a thick swatch of trees. A brochure the resort supplied said there were woods to the west, the lake to the north, ski slopes on the east side of the building, and the town of Rocky Point to the south. Callie leaned against the table and skimmed the brochure. The resort offered quite a few amenities. Maybe she would try her hand at skiing while she stayed there.

Callie washed her face in the sink and dried her skin with a bleached white hand towel. She hung it on the bar over the toilet and frowned at the water pooling at the bottom of the bowl. "That's great," she muttered.

She needed a working sink. If all the pipes were connected, the bathtub might be affected too, and she wanted to be able to shower in the morning. Or tonight after dinner.

Using the phone on the nightstand, she called the front desk. "I need maintenance."

It wasn't that late in the day, and she hoped someone would be able to come by her room soon. "My sink is plugged and won't drain."

She recognized Sophia's voice. "We'll have Mitch up there right away."

"Thank you."

Callie should have asked to be transferred to room service; she'd changed her mind about that drink. Marnie's suggestion of a bottle of champagne sounded better and better, but she didn't bother calling back.

Even though she was on vacation, she shouldn't drink too much. Her father told her she needed to be in control at all times. What if someone needed her? He always had an example at the ready of a time when he'd been able to help someone.

Service was a calling.

Ace Carter spoke of their occupation as if they were ministers or missionaries.

And he expected her to behave as such.

Someone knocked on her door, and she pushed the thoughts away. This was supposed to be a vacation, and it wouldn't feel like one if all she did was worry about her job and what her dad thought of her. She'd fought hard for it and won, and she needed to make the best of it.

Callie opened the door expecting an older man, balding, wearing a t-shirt and stained overalls carrying a red battered toolbox, and she blinked in surprise at the man only a few years older than she standing in the hallway.

Her gaze traveled from his dark brown hair to his green eyes. Slim but strong with the way he carried an enormous toolbox.

He shifted slightly, and asked, "Did you need maintenance?"

Callie flinched and hid a gasp behind her hand.

The skin on the right side of his face was a mottled red and pink, shiny smooth in places, puckered in others.

Through the crackling of heat in her ears, her mind whispered, *fire*.

His Frozen Heart is the first book in A Rocky Point Wedding Series and is available now in Kindle, Kindle Unlimited, and paperback. Don't miss this exciting new series! Start reading today!

ACKNOWLEDGMENTS

A special thank you to Mark and Sue Knudson, who direct the real Fargo, North Dakota marathon. Through my years of running in Fargo, ND, I learned a lot about the running community, race routes, and the expos. Every year, the Knutsons, and all the kind volunteers, put a lot of work into the marathon, and without their example, I would never have been able to write this trilogy.

Thank you.

Only the running community could rival the writing community in support, acceptance, and loyalty.

It's an honor to belong to both.

ABOUT THE AUTHOR

Vania Rheault has lived in Minnesota all her life. In 2003, she graduated with a BA in English with a concentration in creative writing. When she's not writing, she's reading, playing with her three cats, or going to movie night with her sister.

Find Vania on www.vaniamargene.com and these social media platforms:

www.ingramcontent.com/pod-product-compliance
Lightning Source LLC
Chambersburg PA
CBHW021000120726
47905CB00009B/2777